THE CURE

THE CURE

A BLACK GHOST THRILLER

FREDDIE VILLACCI, JR.

American Big Pharma wants her gone.
China wants her as a bargaining chip to rule the world.
She could save millions of lives.
But now she's fighting for her own.

On the brink of curing cancer, Gracie Green is eager to advance to human trials and share her findings with the world. But the FDA, and special interests in Big Pharma and a host of other people who stand to lose billions if cancer is cured, have other ideas. They hire expert assassin and Ex-CIA operative Jaco Ivanov; with one mission—wipe Greentech from the face of the earth!

Hunted by an expert killer and framed for a terrible crime, Gracie finds herself on the run, struggling to stay one step ahead of Jaco and his vast assets. Caught between a murky world of shadow governments, assassins, and even China's quietly deadly intelligence network, her future hangs in the balance. There's only one thing none of them accounted for—the Black Ghost.

Gracie will need more than luck to find the truth and bring her cure to the world. Can she hope to survive against such powerful enemies, even with the help of the legendary assassin who tops the FBI's most-wanted list...

Or will the Black Ghost finally have met his match?

V

To the scientists who find a cure.
One day, hopefully soon,
cancer will be cured with a simple pill.
Just as today an infection is treated with penicillin.
When that day comes cancer's reign of terror
over the world will be over.

V

1

Two years after Book 1
Early July

Bic tried to steady the pace of his pounding heart as he squeezed his massive body through a skintight hole leading into a death cave of pungent-smelling impenetrable blackness constructed by the Viet Cong. Once he got down there, he'd fire his weapon toward the source of any sound—a drip of water, a flutter of wings against a hard carapace—and each blast would reveal the contours of the cave in strobe relief, and he'd wish he hadn't seen it…

…This is what confined spaces did to Bic Green.

He was a big guy, well over six feet tall; his dark skin tight over thick chiseled muscles—the kind you only get from a combination of genes and hard lifting—and the tight chamber of the MRI machine he found himself in was the latest culprit.

For two years now, since his first collapse on the boat in the coastal waters of Seal Island, he'd been suffering blackouts. Random, without warning, and excruciating; they tortured him until some benevolent switch in his brain brought the blessed relief of unconsciousness. He had seen consultants all over the world, but received no answers.

The opinions varied—allergic reaction, nervous breakdown, post-traumatic stress. One psychologist had the unmitigated gall to suggest Bic had invented the incidents in his mind. But the gob of blood he'd spit up on more than one occasion didn't lie. Something was wrong with him and it wasn't going to go away on its own.

He often wondered if this was God paying him back for all that he had done. If so, that was okay, he couldn't get the pictures of those innocent victims out of his mind. Especially the two he didn't kill, the children of the Braddicks. That eight-year-old boy was just a year older than he was when his mom was murdered. The boy didn't do anything, he was so scared, but he could see it in his eyes that he had wanted to really bad. One day, somehow, he'd hoped to help fix that young boy he'd taken so much from.

He'd been reluctant to return to the states since his assassinations of nine of the ten wealthiest people in the US, but his niece, Dr. Gracie Green, wouldn't take no for an answer. She had arranged a panel of sub-specialized radiologists at the Duchossois Center for Advanced Medicine (DCAM) at the University of Chicago Medical Center in Hyde Park to comb over his entire body, certain that they would find answers.

Two hours later—his head still ringing from the jackhammer pounding of the MRI—Bic sat next to Gracie as she reviewed her notes in a brightly lit conference room at a highly polished oval oak table. Gracie stood slender and tall in her high heels and commanded attention with a confident, watchful demeanor. Her black hair was straightened into a bob and slicked back away from her face to behind her ear, revealing her youthful twenties face and promising never to get in the way of anything. She was wearing cobalt blue scrubs and a tailored white lab coat, which strongly contrasted with her espresso-colored skin.

Her nametag read *Dr. Grace E. Green, Oncology* and her lab coat had an embroidered coat of arms and the words *At the Forefront, UChicago Medicine.* Though she had moved her research work to her private lab, she had retained her admitting privileges and continued to see patients occasionally here at DCAM. She had earned a few chips, and today was a day she was calling most of them in.

She reached over to him, placing her fragile hand on top of his. "You okay?"

He nodded once. "Fine."

"Liar," she said with a teasing smile. "It's okay to be scared, you know. But in a few minutes the doctors will be with us and we'll have answers. That's the first step in a process."

Bic looked at her hand and smiled, "I used to hold you in one arm."

She pulled her hand away with giddy embarrassment. "Cut it out,

Unc."

"Look at you now," said Bic. "A brilliant woman getting ready to put your mark on the world. Your momma would be proud."

"Thanks, Unc, but you're changing the subject."

Both heads snapped toward the opening door as a six-man panel of doctors entered.

"Well," said Dr. Yang, a serious-faced Asian thirty-something with a Beatles haircut. Bic had never much cared for the Beatles look, but this guy pulled it off. "We didn't find any abnormalities."

"None?" Gracie asked. Bic thought she sounded disappointed.

Dr. Yang shook his head. Bic almost expected to hear girlish shrieks as his side swept bangs moved back and forth. "I went over the body scans six times."

She turned to Dr. Samuel, a man with dark caramel skin and dark brown eyes in his forties with close-cropped graying hair wearing a lab coat pressed as stiff as cold rubber. "No abnormalities in the bi-frontal white matter regions?"

"None," said Dr. Samuel. He threw a glance at Bic—what was the look? Reassurance? Pacification?

"You did the flair, T1 and T2 signals?" Gracie asked, clearly perplexed.

"I did. Personally."

"And nothing?"

"Nothing. No lesions. No shadows."

"No lesions," the man echoed. He continued gazing at Bic. Reassurance, pacification... pity...

Accusation...

Malevolence...

The man's face distorted into a wooden mask, drawn taut and lightening in hue, with black grains and knots appearing there. The eyes glowed from behind the mask in a familiar, dope-stained red and a voice barked out from behind it "*I see you.*"

Bic jerked back in his seat as if jabbed with a cattle prod.

"Mr. Green? Are you okay?" asked Dr. Samuel, his appearance completely normal.

Bic nodded slowly, his breath coming in a long, uneasy sigh. "Yeah. Been a long day of tests is all."

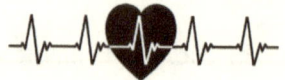

Though he obediently looked around as Gracie showed off the building they exited, Bic barely noticed the beautiful, clear day illuminating the impressive four-story atrium. It even smelled light and summery. Until they stepped outside. The full impact of the heat and humidity of a city set next to an enormous body of water hit him and roused him a bit. As they moved through the facility parking lot, Gracie's voice sounded oddly distant as it reverberated, even though she walked right next to him. "Unc, I'm so sorry to put you through all that for nothing. I thought they'd have some answers. Or at least know what questions to ask next."

"I appreciate you trying," he said. "I was proud of you in there. Half the words you said, man, sounded like Martian to me."

"I'll figure out what's wrong with you, I promise. We still have the bloodwork to assess. I've been corresponding with a hematologist in Boston who specializes in rare blood diseases."

They stopped in front of her Nissan Maxima.

"Thank you," said Bic.

"Unc," she said, "are you serious?"

"You're a busy girl. You don't have to do this."

"I don't want to hear any more *thank yous* out of you. It's insulting," she said with a smile. Gracie stopped, "Hey, why don't you come with me to see our lab building? It's not every medical researcher who gets the funds to build her own private lab. I want you to see all the cool stuff we're doing and meet everyone."

"I'd love to, but I need to catch a flight."

Gracie frowned. Bic couldn't help but noticing her brow furrowed just like her mother's used to. "You just got here."

"Let me know when I can meet with that doc in Boston. And I meant what I said about you being busy. I don't want you to take your eye off your company worrying too much about me."

Her face beamed for a moment, then turned serious again. "Please tell your investors I have a plan to speed up getting our drug advanced into Phase 1 human FDA trials." With a proud smile, "We cracked it."

"Since you were five I believed with all my heart you'd find the cure," Bic said emotionally. "The only way I can sleep at all at night is knowing the good you're going to do for so many." He enveloped her in a big, long hug, then gave her a couple of pats on the back and released her.

"I miss these," she said tenderly. She put her hand on his arm. "You have to promise me I'll see you again before another two years pass, okay?"

"I promise," Bic said, as he opened Gracie's door for her.

"Really," she said, getting in.

"Really."

And closed the door.

2

Bic made sure Gracie exited the garage before he left his car to reenter the center. He moved calmly, though his hands trembled. He hadn't had a desire to release his darkness since he had released that same anger by feeding Congressman Tidwell to the sharks. But seeing that hallucination of that mask triggered something primal inside of him. His successful suppression over the last two years of his rage had suddenly sprung back to life. But why? He didn't *need* to kill anymore. He didn't need a raw piece of meat to drop at the scene as he looked into the eyes of his victim to say the last words they'd hear on this earth. Those were the traits of a serial killer. That Bic was no more, or so he thought. Now he realized *that* Bic Green hadn't died inside him, but had merely gone to sleep. And now, like a recovering alcoholic is drawn back to the bottle…

Bic wandered the hallways near the conference room until he spotted Dr. Samuel walking at the opposite end of a corridor. The doctor turned into an office. A third Bic Green—the hunter—was awake. And the hunter wanted answers.

Bic entered the office, shutting the door behind him, and took a seat. The blinds were shut, blocking out the beautiful Chicago day, but also blocking out the heat. Most of the room was immaculately tidy, but his desk and the table behind him were stacked with files. Dr. Samuel looked up from the stack of case files that covered his desk, his computer monitor glowing to his left, brightening that side of his face.

"Bic, can I help you?"

"You don't seem surprised to see me."

Dr. Samuel hesitated, then replied, hints of Southern roots barely noticeable. "I'm sorry I didn't have any answers for you."

"I think you do."

"I'm not sure what you mean."

Bic blinked once, letting the silence stretch just a little too long. "Something happened to your face."

The man cocked his head. "My face?"

"I've never experienced it before. I felt like you sensed it too."

"Bic... are you ok?"

"Who are you?"

"I'm not sure I understand..."

"I saw a wooden mask on your face. I heard a voice."

"A mask... on my face..." Dr. Samuel's eyebrows furrowed together as his eyes darted to the closed door then back to the man seated before him.

Bic nodded slowly.

The doctor turned his head slightly, keeping his eyes trained on Bic the whole time. He extended his open hand. "Why don't we move to the conference room where there's water and more comfortable seats, and we'll talk about this, ok?"

"I'm not crazy," Bic said, straining against the words.

"I never said you were, Bic."

"I know. I know because it's written all over your face: you *know* I'm not crazy."

"So... you're saying you experienced some sort of... hallucination? What did you see?" asked the doctor when Bic didn't reply initially.

"I told you. Your face became a mask. Aged wood, very stylized and carved to look like a long face, dyed brown."

"Sounds like you saw a Dan mask."

Bic looked on for an explanation.

The doctor leaned back in his chair. "Refers to the Dan people of Liberia. It's a sacred object used for protection and as a channel for communication with the spirit world."

"Does this have something to do with what's wrong with me?"

"Could be a side effect of the meds Dr. Green gave you. Sometimes it takes a while till we can regulate dosage. She should have gone over that with you."

"You're a bad liar, doctor."

Dr. Samuel smiled awkwardly. "Excuse me?"

"You have what poker players call a tell. You blink a lot when you lie." Bic said matter-of-factly.

8

The man's face froze and he blinked a couple times.

"What are you holding back?" Bic asked with a sigh, shifting in the uncomfortable seat.

"As a doctor, that is, as a member of the medical profession who's sworn to do no harm, I'd say I'm holding nothing back. But as a man who can plainly see that you're not going to leave this office—or let *me* leave, for that matter—I can tell you about my Auntie Elodie and what she did in the Bayou when I was a young boy. And though my medical mind wants to say that she did some stuff medicine will eventually explain, I can safely say that it hasn't explained it yet." He paused, watching Bic. "That's between you and me. Understand?" Dr. Samuel spent the next few minutes talking about his ancient aunt, and what she did with masks, rituals, and powers that no one understood. How the darkness ran deep with blood. He finally trailed off.

"You didn't blink once. Thank you." Without another word, Bic rose and left the office.

When he got to his car, his hands were trembling. The rage was back. The other Bic, the killer, was awake and thirsty.

He put his head back onto the headrest and closed his eyes, feeling the hate wash over him like water from a baptismal font. Darkness *did* run deep with blood, and he had come to a realization.

"He's not dead," he said out loud. "The bastard's not dead."

Thoughts of his father revved the engine of bloodlust within him.

3

J aco Ivanov climbed the metal steps of the Gulfstream G650, his face a carefully schooled mask of respect. He paused and glanced at his yellow gold and stainless-steel Rolex and silently nodded to himself and continued. His pearl-white Savile Row suit, which contrasted strongly with his bright blue eyes and brown eyebrows, matched the corporate jet in both color and sleekness. The aircraft itself, hangered at a private airfield twelve miles outside of midtown Manhattan, bore a royal blue corporate-stylized 'V', logo of Vintigen, the largest drug company in the world, coveted for its extensive line of anti-cancer drugs.

The cool, conditioned air inside the cabin pulled the muggy July heat away from his skin. A well-built man dressed like a Secret Service agent met Jaco and motioned to him to raise his arms for a pat-down. Jaco removed his aviator sunglasses, placed them atop his bald head, then smirked as the young, blue-eyed man with the dark hair patted him down. The agent caught the smirk.

"Ticklish?" Spoken with a sneer.

"No," said Jaco, "I was just thinking about how you remind me of me, maybe 30 years ago. You sure you're not my bastard son?"

Jaco caught a glimpse of a SIG Sauer P226, the standard sidearm of a Navy SEAL, beneath the other man's sport coat.

"Got tired of burning garbage in the desert?"

The agent stopped and looked at him quizzically.

Arms still up, Jaco motioned with his head toward the man's weapon. "Who does a Navy SEAL have to hump to get this cushy job?"

Ignoring him, the agent finished the pat-down and nodded.

Jaco lowered his hands. "Thank you for your service."

The front section of the plane's interior was plush, with four oversized off-white leather captain's chairs arranged in a conversational grouping. Jaco smiled. He might steal this design for his own plane, substituting his family crest for the V logo stitched on the back of each seat.

"Have a seat," the agent called to him. "You'll be taken to the back cabin once we're in the air."

"Yes sir, sir, yes sir," Jaco said under his breath, surveying the finer details of the plane's interior.

He fell into one of the captain's chairs, the young agent beside him. Jaco closed his eyes. He didn't care to know the kid's name. To him, names, like the people they were attached to, were unimportant unless they came with some intrinsic value that would benefit Jaco Ivanov. He ran through various scenarios he might encounter once the meeting began, and their outcomes. He hoped it would be something he could take care of alone. He didn't want to involve more people than necessary. Pies were better whole, not split.

About 30 minutes after takeoff, he opened his eyes and looked out the nearest window. All he could see was the vast Atlantic Ocean. They were a couple hundred miles offshore by now. The young man sitting next to him had his right index finger on his earpiece. He nodded and stood. "Sir, they're ready for you in the back room."

Jaco stood, then proceeded through the eight-panel door leading to the rear section of the plane. The space was about three times larger than the front cabin, with four captain's chairs identical to the ones up front occupying a small foyer. Beyond was a massive, walnut oval conference room table with a dozen chairs around it.

Two men sat at the table, wearing collared shirts. Suitcoats hanging on hooks at the end of the room emphasized the backroom feel of the meeting. One was Colton Nash, the CFO of Vintigen. Colton was one of those guys who had a boyish face that make them look twenty-nine for decades. As long as you didn't know him when he was twenty-nine. He was tan, short, chubby, blue-eyed, and he had his blond hair like Robert Redford in *Three Days of the Condor.* Tasteful but expensive jewelry shone from wrist, fingers, cuffs, and collar, including a tie pin and a collar pin. Jaco thought maybe that was the rich man's version of suspenders and a belt.

The other was Peter Rains, a CIA operative in charge of the black ops assets operations. His look was pretty much the opposite. Dark hair and eyes, tall, trim, dark suit, and no jewelry except a watch, and not an expensive one. Peter was his handler some five years back, before Jaco had gone rogue. Jaco knew that in Peter's world, when he was going to do something on US soil for the "good of the country," using hired guns from the criminal world was part of the playbook. And if one gets caught, one merely exterminates the problem, and life goes on.

Peter stood and extended his hand. "Jaco. Good to see you again."

"Likewise."

Peter motioned for him to sit at the head of the table.

Jaco pointed to the 30-year single malt bottle of Glenfiddich at the bar. "That for little old me?"

Rains smiled. "Thought you might like a drink once the deal is done."

Jaco sat, "I'll admit it's a nice touch, Peter, but don't think a fine bottle of scotch is going to get you a discount."

Nash cleared his throat. "Now that you mention it, can we get down to business?"

Jaco glared at the man with a deeply calm smile, "By all means."

Nash opened a file folder for Jaco to see. "Mr. Ivanov, I'm going to cut right to the chase. There's a small biotech company called Greentech. It's getting in the way. We'd like very much for its founder, its scientists, and all of its research to... *not* be in the way anymore."

Jaco scanned the file, taking his time about it.

"Our people will take care of the research submitted," said Rains. "The patents, the FDA crap. We need you to take care of the rest."

Jaco clapped the folder shut. "What's the pay?"

"Two million." Rains said.

Jaco snickered. "I mean in total."

Rains and Nash exchanged glances.

Jaco leaned forward. "Gentlemen, you wouldn't have hired me if this company wasn't a really big problem for you. So, tell me, what are they on the verge of curing this time? Diabetes? HIV?"

"It's no different than any job in the past," said Rains.

"Sure it is. I can tell by the scotch."

"The Powers That Be want the company taken out," said Rains. "Leave it at that, Jaco. Are you in or out?"

Jaco sat on his thought for a moment, then smiled. "I'll be

damned. It's cancer, isn't it?"

So it was a problem after all. Over 75 percent of Vintigen's revenue came from cancer treatment drugs. "Which type of cancer we talking about?"

"According to our guy at the FDA, all of them," said Nash.

"You don't need me," said Jaco. "Seems like you could buy this startup company for two million. Sorry, gentlemen, but you wasted your scotch money."

"We've made an offer," said Nash. "They're not for sale."

"*Everybody's* for sale," said Jaco.

"Not this broad," said Nash. He pulled out the second page in the packet.

"And who's this?"

"This is Grace E. Green, known as Gracie," said Rains. "She's the founder, head scientist, and private owner of the company."

"And your chief target," added Nash.

The picture of the young woman made him smile. Her skin, her cheeks, her full lips, her brown eyes kind and intense at the same time. She reminded him of the first time he'd seen Halle Berry on the big screen. He tapped the photo. "I don't kill kids, it's bad business."

"She's no kid," Nash sneered. "She's 31 years old. A Ph.D. and M.D."

Jaco looked at Rains, and then back at Nash, distracted for a moment by the chunky ring on Nash's right hand.

"What's with this guy and his silence?" Nash said.

"Relax Colton. Jaco, we're prepared to erase your debt on that failed hotel you dumped your life savings into in Miami. We'll buy it for one million more than you owe."

"The swimming pool is worth more than that. Speaking of money, who's backing the company? Family? Hedge fund?"

"She doesn't have any family," said Rains. "She was orphaned at the age of five when her mother died. She comes from nothing. Common as dirt."

"You didn't answer the question." Jaco enunciated, "Where's the money coming from?"

"She's scrounged up a couple of grants here and there, plus a minority female business loan."

"Uh huh," said Jaco. "Mr. Nash, to answer your question earlier, my silence means I like to mull over the facts. That's how I am. I treat every problem in life the same way. Traffic jams, papercuts, and your little rodent problem." He jabbed a finger at the man. "You're here risking everything because if this drug hits the market, your company would be bankrupt in a month, the hospitals in 5, the States in 10 from Medicaid, and the government in 20 from Social Security and Medicare."

Rains took a deep breath and nodded his head.

Jaco continued. "As a professional staying in my lane, I'm going to go light. Pigs get fat, hogs get slaughtered, right?" He made deep eye contact with Rains, then landed on Nash. "Gentlemen, forget the hotel. Add another 19 million to my contract. I assure you, when I'm done, Miss Green and her company will stink so much that people will think they're selling fertilizer."

After a moment, Nash nodded to Rains.

Rains put a flat palm on the table. "Let's drink some scotch."

4

Two Months Later

The Slutty Dragon was filled with the finest elements of the New Orleans populace that three AM had to offer. Bic could only guess what smells the overwhelming Febreze scent covered as he scanned the patrons. Half of them were C-level street thugs barking all sorts of degrading slurs at the strippers—acting like they owned the place. The other half were men in dirty work clothes, still there nine hours after the job was over. The only difference between the two types was the costume; nasty behavior was universal.

Behind his sunglasses, Bic scoped out the drug element. These were the fixtures of the place. They matched the carpet, the scarred furniture, and the cigarette burns in the upholstery, and the tattered soul of the place.

He spotted Hawk cheering along with the rest of the crowd as a drab stripper with silver chains hooked to bondage rings on her g-string and a red bra studded with rhinestones swung her bleach-blonde hair, working the pole to Warrant's *Cherry Pie*. Bic locked eyes with his best friend, a man he'd known since Vietnam. Hawk fit this environment, still dressing like it was 1980, when he rode with a Texas biker gang, hanging onto his greasy steel-gray locks with their business up front, party in the back style.

"What, I'm not allowed to enjoy myself?" Hawk smiled, then pulled out a fiver and contributed to the spray of bills raining down at the dancer's feet.

Bic turned and spotted the group he was looking for deep in the corner of the club. Two high-level scumbags that had four girls, all of a type, blonde and extra buxom, giving them lap dances. That wasn't unusual. The cocaine being snorted out in the open? That was unusual.

Bic walked up to the table. The bald white dude had arm sleeve tattoos on both arms and a sleeveless black shirt that showed them off. The smaller black dude had a tight fade, sunglasses that looked like Neo from *The Matrix* had loaned them to him, and a crisp, white designer shirt with subtle texture and white buttons. These guys were working really hard to look a level of cool they weren't.

Bic stood over the men for a long moment.

Mr. Matrix caught his eye. "Yo, get your own, man." He waved his fingers. "Run along, bro."

"I'm looking for the priest," Bic replied.

"You what?"

"You wanna buy?" said Mr. Sleeve Tattoos. "An eight ball's $150."

"I don't wanna buy," Bic said flatly.

"Then it's best you run along boy," said Mr. Matrix, "before someone gets hurt."

"I don't want any trouble," said Bic.

"Oh good," returned the man. "Then you'll understand that I'm a little busy here."

Bic stepped forward and gently swung aside the ladies entertaining Mr. Matrix like a pair of western doors. "I said I don't want trouble."

"Oh," he pulled down his sunglasses, "you see, that's funny, because you just found trouble."

Mr. Sleeve Tattoos tossed his two strippers aside and stood up. He was roughly the same build as Bic. Before he could make it fully upright, Bic landed a punch to the throat. The guy dropped, gasping for air. One of the strippers screamed as the other dealer pulled a 9-millimeter out from behind his back. The ladies ran for cover.

A shiny silver .357 Magnum came up from behind the man. It was Hawk, who stuck the barrel into the dude's ear before he could do anything else. "Hand over the hardware, Bobby Brown," he purred, as he cocked the hammer, "unless you want me to blow a hole as big as the Belle Chasse tunnel through your head."

"You don't know who you messin' with," Mr. Matrix spat as he handed Hawk his gun.

"I think I'm messing with," Hawk half-sang in a high-pitched voice, following the tune with a laugh to himself. "the idiot with a .357 acting like it's a Q-tip in his ear."

Bic stepped up to the man. "The priest. Where is he?"

"Oh boy, someone better call 911 for little Bobby," Hawk sang out.

The man on the floor attempted to get to his knees, but Bic threw a ferocious forearm into the man's jaw. He dropped back down to the floor unconscious. Bic then grabbed the man sitting by his shirt and pulled him to his feet.

"Where's the priest?" he roared holding the man off the floor.

"Please don't kill me."

"Where?" Bic shook him like a rag doll.

Urine soaked the front of the drug dealer's pants as he stammered, "he's in the VIP room."

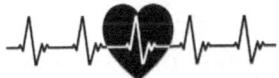

"This here room is taken," an older black man wearing the familiar tab collar priest shirt said, as he snorted a line of cocaine through a rolled-up 100 off an Asian girl's stomach. She ran her fingers through the back of her hair and moaned as the priest snorted.

The priest glanced up in annoyance and saw Bic. Even though he was high as a kite, seeing the big man sobered him right up. "I—I can explain!"

Bic clenched his jaw and his nostrils flared as he repeated his performance and grabbed the priest by the throat, fighting back his instincts to crush his windpipe. The stripper's eyes went wide and she bounced up, sending white powder flying as she fled the room.

"Where is Clarence Green?" Bic growled.

The man gasped by way of reply.

Bic relaxed his grip.

"There must be some mistake, I swear in front of God Himself."

Bic put a vice grip on the man's throat. The man's eyes bulged.

"Your life depends on your next words."

The man panted for his life. "I'll take you to him!"

Bic released his grip.

The priest fell to his hands and knees, gasping in a full breath of air until Bic blasted him with a haymaker to the jaw. He slumped to the ground, unconscious.

"That's what you get for lying, Pinocchio," said Hawk, coming up behind him. He had given Bic a moment alone while slipping the bouncers and management a stack of hundreds to ignore them. "Think this douche really knows where your old man is?"

"He showed me his grave, gave me a letter from him, trying to make amends for what happened." Bic looked into his friend's eyes, feeling the sour burn in his own. "Somehow, that letter gave me a sense of inner peace; it made it so I was able to let go of all of it." ·

"Sorry brother, I hate the man and I never met him."

Logic took a backseat to rage as the repeated thumps of his father smashing his mother's skull with a black iron pan stuck in Bic's head like an earworm.

Bic muttered to himself the last words his father ever spoke to him after he jammed a raw pork chop into his mouth, choking him unconscious, *It's pork chop-eatin' time.*

He dragged the priest out of the room by one foot, the head dragging and thumping along the floor. He said nothing. Action was going to be the only words spoken from here on out.

5

Today's the day, Dr. Gracie Green thought to herself, tossing the latest research report in the center of her desk next to her oversized flat screen monitor. She smiled at the only other item on her desktop: her favorite childhood picture with her mother. The rest of her office was clean, simply furnished, with the kind of store-bought furniture that comes in pieces you have to assemble yourself. The desk had a hutch and small wardrobe closet where she could keep her lab gear. She turned to her conference table, a small, square table pushed up against the wall, where the blueprints of her grand plans were on display.

Gracie smiled as she thumbed through them, thinking fondly of how she came from nothing—like so many in her neighborhood. And now, here she was on the brink of something that could help revitalize her community while impacting lives around the world. What a long journey it had been since her mother died of ovarian cancer, when Gracie, aged seven, vowed she'd find a cure.

So far, she'd renovated only a small fraction of the building: a reception area in the front that led to a work area serving as a research lab. All the lab equipment was top of the line and was where virtually all her sole investor's money had gone. Behind the laboratory were four offices, one of which was her own. Once she received FDA approval and started the march through the human trial phases, she was going to turn her abandoned 450,000-square-foot auto-parts factory into a state-of-the-art drug production facility.

The data from her latest series of experiments had confirmed it. Greentech, her two-year-old biotech company, really *did* have a cure for all types of cancer—and a quick one at that. Even though they had met every single criterion to begin Phase I human trials, the FDA had not approved their applications. Once again, bureaucracy and innovation were proving to be deadly enemies.

After her third try with data showing that lab mice previously loaded with cancer cells were cancer-free within two weeks with no side effects, the FDA sent her a letter stating their concern that her drug compounds may actually do more harm than good, citing the potential that the cure may create toxins in the blood stream that would likely result in brain damage. It was complete speculation, of course, and backed by no empirical evidence. The rest of the letter recommended she spend a ridiculous amount of money on new experiments to meet these fabricated toxicity requirements and reapply after trials were independently verified. Best case, they were costing her a year.

With a cure she believed was going to be as much of a game changer as penicillin, Gracie had taken matters into her own hands. In a couple of hours, the mayor of Chicago would be visiting. It was a natural solution. The mayor would get his press footage showing he cared about the South Side of Chicago for the up and coming election. After all, what better photo-op than a young black female starting a biotech business right in the heart of what others deemed a war zone? Yes, she knew why he was there, but if she impressed him enough and converted him to a true believer in her company, she'd have a powerful ally with enough political clout to cut through all that FDA red tape with one phone call.

She went over to the hutch wardrobe, opened the door, and looked at herself in the mirror. Across the bottom of the frame the word *BELIEVE* was etched.

She took a deep breath, then said to herself, "You got this."

Her hair was long, full, and dark, with tight curls, her face accented with just the right touches of makeup. She approved. Clean and simple. No visible jewelry, though underneath her blouse she wore an emerald heart pendant Unc had given her for her high school graduation.

She'd treated herself to a shopping trip the week before. The dark navy suit pants felt tight now for some reason. The vibrant but conservative blue silk blouse was sticking to her. Thank God she got her tailored lab coat pressed, professionally covering it all up. She ran her finger along the stitched name: *Grace E. Green, Ph.D., M.D.*

She smiled at the confidence this simple, tangible evidence of her success brought. She was ready.

"Gracie, like, quit daydreaming," said a woman in the doorway. "And, oh my god, you look fabulous."

Gracie laughed as she turned to look at her best friend, Dr. Anna Graham, a tall California blonde. "I still can't believe it's finally happening." She pointed toward the plans they'd sat and discussed with each other so often. "It seems like yesterday we were studying in the Stanford library, worrying about our biochem exams."

Anna came forward and embraced her friend. "You got this. And tonight, we're gonna do margaritas and dance like idiots." She waggled her hips then winked.

Gracie laughed, "this is for your mom. I'm not going to let happen to her what happened to mine."

"You're not going to miss with Mayor Linstrom today. We're gonna nail Phase I trials, and get it *right*."

"I'm pretty good, huh?" Gracie said, with confidence.

"Um, the girl who graduated summa cum laude from Stanford and went on to cure cancer? Hellooo?"

"Yeah, we're not there just yet. We've still got the mayor to win over."

Anna straightened her friend's collar and began dusting the shoulders. "We're *gonna* win him over. I mean, come on. We're promising him a biotech company on the South side of his miserable city."

Gracie's brow furrowed, "Yeah but, we don't have human trials. No one cares about mice. They want to see humans. It's not a done deal yet."

"Just stop it," said Anna.

Gracie took a deep, cleansing breath and shook her head. "Yeah, okay. You're right. I don't know what I'd do without you."

"You'd pay for your own darn margaritas. Come on, you need to get your stuff together. Let's go make this happen. Shall we assemble our big, expensive staff?"

Gracie giggled, then called out, "Steve? Alice?" The 'entire' staff was more like a family at this point, calling each other at all hours as breakthroughs were made and becoming slow but sure confidants as they spent more hours together than apart.

Steve Cotwell, a slight man with straight brown hair and wire-framed granny glasses, was the first to arrive. "You called, milady?" he said with a courtly bow and an obviously fake London accent, though he tried. Steve was a frequent attendee of Renaissance festivals and it showed. Despite the mild social awkwardness, he was invaluable.

"Are all the sequences and analytics ready?"

"Yes indeed." Steve looked at Gracie with googly eyes, as he always did. She was amused by his eccentricities and he knew it. He was a genius who had dropped out of the University of Chicago the day after answering her ad for a genetics expert in the paper. No big deal. He already had two doctorates.

"You've got coffee on your coat," said Gracie as she pointed to the stain on his boxy white lab coat.

Steve looked at his chest in chagrin. "Aw man," he said, breaking British character, "I don't have another one here. Still, better than mustard, right?" He was a frequent eater at the food truck that parked a couple blocks away.

"Go look behind the door in your office," said Gracie. "I had one dry-cleaned for you."

Steve put his hands together in prayer position and bowed again to Gracie, saying, "Gratitude, milady."

Alice Casselshouldt had entered the room in the midst of this, the shortest one of the crew by far, sporting the perma-ponytail she kept her long brown hair in. Gracie had never seen her hair down, ever. She was almost a polar opposite from Steve. She didn't waste time with flagrant activities, eschewing them in favor of puzzles and personal growth. She often made it known that if she was going to spend time away from her life's purpose, it was best spent doing things like the crossword to refine her mind and contribute to being sharper and better. Somehow, despite the vast chasm of difference, Steve and Alice had become besties.

"And you, my MIT renegade and computer guru. Everything ready?"

"Yep. All the programs are set to run simultaneously in five-minute increments. You'll be able to take the mayor to all four testing areas on the lab floor. Each is set to present the results of our cancer cell markers and virus release in the sequence we discussed." Serious hazel eyes looked at Gracie through very trendy black-rimmed glasses.

Anna pointed. "Mice loaded with cancer." She pointed to another section of the lab floor with mice moving vibrantly about in their cages. "Cancer free mice. Case closed. Human trials, here we come."

"Amazing work."

Alice shrugged her shoulders and gave an awkward smirk of a smile. "No biggie."

"Unstoppable!" Anna added, pumping a fist in the air.

Just then, the phone rang in Gracie's office. She trotted over to it. *Unknown Number.* She picked it up hesitantly. The line was dead. "Huh," she grunted.

As she rejoined Anna and Alice, they heard Steve call out.

"M-miladies," he said in a trembling voice.

6

Gracie hurried out of her office with the other two women in tow. What they saw made them stop short.

"Who the hell are you?" Gracie demanded of the man with the backpack draped over his shoulder—the man who was holding a silver handgun to Steve's head.

There were four men she had never seen before, three of them pointing their guns at her, Alice, and Anna.

The man with the backpack was older than the others but not old, with salt and pepper hair and an untrimmed beard. He said something in another language to the three other men with him. Given the way they looked, she supposed it was Arabic or Farsi. What she did know is that they had the stereotypical look of Middle Eastern terrorists— so perfect it almost looked cultivated.

It's funny, the details you notice when fight or flight kicks in… was the only thought Gracie could muster initially.

Using their guns to communicate, they had all three women put their backs to the wall.

The older man, who seemed to be the leader, holding the silver gun to Steve's head spoke again, slightly shifting the backpack he was wearing. One of his men, who was young and the only one who was clean shaven, as well as the only one using a rifle instead of a pistol, continued to hold the three women at gunpoint with a modified RF-15 knockoff of an AR-15. The last one holstered his weapon and went to the leader, removing his backpack. This man had dark red hair with a beard and lighter eyes. He opened the backpack and began to bring out what appeared to be bricks of off-white clay. Within seconds there were 20 bricks on the desk, whereupon the fourth man, who was very short, had remained closer to the doorway, holstered his gun and went over to the desk. He also had a backpack, which he set down next to the desk. He and the redhead began deftly inserting slim metal cylinders into the clay.

The leader barked additional instructions, waving his left hand toward the offices, while keeping the silver gun pointed directly at Steve's head.

The redhead working on the bricks stopped and went into Gracie's office. There was a series of quick, sharp snaps, and then the hard drive of her computer flew out of her office and crashed into the hallway. The man repeated this in the remaining three offices. He then went into the sturdy metal cabinet next to the lab equipment and began opening drawers until he came upon one with the supply of drugs marked for human Phase I trials. He tipped the drawer onto the floor. About 20 bottles bounced and clattered about. The man reached down and opened one, dumping the red and blue pills in his hand.

The short man at the desk finished his work with the bricks and began placing them throughout the reception and office area.

Speaking very quietly out of the corner of her mouth, Anna whispered, "Oh my God." Her voice was a trembling mess. "I know what that is."

The young, clean-shaven man with the black gun snapped to her.

"That's enough C4 to blow up the Pentagon," said Anna, her voice high-pitched and panicked.

The man screamed, waving the RF-15 at her, clearly demanding silence.

The shock hit Gracie hard as she realized that her company would be utterly gone as soon as the C4 was detonated. The short man working the explosives flipped a switch on the small devices planted in the bricks immediately after he'd carefully placed each one. Not that she knew how this type of stuff worked, but it only made sense that most of the explosives, except three that were placed at the front lobby door, were planted in a way that would completely wipe out every physical trace of her life's work. Several weeks ago, after Steve had found their anti-malware program and firewalls had been disabled two consecutive days from a remote location in Beijing, he convinced her to not back up any of her formulas on the Cloud or any external servers of any sort. Everything they worked from, and saved to, was on the premises.

The leader barked out additional orders.

The red-headed thug who had dumped the bottles went to the second backpack. Here he extracted plastic zip ties, a syringe, and a vial of clear liquid, placing each gingerly upon the desk. Gracie looked from Anna to Alice to Steve. It was about to hit the fan. Steve had an insane phobia of needles. She could see the horror in his eyes and the perspiration dripping from his forehead. The gun at his head was nothing to him compared to the thought of what they might do with the needle.

Her mind raced. The four men probably had combat training. Under her desk was a panic button, part of the alarm system. If she could somehow get to her office. But how?

In the midst of this, Steve's eyes darted between his coworkers, landing on Alice. "Goodbye." He mouthed the word to her.

The short terrorist who had placed the explosives—they *had* to be terrorists—grabbed the zip ties and walked toward Steve, while the leader slid his weapon into an underarm holster. He grabbed Steve's arms and was about to shove them into position when Steve charged the man with all his might, yelling, "Run!" as the short man and the leader went tumbling to the floor.

Several things happened very quickly after that. Anna made a mad dash for the lobby. Alice followed, but was grabbed and violently thrown to the ground by the clean-shaven terrorist. The redhead sprung quickly over from the desk, pulling his gun and savagely pistol-whipping Steve in the back of his head. Steve went sprawling as the blow landed with a sickening crunch, knocking him away from the leader. The short man, still on the ground, pulled out his pistol and tracked Anna with it.

The shot was deafening. Blood spattered across Gracie's cheek.

Anna's body fell to the floor.

Like a tailback trying to break a run to the outside, Gracie sprinted for her door, hoping to reach the panic button under her desk. She shot past the young man who had tackled Alice, but he leaped to his feet and chased her into the office. Gracie dove over the top of her desk and, as her hand cleared the top edge of the desk, she curved it underneath and hit the panic button for as long as she possibly could.

The clean-shaven terrorist yanked her up from the floor and bear-hugged her from behind with his wiry but very solid arms. Though she managed to get in a few solid kicks on his shins, they weren't solid and her breath was hard to inhale through the crushing pressure on her ribs. He dragged her out of the room, back into the hall.

Alice was still on the floor leaning against the wall, now zip-tied, weeping and shaking. She hadn't moved from where she'd gone down. Anna lay in the center of an expanding puddle of blood. Steve was on his knees with the redhead and the leader pointing their handguns at his head, blood on his hair and lab coat. The short man was walking toward Alice with his strange tan pistol pointed at her. The leader holstered his gun and said something quick and stern.

The redhead, who was holding his gun a foot from Steve's face, pulled the trigger. The bullet burst into Steve's head, cratering his forehead, but his eyes never blinked, and he never lost his defiant look. Then the spark of light in his eyes was extinguished and he fell face-first to the floor. The leader then pointed at Alice, still on her knees up against the office wall where she'd been thrown. He said the same stern words he'd said a moment before, and the redhead moved away from Steve, toward Alice, his arm fully extended at Alice, and pulled the trigger. The bullet popped into her skull with such force her head snapped back and cracked into the wall behind her.

Gracie screamed as she flailed like a crazed animal to break free from the clean-shaven man's grip, using everything in her power. If she were going to go down, she'd do it with a fight.

The man tightened his grip, locking her body into position. Then came the duct tape.

Why aren't they killing me too? She wondered.

7

The tape sealed her mouth shut. The windowless cargo van reeked of her four captors, who apparently had only a passing acquaintance with soap and water and none with deodorant. The fast food wrappers and assortment of miscellaneous garbage on the floor didn't help the smell either. From the looks of the torn-up seats, the van had to be at least 10 years old.

She tried to move her arms but her body was securely tied to one of the two rear captain's chairs. She did, however, have a clear forward view of the front of her factory building, two blocks down the street. Thinking of the brutal slaughter of her friends, her chosen family, Gracie couldn't help but wonder again why they hadn't killed *her*. Was she to be ransomed, or did they have some special fate in store for her?

That thought quickly turned to shock as Mayor Linstrom's black Lincoln Town Car pulled up and parked on the street in front of her building's simple glass entrance. Behind him was a Chicago PD car and three news trucks. The other shoe had finally dropped as she realized what was happening.

She tried to yell, straining to break free, but she couldn't even make enough of a fuss to draw the attention of her captors.

The leader, who was in the driver seat, said something to the short man, who was sitting in the front passenger seat, who then handed the leader a small black device similar to a garage-door opener. Pressing a button, the leader seemed grimly satisfied when a small red light on the trigger mechanism turned green. Then he held his thumb over the trigger button as he watched the mayor step out of the rear passenger side of the Town Car. The mayor's assistant and the press crews followed him as he walked toward the entrance of the massive old building.

Leading the pack, making expansive gestures and talking over his shoulder as he went, the mayor placed his hand on the door handle. Then his assistant waved for his attention and he paused, let go of the handle, and started to walk away from the building.

Growling, the leader moved his thumb to the top of the trigger button. He leaned toward the windshield. Gracie tried to scream.

The mayor stopped 10 feet from the front door, and his assistant signaled for the news crews. They got into position as the Mayor appeared to make some sort of speech in front of her building. Thank God for politicians.

The short man slammed his hand on the dashboard and said something in an annoyed tone. The leader quickly replied, then all four men began speaking very fast to each other. She didn't know the language, but it was clear they were fighting over whether to hit the trigger right now, probably not knowing if the mayor would actually enter the building. Maybe their intel was bad, and any second now he would be done with his interview and would leave without ever entering at all.

Suddenly, the sirens on the top of the squad car lit up as both police officers exited the vehicle. The speed with which they did so suggested that they now knew something was seriously wrong.

As both police officers waved their arms and sprinted towards the mayor, some of the news crew scattered and some stayed put, ducking with their cameras pointed. Then one officer reached the mayor and grabbed him. His partner had his gun drawn and pointed upward as he scanned in all directions, ready to protect the mayor and his partner from whatever might occur. Just then, the redhead in the captain's chair next to Gracie pointed toward the windshield and yelled.

The leader, who'd been facing the rear of the vehicle at the time, arguing, swung around and saw the officers hustling the mayor away from the building. Spitting something that sounded like a curse, he pressed the button on his device.

An explosive pulse of energy from Gracie's lab shook the earth below the van and windows along the building's wall shattered outward. A bloom of fire rose from the site, then blanketed everything, igniting the vehicles, while the shock wave flipped them side-over-side like tumbleweed. In the blink of an eye, everything was engulfed in flames, and the combination of smoke and dust created a dense, dark cloud, cutting visibility to zero.

The van rocked as bits of debris starred and cracked the windshield.

8

Her best guess was that they'd been driving for at least eight hours. They hadn't been stopped as they fled the scene of the explosion, and by now had already traveled west out of Illinois, through the southwest corner of Wisconsin and southeast corner of Minnesota, where the interstate literally cut through hills and forest land. For the last several hours, they had been making their way through the long stretches of fallow harvested farmland and the timid greens and yellows of the soybeans and winter wheat, the intermittent stands of deciduous trees with their color-drenched fall foliage and imposing evergreens that blanketed the southern third of Minnesota along I-90. The last few road signs they'd passed had indicated that they would soon be crossing the state line into South Dakota.

The men had barely spoken a word to one another since the explosion not even acknowledging she was in the van. That would have to change soon if they didn't want her to soil herself. For hours, she had exhausted herself wondering how this had happened—in fact, what exactly *had* happened? Her mind worked the puzzle.

How could they even know the mayor was coming to visit her that day? They hadn't publicized the visit. The fact that her captors hadn't bothered to blindfold her meant they probably intended to kill her, but her still being alive meant they needed her for something.

But what?

She imagined herself reading some terrible propagandist's creeds at gunpoint in a live internet feed, begging for her life right before they executed her in front of the whole world. The corners of her eyes started to water and she had to blink back the forming tears.

She couldn't get caught up in what *hadn't happened yet*.

Instead, she turned her focus to what she knew and what she could deduce. The only thing she'd concluded was that this thing—whatever the hell it was—had been methodically planned. The confident execution of the strike proved that. From the second they'd entered her building to the moment they left the disaster site, there was zero confusion among them—save for a momentary lapse in the van right before the explosion. That notwithstanding, they *must* be following a script.

No one had eaten or drunk anything since the explosion. The only change was that the men in the front seats of the vehicle had put on Green Bay Packers hats and sunglasses when they were driving through Wisconsin, and when they crossed the border, they'd switched to Minnesota Twins caps—simple disguises, but effective enough.

She asked herself, *how many damn caps do they have?*

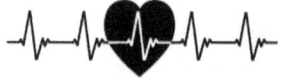

Minutes after crossing the border into South Dakota, they finally exited the highway onto a narrow dirt road. On both sides of the road, rows of mustard yellow soybean plants stretched as far as the eye could see—so far it almost seemed as if the plants reached up into the sky and touched the white, puffy clouds at the horizon, where sporadic beams of sunlight pierced random gaps in the overcast, tinting the sky in shades of violet, gold, and purple.

After a couple of miles of bumping down the road, they pulled up to an old farmhouse surrounded by massive oaks and evergreens. The density of the trees and their thick branches hid the house well. From a distance, one might think it was just another of the dozens of copses that dotted the soybean fields.

The redhead seated next to her pulled out a box cutter and jutted it playfully in her face, letting forth little wordless chuckles as she flinched and squeaked in response. Then he uttered something in a lascivious tone and cut her free from the captain's chair, leaving her arms zip-tied behind her.

The four men escorted her up the front porch. The typical white-painted, wooden turn-of-the-century farmhouse was well-built and had character, but showed signs of wear, mostly due to its age. It was a run-of-the-mill country home, complete with an unlocked front door with peeling apple red paint.

This front door opened into a shabby living room. The leader flipped on the light switch at the entrance, and a dark wood blade ceiling fan with a dome light spun to life, lighting a small, sparsely furnished space. They forced Gracie into a sitting position on the sofa along the wall, opposite an old tube-backed TV in the corner and a large picture window directly across from her. It was nearly dusk. The only things Gracie could see outside were the scattered trees that hid the home from anyone who didn't already know it was there.

The redhead joined her on the couch. Once again, he smiled that disgusting smile of his and uttered the same filthy sentiments in the same filthy tone. Gracie could see the dark metal butt of his gun poking out of his underarm holster, the instrument of death that had taken the lives of Alice and Steve earlier that day. How many other fragile existences had been extinguished by this thing?

The leader turned on the TV to crackle of static, and a minute later, a picture faded in. It was clear that there was no cable, as he played with the silvery V-shaped antenna in the rear of the television to clarify the snowy image. After a couple of attempts, the screen cleared up enough to pick up KDLT News on NBC out of Sioux Falls. The three men stood with their arms crossed, staring intently, waiting to see the results of their work.

It was no surprise to Gracie to see that there was special ongoing news coverage of the terrorist attack. The news anchor recapped the horrific details in scattershot newsworthy improv.

The scene cut to an aerial photo of Gracie's building. The entire structure had been cratered. All that remained was a stark pile of blackened, smoldering debris partially collapsed into the foundation.

As the shot continued, the anchor spoke off-camera: "Again, it has been confirmed that Chicago Mayor Charles Linstrom is one of eleven dead in the aftermath of the horrific explosion at the former site of Greentech Laboratories, a biotech start-up firm. And we do have word that the White House *has* confirmed this to be an act of terrorism. They confirmed it about one hour ago. We are as yet awaiting a statement by the President, we are told…"

Her mind raced at this point. Whoever knew her undoubtedly thought she was dead. She sprung back to attention when her own face—a photo taken from her company's website—flashed up on the screen.

"And we want to reiterate, we are getting word now that the woman you see here, Dr. Grace Green, the owner of Greentech, *was involved* in the plot. Sources at the CIA have confirmed discovery of a series of encrypted emails that reveal Dr. Green's ties to ISIS, and that the attack on Mayor Linstrom was in fact a coordinated hit. Apparently, the biotech firm was something of a front, a shell company created and operated, uh, for the sole purpose of maintaining a headquarters for ISIS. Excuse me, we're getting word that the CIA has traced all the funding for Greentech—am I reading this right? —yes, to a single source, an overseas account confirmed to originate from a known terrorist sponsor. We'll have more word on that as details emerge and more of course on this operative known as Dr. Grace Green…"

Cold washed over her as the blood drained from her cheeks. Gracie fought to not puke and pass out simultaneously. She felt the sting of salty heat in her eyes. Her mind clouded with pain, stabbing for answers.

9

ichaelson's Auto Salvage just outside of D.C. looked like the parking lot for the Apocalypse. The sun had begun to dip, tainting the abandoned heaps with the color of hopelessness.

Jaco Ivanov flicked a bit of lint off his cuff as he strode through the lot. What a wasteland. Hoods gaped at him like toothless mouths. He sneered back in disgust.

One vehicle stood out among the wreckages, parked within a stack of junkers as if they themselves had made room for it—a black Suburban with tinted windows, which flashed its headlights at once, as if he wouldn't have known otherwise that this was the car. Idiots. Why don't they just put an ad on Facebook?

He had barely lifted himself into the front seat and closed the door when Peter Rains started in on him.

"Are you out of your blasted *mind*? The mayor of Chicago? What the heck is wrong with you?"

"I thought it was executed flawlessly... as they say; *Problemy resheny*" Jaco returned. "Problem solved. You're welcome."

Rains could barely get the words out without spitting first. "Execut—You psycho! You orchestrated an ISIS terrorist attack on U.S. soil."

"I removed the mayor of Chicago, is what I did. Besides, there's oversight there."

Rains clenched his fists. "*Assassinated* him, you sadistic monster!"

Jaco pointed at the man's hands. "I'd watch myself there, friend. And the labor was free, by the way. Moreover, it gave cause to the explosion. If there was no cause, it would have drawn a different type of attention. Now, thanks to yours truly, the story is about a terrorist attack and not about the out-of-the-blue destruction of a promising new cancer drug company. Now, the leader of said company is a deplorable terrorist—ahem, not yours truly, thank you—and said company was a front. Personally, I think it was an elegant solution and I haven't heard one word of thanks from you, Peter."

"There are certain lines you don't cross." Peter said, jabbing a shaky finger at the air.

"You mean it's acceptable to murder your friend's competitors, but taking out any part of the good ol' boy network is off limits, yeah? I guess all those poor people who will suffer and die from cancer every year are within limits?"

"Linstrom was a good friend. And he was important to us."

Jaco tried not to smirk but couldn't hold it back. "Not anymore."

Peter stared at him for a long moment before the light dawned. "Oh, I should have known," he growled, his voice rich with loathing.

"Yeah, you should have."

"You *petty amateur*. You killed Linstrom for what he did to your special ops team in '10 when he worked for the White House."

"Like I said, an elegant solution."

"I thought you were a professional. Professionalism takes precedence over petty crap that happened years ago."

"Depends on your definition of petty." Jaco figured he had toyed with Rains enough. "Alright, let's get down to business. Have you seen the news lately?"

"Of course," Rains snapped.

"How about the intelligence flying throughout the agencies?"

"Yes."

"Okay, then. Let me ask you, is everything working perfectly?"

"That's not my point."

"It's *exactly* the point, Peter. Why are you so blind to the outcome? You can tell the powers that line your pockets that my methods work to everyone's advantage. Yes, including mine, but above all, to theirs."

Rains looked away, hand on the steering wheel, and let out a deep breath. "What's the exit strategy?"

"The terrorists are holed up at a farmhouse in South Dakota. They're going to execute the girl at five AM. You're going to get some intel across your desk. You send some of your CIA boys on the lead, then alert the FBI. We raid the house and kill everyone in the firefight 30 minutes before the FBI arrives. Terrorists killed, justice served, case closed."

"The girl?"

"She'll look like she was killed in the firefight alongside her fellow terrorists fighting for their cause—her time of death will be the same as her comrades. Again, everyone dead, no witnesses, not one clue leading to any other conclusion except terrorists caught and killed. Vengeance is ours, sayeth America, and the threat is gone. People will be rejoicing over their bacon and eggs, everyone gets their own apple pie."

"Anyone gets ahold of these terrorists or the girl before we do—"

"Relax," Jaco said with a dismissive wave. "We're a day from closing this deal, then we can all go to the islands for the extended vacation."

"You'd better be right. No one can know we killed Linstrom—and I mean *no one*."

"The execution will continue like clockwork. Guaranteed."

"You're smug and arrogant. You don't even see your biggest weakness." Rains shook his head.

Jaco tilted his head at the insult. "Relax, Peter. Have a drink. Have two drinks."

Rains twisted his face in disgust. "Cut that smooth-cat indifference act with me. It's fake and boring. Just don't mess this up."

"I go where the money is, Peter, just like you. The difference: I show my face when I come to pick up my check."

Peter conceded a nod, acknowledging Jaco's role in their arrangement. Then, brimming with self-congratulation, the men shook hands, and Jaco exited the Suburban.

10

The TV had been on all night: the same channel, the same horrific newsreel looping incessantly.

Gracie had heard herself called a terrorist so many times now, and with such conviction, that she herself had begun to question the reality of her life's work. After all, who invests all that money after just seeing a thesis paper with no lab research to back it up? Maybe terrorists? This was Rule Number One in medical research: a paper is just a paper. Don't get caught up in the brilliance of an idea. Without experiments and replication, great ideas are fake gems.

Plus, who was Bic but her biggest fan since she was five years old? He was her rock, but he wasn't a scientist. That man could and would convince anyone to believe in her on the basis of love alone.

Hunger gnawed at her stomach. Her throat was parched.

The leader had been looking at his watch constantly since about four AM. According to the TV news, it was almost five o'clock now, and he seemed more anxious than before.

Soon, she thought, someone would arrive for them. Some emissary from whatever head of state was responsible for the cell. She'd soon find herself living in captivity in some cave in the side of a Syrian mountain. The same ugly photo of her would be featured on the news daily—"the hunt continues…"— until the U.S. military hunted her down and killed her like the rabid dog they believed her to be.

The leader looked at his watch again and spoke sharply to his soldiers. The short man turned off the TV, then he and the leader exited the room, leaving her alone with the redhead.

Frowning furtively, this man removed the box cutter from his pocket. Gracie braced herself once again as she looked into the man's dark, soulless eyes. He showed no emotion. She had no doubt that he could slit her throat without a second thought.

The edge of the silvery blade would slice her like a scalpel. The man's eyes widened as he noticed her regarding the knife.

She looked at the front door, only 10 feet away from where she sat on the couch. Four quick strides, by her calculation. Her hands were zip-tied behind her back, which meant she'd have to spin around to turn the doorknob—if that was even possible.

From the other room, the leader barked out orders, his voice impatient.

The redhead turned and grabbed her by the shoulder. Apparently, all that her body had suffered in the last 20 hours had seriously diminished her reaction time. He thrust her forward. Her chest was now pressed against her knees. Her back and arms were completely exposed to him. Calmly, slowly, he moved behind her.

She heard the slice and snap and her hands were suddenly free. Bending around her and smiling, the redhead intoned that same lascivious bit of jargon he had before while brandishing the box cutter.

As he sat her back up, her arms dropped to her sides, full of the pins and needles of returning circulation. There were sharp pains in both shoulders from an entire night's worth of restraint. Instinctively, she raised her hand to pull the sticky gray duct tape from her mouth. Her eyes locked on the redhead, waiting to see what would happen. He smiled at her, retracting the box cutter's blade and placing it on the end table. He continued watching her. He wanted to see this, she thought. She'd try her best...

She began to pull the corner of the tape off the right side of her face, pausing when it stung. She peeled the tape completely off, and gasped air through her mouth for the first time in over 20 hours.

The man licked his lips, his eyes an emotionless sea of dead, light brown.

The other three men entered the room then. The leader had a large glass of water and a slice of white bread. The clean-shaven young man had a change of clothes for her: a pair of jeans, a red Stanford T-shirt, and shoes, all in her size. In fact, they were *her* clothes, collected from her condo. She couldn't believe it.

The leader handed her the bread and placed the glass of water on the end table. Gracie, still sitting on the couch, looked up at him, her eyes full of questions. He pointed at the food and motioned to his mouth.

She nodded quickly. A couple of bites were followed by a quick wash-down with the water, and she repeated the activity until both bread and water were gone. It could have been a five-course meal. Wonder Bread never tasted so good.

The leader grabbed her by the arm and pulled her to a standing position. At five-ten, Gracie was taller than three of the men, but about the same height as the leader. He said something in Arabic, and the man with the folded stack of clothes handed them to her. The leader gabbled at her, obviously giving her instructions to change.

When she took the clothes and started to walk toward the bathroom, the leader grabbed her arm roughly while pointing for her to stay put.

"Come on. You gotta be kidding," she said, strengthened by the slight relief of her hunger and thirst.

The man pointed at her and yelled again. He then looked at his watch pointedly. Gracie looked over at the news report. 4:55. She stayed put, eyes narrowed.

The leader spoke again with the same aggressive tone, and the clean-shaven man yanked off her white lab coat.

"Okay."

She quickly slipped out of her black slacks, grabbed the pair of jeans and slid them on sloppily. Whipped off her blouse and threw on the T-shirt. Sat down and put on her gym shoes.

The short terrorist grabbed her old clothes and shoes off the dingy floor and went into the other room with them as the leader looked at his watch again. Then he snapped out another order. Gracie didn't know the language, but she recognized the phrase. It had been etched into her brain forever: the same phrase the leader had barked out when he gave the order to kill first Steve, then Alice.

The redhead stood in front of her, pulled his gun from his holster, and pointed it at Gracie's head. Gracie couldn't find a trace of empathy in his eyes. It seemed like, to him, this was just a transaction. The other three men around her backed away, stepping toward the front door behind them both. Clearly, they were moving out of the way to avoid any blood and brain spatter.

There's no point in screaming, she told herself as she looked up at the only source of light in the otherwise dark room—the dome light beneath the ceiling fan. Looking at that brightness, she prayed she would be lucky enough to soon see her mother in Heaven. A small sound escaped her throat involuntarily. She hated that they heard it.

With the explosion of a loud gunshot, the light blinked out, and she wondered, for an instant, if she were already dead, as she felt a warm mist on her face. Not sure if she was wounded and still half alive, or completely dead and just having some sort of out-of-body experience, she watched what appeared to be happening in front of her in the pre-dawn grayness of the northern morning.

A shadow leapt across the room, huge and dark, with the stealth of a panther. There were nauseating sounds of bones being cracked and broken, and terrible sounds heaving from human chests. And then there was silence, punctured only by the dim sounds of the T.V. in the background.

11

The black Suburban tore down I-90 toward the South Dakota state line. Four highly-trained and battle-tested men rode in the vehicle as it cut through the cool predawn air. Jaco Ivanov rode in the front passenger seat, his teeth grinding in gleeful anticipation as he checked his watch. Just after five o'clock. The scientist should be already dead. All that was left now was to exterminate the terrorist vermin he'd brought into the country.

After receiving his 21 million-dollar payday, he'd be able to finish his negotiations for the castle he'd put an opening offer on last week. One of the wealthiest families in his parents' home country owned that magnificent property, but found themselves in dire straits, needing to sell. Owning it would give him and his only sister, who had moved back to Bulgaria, oligarch-like status. It was time for him to start living like a king. With this payday, he'd have the finest of everything for the rest of his life.

He and his men were dressed in full body armor, armed with an arsenal of weapons ranging from pistols to close-range combat machine guns and explosives. Jaco had made sure his team was prepared to take the terrorists down fast and hard. It wasn't his style to mess around in these situations.

At 5:03 AM, as scripted, Peter Rains' intel specialist at the CIA uncovered intelligence that revealed the location of the terrorist safehouse, and their plan to escape the country in a soybean container headed to the Middle East. Everyone needed to be dead by the time the FBI got there. Upon their arrival, Jaco and his team would surrender the mission to the Feebs and disappear into the morning sun, never to be seen again. By midday tomorrow, 21 million would be deposited into his offshore account. And not that he cared, but he and his team would be instant heroes for taking down the bad guys he had brought into the country.

He just loved the irony of his plan. It made him feel almost as special as the money.

12

The dome light flared to life to reveal the redhead, who had killed Steve and Alice, lying dead on the floor next to Gracie, a single gunshot wound drilled through his skull. The short terrorist who had killed Anna lay motionless with blood pooling around his head. The leader and the clean-shaven young man were on the ground, unconscious.

"*Unc?*" Gracie cried out, astonished. She scrambled to her feet and ran to him.

Bic hugged her. "There's blood in your hair." He pulled away. "You alright?"

"Everything…" she began. "Everyone is gone."

"You're safe now."

She fumbled around her words. "The world… thinks I'm a terrorist."

"Gracie…" he paused looking hard at the men he'd just taken down. "*These men* are terrorists. Someone went through a lot of trouble to set you up."

"How did you even *find* me?"

"I have resources," he said, turning away.

"These men… the money…"

He looked back at her. "Gracie, please, I can see it in your eyes. Whatever you're thinking, don't."

"Seriously, Unc, how did you find me in the middle of nowhere?" Any answer would have only prompted more questions.

Bic looked down at the emerald heart pendant he'd given her for high school graduation. He took it gently in his fingers.

"You remember when I made you promise you'd wear this always?" There was no fondness in his voice.

"Y-yeah… of course I remember."

He looked at her like he was waiting for something to click. "Always," he said. "You do wear it always. I know you do."

And the reality hit. "You gave me a pendant with a *tracking device* in it? *You lojacked me??*"

"To keep you safe." He shrugged.

She didn't have time to register the meaning of the act, feeling only betrayal. But she glanced around at the corpses strewn at her feet, and she clasped the pendant. It was more than a mere token of his love for her. It was life itself. A surge of raw emotion made her tremble.

"Unc, what are you not telling me? Oh my God, I can see the lies all over your face."

"I promise you, I had nothing to do with this, Gracie—why would I ruin our dream?"

One of the men on the floor started to come to. Bic put his massive leg on the man's chest to hold him in place.

She stared in disbelief. "I need you to *answer me.*"

Bic stared down at the writhing figure who struggled to speak.

"Was my company funded by terrorists?"

"No," Bic said firmly, staring at her with his white eyes.

"Where did all those millions of dollars come from?"

"Gracie, the money has nothing to do with terrorists, I promise."

"Then where'd you get it?

"There's nothing in this world more important to me than you. I would never hurt you." He kept dodging.

"This isn't a hard question to answer. Where did the ten million dollars come from?"

"The money came from me."

"Really. Your consulting business? God, how could I have been so stupid?"

"You want to know about my business?"

"I'm a wanted terrorist. I deserve the truth."

The man from the floor reached out for Gracie's leg.

Bic lunged down, immediately binding, then gagging, the man.

He looked up at Gracie. "I promise I'll tell you everything. Right now, we have to leave."

"I'm calling the FBI. I have to clear my name. You have to explain to them where the money came from."

He spoke sternly. "Gracie, I understand you're confused, but turning to the government would be no different than giving yourself back to the terrorists. Right now, as we speak, there are men on their way here, very bad men who are coming to clean this mess up. I'm sure of it."

"How could you possibly know this?"

"I've dealt with these situations before. They don't care about the lives, they just want to discredit you. Killing you is part of that."

She let out a slight chuckle of disbelief. "Unc, if this is really you, then you'll understand. I'm sorry, but you always taught me to be honest and tell the truth. It's always served me well, so that's what I'm going to do. You gonna try and stop me?"

He gently placed his hand on her arm. "Gracie, wait. Think about the news. How quickly the CIA leaked all that evidence to the news about you being a terrorist. There's only one reason they'd bother to frame you instead of just killing you with everyone else."

"You keep saying 'they'. Who the hell is 'they'?"

"People who want you dead because of what you have."

She thought for a moment. "The cure?"

"Terrorists don't frame people and give them credit for their acts of terror. They're usually pretty quick to claim that glory for themselves."

"What in the world am I involved in here?" She said as she sank down on the couch, her face in her hands. "How can you be sure your 'consulting business' isn't part of this?"

"I have nothing to do with any of this and neither do you—that's the point. Well, other than your cure. You have to trust me. This was all premeditated, planned down to the minute." His mannerisms quickened. "We have to go *now*." He bent down and finished binding and gagging the other two men on the floor.

"You do that awfully well," she said flatly.

He looked at her pleadingly. "I'll explain everything. Yes, I'm not exactly who you thought I was—but just in my job. I am and always will be your Uncle Bic who loves you dearly and wants nothing more than the best for you. And that's why we need to go."

"Please, let's just call the FBI and explain," she pleaded.

"They will lock you up and throw away the key, and that's the best case scenario. Worst is you die during transport to the field office."

She watched in disbelief as Uncle Bic yanked the two bound men from the floor by the backs of their shirts. It was like watching a guy heft his luggage.

"Running is what guilty people do," she said, rising.

"And survivors," he said. "Come on."

13

The black Suburban drifted down the narrow dirt road at about five miles per hour with its headlights off. In the distance, with the faint gray backdrop of the eastern horizon, Jaco could just make out, above the fields of soy, the clump of thick trees surrounding the terrorists' safehouse.

"Pull over right here," he said when they were about 200 yards away from the trees. He glanced at his watch: 5:25 AM.

The driver pulled off the road at a 45-degree angle. Soybean plants snapped and crackled under the tires as the vehicle slogged into the field, sinking a good four inches into the loosely-packed soil.

"We're gonna need our NVG's, boys," Jaco said quietly.

One of the men in the rear seat, whom Jaco knew only as Herzer, reached into one of the equipment boxes in the back of the Suburban for the night vision goggles. The men finished their prep by sliding high-capacity magazines into their sidearms and MP5 submachine guns, making sure each firearm had a round chambered.

The team stepped out of the vehicle into the thick, fuzzy-leaved plants. The vegetation was thigh high and reeked of wet earth. A slight breeze shook the leaves of the plants ever so slightly, giving them the appearance, in the eerie green of the NVGs, of a sea of hands waving in the air, like a stadium at a sold-out rock concert for aliens.

Two men exited the rear of the vehicle then worked quickly to throw a mesh camouflage net over the vehicle.

Jaco gave the signal to move toward the trees. They crouched low as they made their way toward the target. The only giveaway of their approach—if anyone had the senses to detect such a subtle hint—was the quieting of the grasshoppers jumping out of their paths as they cleared row after row.

At the tree line, Jaco got his first visual of the front of the house. He noticed two things instantly: the picture window of the family room, brightly illuminated from within, and the terrorists' nondescript white cargo van parked in the driveway.

Jaco put his fist up and signaled to the team: two in front, two to the rear. The men going to the rear of the house stayed within the coverage of the tree line as they moved toward their position. Jaco waited until they had time to take their places before gesturing the final man, the mercenary Herzer, forward. They slid to the rear of the van for coverage. As Jaco knelt behind the vehicle, he caught a glimpse of something from the corner of his eye.

He pulled out a mini-flashlight and pointed it at the dirt next to the van.

"What in the hell?" Herzer breathed as he crouched low behind the van, anticipating gunfire in response to Jaco's reckless action.

As quickly as Jaco had turned the light on, he turned it off. He glanced at Herzer and whispered, "There was another vehicle here."

"You sure?"

"Yes. Be ready for anything," Jaco said as he flipped off the safety on his MP5, prompting Herzer to do the same. They darted toward the front door with their weapons at port arms, ready to unload the 30-round magazines into anything that moved.

At the door, out of the line of sight of any of the windows, Jaco gave the signal. Herzer, who was crouched under the living room's picture window, pulled out a flash-bang grenade, pulled the pin, and paused—a lot longer than any sane man would have. Then, without looking, he heaved the grenade through the window above him.

It crashed through the window and landed with a loud metallic thud on the floor. An instant later, a deafening bang sent a pulse of light throughout the house. Jaco didn't even bother to see if the door was open as he drove his heel into it, knowing he had a good 5 to 10 seconds of complete blindness and disorientation on the part of his enemy for easy kill shots once he busted through.

There was nothing to shoot. One terrorist, shot through the head, hung by his wrists from the ceiling fan in the middle of the room, his feet dangling two feet off the floor. No sign of the others. *Not good.*

"The rest of the house is clear," announced one of the two men who'd come in the back.

"I thought this was gonna be an easy job," Herzer snarled as he looked at the dead terrorist hanging in the air, his MP5 still in a combat position as he scanned all possible points of attack. "Already dead is too easy or too hard."

"Sometimes you actually have to *earn* the money I pay you," Jaco snapped as he noticed a small, square piece of paper tucked under the dead terrorist's right bootlace. Scowling, he snatched it up. As he unfolded it, all he could think of was how badly he was going to hurt whoever had foiled his perfect plan.

In black ink, all caps, the note read: IT'S PORK CHOP EATIN' TIME!

"Cut the lights, now!" Jaco shouted as he flipped down his night vision goggles. "Exit as you entered." He let Herzer go ahead of him, just in case an ambush awaited. When it was clear nothing was going to happen to the merc, Jaco followed with extreme caution, his senses on high alert.

"Someone's running through the field to the north," one of the rear-entrance men reported by helmet radio.

"Track him down and take him out," Jaco replied. "We're right behind you."

He made his way quickly along the tree line in a zig-zag pattern, making sure to use every tree possible to block potential sniper fire. Herzer followed on his heels. Once he made it to the rear tree line, he peeked around the trunk of his cover and saw the pursuit: his men were running full tilt after a single man who had a 300-yard lead.

Close enough.

Jaco nodded to himself, then gave the order. "Clear to engage."

The chatter of automatic weapons fire rang out, even as the commandos continued to dash toward the fleeing man. He watched confidently as they quickly adjusted their fire to drop the runner.

He went sprawling like a bag of rocks. After he dropped, Jaco's men slowed to a jog, MP5s still braced against their shoulders and at the ready, advancing toward the location of the man they'd just hit.

"Status," Jaco said into the radio clipped to his shoulder.

"This guy's ankle was tied to a stake in the ground, with enough rope slack to run in a small circle. Threat is neutralized."

"Ignore him for now," Jaco replied, "There were four terrorists. We have two left and the scientist. Keep your eyes open."

"Behind those trees on the left," Jaco heard one of the men say through

the radio.

The men with their MP5's drawn walked toward the tree.

Approximately 20 yards from where they'd dropped the target, a massive form surged upward from within the camouflage of the soybean plants like an enormous wolf spider leaping from its den. Before the operatives could react, the large man simultaneously jabbed large combat knives into each man's gut. The massive man lifted them in the air, one in each hand, before dropping them to the ground. The whole spectacle was eerily silent, the smooth death of two men without disruption to the predawn quiet.

Jaco stared in awe. The two long knives gleamed in the waning moonlight like the fangs of some terrible beast.

The figure vanished, as silently as he'd appeared, almost leaving Jaco to wonder if it had been an optical illusion. There was another hired gun at the scene.

Jaco's lip twitched into a half smile. This was starting to get fun.

14

A thousand yards south of the farmhouse, concealed behind a massive pair of burr oak trees within a vast sea of soybean plants, Gracie sat in the old pickup, arms wrapped around her torso and shivering, her brain laboring to keep pace with her pounding heart.

None of this made any sense.

No more than a couple hundred yards away she had seen Bic just pop up and kill two men like he'd been doing it all his life. She loved Bic Green, her uncle.

But Bic Green was kind, her benefactor and biggest fan. This man... he was a murderer. What she saw stained every moment of family and closeness she had felt since her mom died. She hated this monster.

She couldn't handle this. Anger, fear, and a cold, calculating detachment took over.

She started the pickup and accelerated out from behind her cover, plants snapping and thumping as she plowed through.

She gazed through her rearview and saw Bic spring from the cover of the soybeans. He was now heading in a full sprint toward her, his mouth open, roaring something she couldn't hear.

Gunshots cracked into the passenger side of the truck. The window blew out.

Cutting the wheel to the left while ducking her body below the window line, she kept her body low, foot glued to the gas. Bullets popped and rattled into her vehicle.

She was going to make it to the road even if it killed her.

15

Bic sprinted at an angle to cut off the two gunmen's path to Gracie, a smoke grenade spewing thick clouds of gray in one hand, a blazing 9mm in the other. The gunmen retreated into the tree line surrounding the house, vanishing into the woody predawn shadows, and as Gracie continued to drive toward the road, they turned their fire on Bic. Only their muzzle flashes gave them away.

Mission accomplished, as far as he was concerned. Gracie was out.

He chucked the grenade to create a wall of cover while unloading the remaining rounds of his Glock 19. He reloaded while in full sprint, then set off another grenade and threw it into the tree line of the house. This new wall screened his path to the front of the property.

Random slugs shredded the plants around him. Judging from the spray, he could tell they were just guessing at his position. The problem was that he didn't have a good visual on them either. Moonlight was fading and the creeping sun on the horizon was in that stage where the bright gold line just made everything else darker. No use firing his weapon at this point. It would only give away his location.

Decision time: kill these men or catch up with Gracie? He knew she'd be heading back to Chicago, which was a huge mistake. And if he didn't find her in the next couple of hours, a score of backup men would find her. Killing these two men wouldn't make Gracie any safer.

He hurled his final smoke grenade in the opposite direction, hoping they'd figure he was creating coverage to gain entrance to the back of the house.

After back-tracking to the front of the house, he was able to enter the cargo van where the two remaining terrorists lay unconscious, still bound and gagged.

Bic twisted the ignition and floored it, glancing in the side mirror to see flashes of light from within the smoke. Bullets riddled the rear of the vehicle. The rear wheels spun hard before gripping the soil, and the van took off like half of hell was after it—Bic was the fool leaping where angels dare not tread. The pursuers unloaded their magazines. The metal projectiles ripping apart the back of the van as he drove off.

Two hundred yards up the road, he locked up the brakes, stopping next to the black Suburban. Extending his Glock out the window, he blew out the two driver's side tires, finished emptying his magazine into the front grill, then took off down the drive and onto the road.

16

Jaco tapped his knee in frustration. "We have a problem," he said into his encrypted cell phone.

"Is the girl dead?" Peter Rains replied dryly.

"What do you think?"

Peter was silent for a long moment, save for the thick sound of his breathing. "Where is she?"

"I don't know."

"You're telling me you couldn't hold on to that little girl?"

Jaco rolled his eyes. "She wasn't here when we arrived."

"Are you kidding me right now?" Rains screamed into the phone, "Tell me there aren't four terrorists and a scientist grocery shopping in Sioux Falls!"

"Easy does it, there, killer," said Jaco. "There's another mercenary involved. Someone got here before I did, killed one of the terrorists, and used another as a decoy to kill two of my men."

"And where is this other mercenary?"

Jaco ground his teeth, partly embarrassed and partly enraged. What he wanted to do right now was carve out Rains' heart with a spoon. "Not exactly sure. But he did leave us a nice note."

"Terrorists don't leave notes. What kind of clown show are you running over there, Jaco? I had your assurances this would be smooth."

"It was stuck in the bootlace of the terrorist hanging from the ceiling fan in the living room with a bullet in his head."

"Ceiling fa— You know what? I don't want to know. What did the note say? It wasn't about the mayor, was it?"

"No. It was about eating a pork-chop."

Several seconds passed with no response. At first, Jaco thought

Rains had finally ran out of responses, but then the silence grew longer, the breathing fainter.

"You said he killed two of your men?"

"Yeah, you know this guy?"

"Did you get a good look at him?"

Jaco visualized the large, dark figure standing while holding up two of his men with knives in their bellies. "Black guy. I think. It was dark. Huge though."

"This is DEFCON 5 bad."

"Who is he?"

"I knew that savage was still alive."

"Peter, stop tip-toeing around and tell me who this guy is so we can work out a plan here."

"It's the assassin who was responsible for all those billionaires a couple of years ago. He's known as the Black Ghost. This is on you Jaco. This was your plan."

Jaco sighed as he pinched the bridge of his nose, closing his eyes for a moment. He finally replied, "And I will fix it, Peter. What's his angle?"

Rains' voice cracked. "What do you mean, 'what's his angle'?"

"Did someone hire him to protect the scientist or get revenge for Linstrom?"

"We need more assets," said Rains. "You clearly can't handle this alone."

"Pardon me?"

"We're gonna need the Farmer."

"Are you kidding me??" Jaco felt his blood sizzle. "I'm not splitting my fee with that homicidal maniac."

"Hogs usually get slaughtered, Jaco, don't get greedy. But don't worry. I'm pretty sure you can get him for free. Just know this, you're not getting a penny if this ocean of crap isn't cleaned up."

Rains hung up without another word.

17

racie's heart raced as she sped east along I-90 in the old Ford pickup. A decent sized piece of a soybean plant, stuck inside the grill, rattled annoyingly in the wind. A tornado of emotion ripped through her insides. Horror, betrayal, loss, confusion, and anxiety swirled in the bewildering mixture. Unanswered questions screwed into her brain like some medieval torture device, ramping up her fear to primal levels.

Every inch of fear made her angry too. How many lies had there been?

She needed to maintain her cool. Every car on the road seemed like it was coming after her, every driver a potential shooter. A new horror reared inside her: As far as the world was concerned, she was a terrorist. Anyone who killed her would be celebrated as an American hero.

Pushing the boundaries of her self-control, she eased her foot off the gas pedal a bit and let the truck slow to the speed limit.

A tear rolled down her cheek. The most stable person in her life, her rock, was more than just a stranger—he was a killer for money.

She turned onto the exit heading north toward the Mayo Clinic's Rochester, Minnesota campus.

She stared out at the blossoming horizon, watching the rays of the rising sun light up the scattered puffy clouds in the sky ahead. Just moments before, they'd been dark and dingy. She used to enjoy scenes like this. Now, it was merely a reminder of the reality of her existence.

She would die, and nature would go on as if she'd never lived at all.

18

Back across the state line in Minnesota, just off I-90, Bic pulled into a deserted parking lot full of weeds. This was the abandoned hotel where he had instructed Gracie to hide and wait for him if, worst case scenario, somehow, they got separated. He was heartbroken over that look of disdain she had given him back in the farmhouse when he told her what he did to fund her company. With no sign of her, he feared she had pulled off at one of a hundred exits and called the authorities to plead her case. If she did that, their enemies would have her within the hour.

Bic pulled the heart shaped locket out of his pocket and looked at it. Uncontrollable anger grew within him, a fiery seed taking root in his chest. He tried to take a deep breath, but the thought of what was going to happen to Gracie if he didn't get to her first was more than his heart could manage. He was only a boy when he lost his mother. Unable to stop his father from beating her to death... If something happened to Gracie it was on him.

A noise grabbed his attention. He turned and looked with narrowed eyes at the two rats he had zip-tied in the back of the van. One of them was kicking the side of the van in an attempt to gain the attention of someone outside it.

"It's time to talk," he said, then stepped out of the van and walked to the back. He swung open the rear doors of the vehicle and pulled one of the men out by the hair.

The terrorist hit the ground jaw-first. Squirming, the man tried to say something through his gag. Bic grabbed him by the hair again and yanked him up to his knees. Something in his pocket rattled like a box of Tic-Tacs.

Bic suspected, considering the age differences in the two men, that the younger one on his knees, a skinny, sullen 20-year-old, might know some English. He was clean-shaven, his hands soft, his nails clean and cut. No signs of a committed life hiding out in caves—unlike the man in his forties lying in the back of the van. Bic was sure after one glance in the older man's eyes that he would take death before speaking.

Bic bent in front of the young terrorist. The young man with the bleeding jaw did not look up at Bic, even for a glance. Bic untied the gag and removed it from the man's face. The terrorist took a quick breath and spat a gob of pink spit.

Bic pulled out his pistol, then, in a slow mechanical motion, buried the cold black steel under his chin and used the barrel to raise his head until their eyes made contact.

He could tell by the man's expression that he'd glimpsed what so many of Bic's enemies had glimpsed right before their death: those intense, cold, piercing eyes. The eyes of something otherworldly—whatever evil his people feared—a djinn, a demon of the desert, or something far, far worse.

After a couple of seconds, Bic asked slowly, "Who brought you here?"

The man replied in a foreign language.

Bic smacked the bloody jaw with a flat palm. "English!"

The man spat out a string of words in the same language as before.

Bic grabbed him by the throat and lifted him to his feet. With the barrel of the pistol no more than a foot from the man's face, while squeezing his neck with his left hand, Bic moved the barrel and pulled the trigger, sending a bullet tearing into the van's metal, and scorching the side of the young man's face.

The man wailed.

"English," Bic growled as he pulled the hammer back, "or the next one is going through your eye."

The man again said something in the foreign language. With the precision of a surgeon, Bic shot the man with a glancing blow that tore a layer of skin off his upper cheekbone.

The scream was excruciating to hear.

"English, or we repeat this again." He sat the man on the rear bumper, still holding onto his throat. The terrorist whimpered like a kicked puppy.

Bic waited just long enough for the man to regain his senses so he could clearly comprehend what was about to happen next.

He pointed his nine at the man's left kneecap, placing the end of the barrel flush to his bone. Bic then cocked the hammer again, looking the terrorist in the face. "Should we try again?" he growled.

The young man's eyes darted to the rear of the van. The older man glanced at the younger as he said, "Allahu Akbar," which seemed to instill a fear even greater than getting shot in the kneecap.

"So be it," Bic said, and rattled off two shots into the older man's chest. He pressed the smoldering barrel right between the young man's eyes, "An English word is the only thing that can save your life."

The man stared blankly at Bic.

"Who brought you here?"

The man smiled defiantly.

"What about the girl?" Bic cocked the hammer.

The man spit at Bic.

Bic let go of the man's throat. He lowered the gun, pulled up part of his shirt, and wiped the spit off his face. When he was done, he raised the gun again.

And put a bullet into the man's skull.

After searching the men, he dumped the bodies onto the cracked tarmac and headed back toward the van.

He speed-dialed Hawk.

"What's shaking, m'man?"

"Hawk, I need your help, ASAP."

"Are you sure, brother? I'll have to let the priest go."

"Black ops guys are involved, and they're going to kill Gracie if they get to her first. My father doesn't matter right now."

"Where is she?"

"She took off her pendant."

"Not good. I'll call Tony."

"Let me know what he can find out," Bic said as he pulled back onto I-90 and headed towards Chicago.

19

Gracie parked on the street in front of the Jacobson Building on the northeast edge of the Mayo Clinic's Minnesota campus at Rochester. A new structure, its high-tech two-story architecture separated it from several of the brown brick massive structures of the main hospital. It shone in the early morning light like a gem.

Inside the building were four state-of-the-art proton beam treatment rooms capable of operating an amazing 12 hours a day. In the fight against cancer, the proton beam was developed as an alternative to traditional X-ray radiation treatment, which not only killed cancer cells but also the healthy cells in front of, and behind, the tumor. These machines made older radiation therapies look like a cave man's club.

Before the proton beam, an oncologist's chief concern was how to balance killing cancer cells and preserving the healthy ones. And up to now, standard operating procedure dictated the following: Due to the potential of extensive damage, especially when organs were in the line of fire, the X-ray radiation dose had to be reduced below the optimal levels required to kill the cancer cells. Now, with proton therapy, most of the energy to kill cells can be released within the tumor, which allows the doctor to deliver higher effective doses.

Walking into the spacious main lobby, her head down, Gracie immediately turned right and grabbed a surgical mask that was at the entrance for patients whose immune systems had been beaten down by chemo, for even a common cold could kill them.

Behind the surgical mask, she went up to the front desk. "I need to see Dr. Clink,"

The receptionist clacked away on her keyboard. "Do you have an appointment?"

"No, I'm an old friend and only in town for a few hours."

"I'll see what I can do. What is your name?"

Gracie realized using her real name was risky, as it could be in the news. "Rosita Stanford."

The receptionist walked back into the facility.

She hoped he would remember the name. Back at Stanford University, she, Thomas, and Anna had dubbed their study group "the Stanford Dance Trio," with each taking a different name. Anna was Marcella, Thomas was Paco, and Gracie was Rosita.

Five minutes later, Thomas came out into the lobby, scanning the room excitedly. Gracie, skulking in the corner, her head turned away from other patrons in the waiting room, took a cautious step forward and raised one finger in the air to get his attention.

"Gracie?" Thomas said with eyes larger than saucers. "You're all over—"

"I didn't know where else to go." She interrupted. "None of it is true."

Thomas slowly looked in both directions, thinking quickly. "Go to the chapel, you can wait there privately. It'll be empty. I'll be there as soon as I'm done."

Gracie took off toward the chapel. She took one look back at her old friend, who watched her for a moment, then turned to go back to work.

20

Gracie sat in the front row of the chapel, head bowed in apparent prayer. A woman came and sat in a pew several rows behind her. She could hear the woman whimpering, asking God to heal her husband. The chemo was too much...

It wrenched her heart.

She had the answer to this woman's prayers, to the prayers of so many that had sat in these pews for the same reason. And someone was desperate enough to ruin her life in order to stop it. No, they weren't just ruining her life, they were blotting it out entirely with indelible marker.

Here in this chapel, she had a modicum of hope. With Thomas, she would have another colleague's voice to go to the authorities to vouch that she wasn't a terrorist, but a respected research scientist.

A flicker of movement caught her attention. A man was walking toward her. She kept her head down, made sure her mask was in place. The figure turned into the pew behind her. He leaned forward, hands clasped in prayer. He smelled like sandalwood.

"Think your prayers will be answered?" he said, his breath on her neck.

She turned her head slightly to the side. His captivating gaze froze her as if he was an angel that had been sent down to save her.

"Gracie Green?"

A hot flush inflamed her collar.

Something appeared next to her head. An open wallet, and a shiny badge. "I'm Agent Quinn, Miss Green. FBI. Please don't run."

Gracie looked up as two more agents appeared before her, rifles pointed. She snapped her head around, the agent stared at her with baby blue eyes. The woman who'd been praying somewhere behind her was gone. Two more agents stood at the exit of the chapel weapons at the ready.

"You can't," she stammered.

"What?" said agent Quinn. "You're not claiming religious sanctuary, are you?"

"Exactly," she said. "You can't arrest me in a church."

"It's not a church, it's a chapel. And yes, we can. The U.S. Government doesn't recognize religious sanctuary. Will you please step out of the pew, Miss Green?"

"Please," she said, her voice breaking. "I'm innocent!"

"Not my call. That'll be up to the judge. I don't want to force you, Miss Green." Agent Quinn stood up. "I can tell you though that innocent people don't run. Turning yourself in right now peacefully would be a start to showing us that innocence."

"You have to believe me, people are trying to kill me!"

"I don't doubt it. You'll be a lot safer if you come with us." He took her by the arm and stood her up. Out came the cuffs. "Gracie Green, you're under arrest for murder and conspiracy to commit acts of terrorism against the United States of America."

"The terrorists killed my team and destroyed all of my research!" Gracie said through tears as the cuffs snapped onto her wrists. "We cured cancer!"

Agent Quinn guided her out of the chapel. "You have the right to remain silent..."

Outside the church, Thomas was standing next to an agent with a note pad.

"Thomas, tell them you know me, tell them about the research Anna and I showed you last year! Please help."

Thomas looked at her with sorrow in his eyes. "Gracie, how could you?"

It wasn't sorrow in his eyes. It was betrayal.

"Thomas... no. Please, think it through. You of all people know this is all a lie."

"Let's go ma'am." Quinn walked her out of the building.

The place looked like a police patrol car parking lot. Helicopters were hovering above, and news vans were beginning to assemble. Two Suburban SUVs pulled up over the sidewalk in front of them.

"I don't know what's happening! I was framed! The mayor was coming to help me get into human FDA trials. You have to believe me!"

Quinn said nothing as he guided her into the truck.

Gracie looked over her shoulder, trying to lock eyes with him. "I can prove it. I've been submitting patents for months. My company isn't a front. *We found a cure!*"

Her gaze into the agent's eyes was long and confusing; there were all sorts of different energies happening there, almost as if he badly wanted to believe her; but then hardness overcame him. "It's really sick to prey on people's hopes. You have no idea."

The agent shoved her into the truck and, as he was preparing to close the door, she saw the agent next to her—and he looked like a stone-cold killer.

She leaned forward. "Agent Quinn!"

He turned, his face cold.

She said, softly, "Someone you love has cancer. Who is it?"

Quinn's eyes narrowed and his jaw clenched.

Fully committed, reading his mannerisms, Gracie continued, "The statistics bear me out. Odds are, someone you love has cancer or has been taken by it."

Quinn regained his composure. "Your mind games won't work on me, Mrs. Green."

"It's *Miss*. And there are no games. Someone is trying to frame me as a terrorist and stop my cure from seeing the light of day." She folded her hands around his, not wanting to let go. In her heart, she knew this man had a legit reason to help her. She pulled him close to her and whispered, "I promise you, I can help. They haven't destroyed everything."

An agent broke them apart and slammed the door shut on her before Quinn could respond.

21

Bic was driving through Wisconsin on his way back to Chicago when his phone rang. It was Tony.

Bic knew that if anyone would know what was happening behind the scenes, it would be his old friend Anthony Parelli, the man who had arranged all his jobs during his career as an assassin. Just as professional athletes had agents, so did elite killers. But with an elite killer, if your agent messed up, you'd wind up dead, so the bonds in these relationships ran really deep. Plus, it didn't hurt that they'd also fought side-by-side in Vietnam.

"Find anything?" Bic asked.

"Yeah. Bad news. The Feds picked her up about an hour ago at the Mayo Clinic in Rochester."

Bic clenched the steering wheel, "Are they going to..." He couldn't bring himself to finish.

Parelli picked up on it. "I wouldn't think so. What I heard, the FBI is clean. It's the CIA we have to worry about. If they get to her, well, I don't even want to speculate."

"Do you know where they're taking her yet?"

"ADX Florence, a federal supermax prison in Colorado. A little over the top pretrial—but hey, crimes against the country, right?"

"Can we get her out?" Bic asked, already analyzing and planning.

"Welll..." he drew the word out in a way that didn't inspire confidence, "they call it the Alcatraz of the Rockies. It's tighter than a clam with lockjaw."

"There's gotta be some way."

"I'm working on seeing who might be friendly to us. An Aryan Brotherhood leader is housed there. I supply them with a lot of their weapons, so I'm seeing if they're willing to work with us."

"Did you just suggest enlisting the help of Nazis to get her out of prison?"

"Enemy of my enemy, Bic." Parelli's voice wavered. "Look. All I'm saying is that we need to do it from the inside."

Bic blew out a frustrated breath. "The CIA will get to her before we can figure that out."

"That's what I'm afraid of. Not sure what they're planning, but I'll let you know if I hear anything."

"Can you get me hired on there as a guard or a cook or something? Or how about getting me in as a prisoner?"

"I can do a lot of things, but that ain't happening."

"Why *not?*" Bic's blood was heating up fast.

"It's a supermax, Bic. As an employee, you're under constant surveillance, and I mean constant. As a prisoner, you're locked in a cell for 24 hours a day, and after six months of good behavior, they'll let you out of your cell in shackles for an hour a day while guards walk around you. Even you can't beat that."

"I'll figure something out," Bic said, and hung up the phone.

It was more than an idea, it was a vow.

22

A lot had happened to Mack Maddox in the past two years, most of it pretty amazing—but the dining room table covered in medical supplies was a constant reminder of something terrible.

The most miraculous thing that had happened was cradled in his arm: his four-month-old daughter, Samantha. It had all happened so fast it had nearly blinded him. But no one ever made him feel the way Caroline did, and after all they'd been through together, their bond was unbreakable.

Caroline was upstairs, resting. He sat on the living room couch of their three-bedroom bungalow in Glendale, just outside L.A., feeding Samantha her eight PM bottle. It was just starting to get dark out, and the temperature was finally dropping—though they kept the windows and doors closed, favoring A.C. as well as keeping out the smell of a wildfire burning in to the north.

He stared into the girl's eyes. They were her mother's, huge and jade-colored.

He couldn't help but replay his favorite love-filled moments with Caroline while gazing into Sam's eyes. With all the complications Caroline had had over the last year, Mack was no longer a field agent, having instead put in for a nine-to-five desk job at the Bureau. He missed the adrenaline rush of fieldwork, but his responsibilities had changed, and he'd made a promise not to put himself in harm's way.

When Sam began to cry, Mack put her over his shoulder, trying to pat a burp out of her as he sang her go-to calming song: *"You are my sunshine, my only sunshine, you make me happy when skies are gray…"*

Sam belched like a tiny 40-year-old beer drinker.

"That's my baby girl," he said.

Someone knocked at the door.

"It's open," Mack said loudly, expecting his father.

Bic Green entered through his front door and strode into the living room in a surreal, seemingly slow-motion clip, wearing those same damned sunglasses he'd always worn, holding a leather binder under one arm.

Instinctively, Mack shielded Samantha and backed away from Bic, who rapidly closed the distance. Mack ran out of room as he back-pedaled as far back as he could, ending up against a desk at the back wall.

"I often wondered if you'd come back to clean up the loose ends," Mack croaked—with his hand behind his back—as he slid open the top desk drawer.

Bic shook his head once, "I've never left any loose ends, Mack."

Mack finally found what he was looking for in the drawer. Gripping the 9mm SIG Sauer tightly, Mack swung the weapon around his body and pointed it at Bic.

The weapon didn't even faze Bic.

"This time there are real bullets in it," Mack said, as he pointed the actual gun he had shot Bic with two years ago, when everything had gone down at the Ralston Templeton estate.

Bic sat down, tossing the dossier on the coffee table. "I'm here for your help. Put that away."

"You got a lot of nerve showing your face here," said Mack. Samantha began to wail in his arm.

"*Get out of my house,*" Caroline shouted coarsely from the stairs. She was standing there in her pajamas, holding a gun in one hand and grasping the banister with the other. She looked different. Her cheeks were sunken and there were dark circles below her eyes.

Bic turned to Caroline, hand still on the table. "I have an offer for your family."

"Your filthy money's no good here," Caroline barked. Her hand trembled as she spoke, her arm struggling to hold the weapon up.

Bic stared at Caroline's obvious frailty. "Not money. I have the cure."

"What are you talking about?" said Mack.

"Get out," Caroline hissed.

Bic shook his head. "You've seen the news. Gracie Green from Greentech?"

"What about her?" Mack asked, drawn in despite his best efforts.

"She's my *niece*." Bic took a deep breath. "When you and I met at Ralston's, Gracie was graduating from Stanford with her Ph.D. in biomolecular chemistry. This is her dissertation." Bic held up the binder.

"Easy," said Mack. Samantha wailed in his arm.

"It's alright. See?"

Mack, with Caroline covering Bic, quickly placed Samantha in her playpen, where she immediately stifled her tears and busied herself with a dog on wheels.

"Just hear me out," said Bic. He held up the binder again. "This describes a new molecular approach to curing cancer. This was her life mission since she was a little girl. She's been curing cancer in mice for months. The FDA has denied her request to begin human trials three times for unwarranted reasons. We've both dealt with evil people in the past who will stop at nothing—"

"Enough," said Caroline. "Like hell, I'm going to let you get him killed for some false hope while carrying out your agenda."

"Mack," Bic said softly, "she's in ADX Florence, and they are going to *kill* her if we don't do something about it. Some very powerful people don't want this cure to see the light of day. They killed the mayor of Chicago and Gracie's research team, wiped out her company, wiped out all her research. All that's left is Gracie. And they're destroying her name and next they'll remove her completely. And when she dies, so does the cure."

"Mack, there *is* no cure. This man is a killer. We both know it," Caroline said. At that moment, she stumbled on the stair, losing her balance and dropping her weapon.

Bic, closer than Mack to the stairs, reacted instantly. He dropped Gracie's thesis and darted toward Caroline, leaping up three steps at once, catching Caroline in time to break her fall.

Mack closed the gap, and had his gun pointed between the big man's eyes.

"You okay?" asked Bic.

"I'm okay, thank you. I need to sit."

Bic helped Caroline to the couch with Mack still tracking him.

Caroline closed her eyes and put a hand to her head. "Mack, put the gun down."

"Not happening."

Bic turned to Mack. "I'm not asking you to break the law, or kill anyone, all I'm asking is for you to keep Gracie alive until I can flush the truth out. They are going to kill her. Everything I have done is in service of her finding that cure."

"What the hell am I supposed to do about that?"

"Go through your channels. You have pull in the bureau. Have Gracie moved under your local office's protection before the CIA kills her."

"Supposing I do. Then what?"

Bic looked down at Caroline. "You'll keep hope alive, not just for you, but for the world."

Mack's eyes glistened as he stared at his wife. "No, no. There's another angle to this. It's not adding up. That girl is a terrorist. I think we've heard enough."

"Mack," said Caroline, "enough."

"You heard the woman," said Mack. "Get out."

"That's not what I meant."

Bic nodded. "I'll leave. But I'll leave Gracie's thesis. And one more thing. There's a woman by the name of Cecilia Graham. Her daughter was Dr. Anna Graham, who worked with Gracie. Cecilia was dying of cancer. My guess is she's not any longer."

Bic walked to the door. "The cure does exist Mack. Save Gracie and you'll keep hope alive."

With that, Bic Green walked out the front door.

Mack lowered his weapon. His wrist was throbbing. He looked at Caroline on the couch. She had a funny look in her eye.

"What?"

"You know damn well what."

"You're not telling me you believe that crap, do you?"

She pointed to the dissertation. "We know people who can give that thing a proper evaluation."

Mack took a steady breath and sat down next to his wife. She was everything he'd ever wanted in a woman, and she was here, and his. And she was wasting away.

She put a frail hand on his cheek. "I like it when you don't shave."

He smiled, took her hand and kissed it.

That night, while sitting in a glider chair in their master bedroom, Mack rocked back and forth as he silently prayed at Caroline's bedside. Sam slept in one arm, his nine-millimeter rested in the other hand, and Gracie's thesis paper lay in his lap as he continued to pray for his wife.

She seemed to be sleeping peacefully, but the thought of what was happening inside her body made him want to scream out loud. A massive invasion was taking place as her body fought the relentless adversary that had spread through her. The dormant tumor had been sleeping inside her for years, hiding in her sternum of all places, well before they had ever met; but last year it had exploded into metastasis. Maybe it was the stress of the pregnancy, but there was no way he could ever regret the creation of the tiny form he held cradled in his left arm. Nor would he ever give up hope for Caroline; but because the cancer had spread to several major organs before she could start her treatment, there was nothing much they could do. She was stage four by the time she gave birth.

She was so stubborn, he thought; she'd been just two months pregnant when they discovered the cancer. She'd had a 50-50 chance then, assuming they terminated the pregnancy and started aggressive treatment; but their child had no chance at all if she did, and she couldn't bear that thought.

Just like that, the decision had been made; and while Mack hated the consequences, he respected the hell out of his wife. Even though her hair didn't shine like it used to, and her piercing green eyes were always tired and bloodshot now, all he saw was the stunner he'd fallen in love with back at the Bureau.

23

Gracie Green could feel the maximum security all around her as she sat in the interrogation room at ADX Florence, an administrative maximum federal prison in Colorado. Shackles bound her ankles and wrists and thick, reinforced steel doors blocked her exit. She hadn't seen a window to the outside since she stepped foot into the facility. And in her heart was the terrible feeling that this was the type of place prisoners never left.

Leaving Bic to go to Thomas, a respected colleague, for help was a mistake. She knew that now. She'd thought one of the few colleagues she'd trusted to share her research with outside her lab would have come to her aid. Instead, he'd bought into the terrorism line.

Two hours later, an agent from the Department of Homeland Security entered the concrete-walled room. He was the G-man from central casting: a standard six feet tall, short, slick hair, athletic build. He placed a manila folder full of paper on the steel table as he pulled his chair from its position across from Gracie over to her right side and sat. His expression was pure psychological torture: A friendly smile.

"Gracie, I'm Agent Jim Kessinger. Can we get you anything? Water?"

"Water would be nice."

The agent nodded to a burly guard blocking the door, who opened it and whispered something to the outside.

Kessinger opened the folder and began spreading the papers out on the table.

"Those are my patents, right?"

"They are," the agent said, reading through them.

"They prove I'm telling the truth."

"Well, let's talk about that."

"I'm not a terrorist."

The agent looked up from the patents and placed his folded hand on top of them. "Gracie," he said, looking her in the eye, "the only way we're going to get anywhere today is if you start telling the truth. Now, I need you to help me to understand why you're here today."

"I don't know," she said.

He placed a flat palm on the patents. "These applications were rejected as non-patentable subject matter. You see what I'm saying. So, that's not a question. There is no question in my mind that you're not who you say you are. I need you to help me to understand why."

"It's... my cure..."

The agent shook his head slowly. "Gracie, you and I both know there's no cure."

"That's not true, I have proof..." Gracie slouched, remembering that all the proof she had was in her office.

"Greentech doesn't have any issued patents on file with any U.S. jurisdiction."

"I'm not a terrorist."

He grabbed the stack of paper from the file. "Gracie, we have folks who go over stuff like this, and they went over it with a fine-tooth comb. I think you know what they found when they did."

"What did they find?"

"Gracie...?"

"I want to know."

"Gracie, you know what they found. These are nothing but a bunch of jumbled thoughts and proof-sources cut and pasted from other scientists' published work on the Internet. It's double-talk."

"That is not true."

"Gracie, I understand why it's upsetting. Maybe you had some other notions about where this would get you. Maybe you were just used by someone. I don't know unless you tell me."

"I... don't know what to tell you."

The detective leaned back and took a deep breath. "Who recruited you, Gracie?"

With tears welling, Gracie shook her hands. The chains rattled like a ghost. "*I am not a terrorist!* They executed my friends and were about to kill me until Bic saved me!"

"Who's Bic Green?"

Her chin fell to her chest. "I already explained. He's my uncle," she said softly.

"Gracie…" His voice was even softer.

She didn't answer.

"Gracie, look at me. You know there is no Bic Green. The man who was your guardian after your mother died was named Forrest Jenkins and he died two years ago."

"What?"

"Gracie, I'm getting tired of this game you're playing."

"Forrest who? I don't even know who that is! Bic Green is my uncle."

The agent shook his head while she spoke.

"Gracie, these patents are garbage, and you know it. Your so-called research is garbage. Your uncle is dead. Come on. Do you think I'm stupid?"

"No, I don't think—"

His voice rose. "Then why are you treating me like I'm some kind of idiot? Because you're a fake scientist? A kid who grew up in the ghetto with something to prove? Always taking crap because she wasn't who she thought she was? You wanted to be a superstar, didn't you?"

"No, stop—"

"You're a smart girl, there's no doubt about that. But you're a little too big for your britches, you know what I mean?"

"That's not true."

"You're not too big?"

"No, that's not—"

"Then why don't you come clean with me?"

Her voice broke. "Can't you see what's happening? Someone's erasing my whole life, changing it to make me look like a terrorist!"

"Why would they do that, Gracie? Why would someone want to go through all the trouble to make you, a little scientist, look bad?"

"My cure," she said defiantly.

Again, the shake of the head. "Isn't that just another example of you thinking yourself more important than anyone else?"

"Not true."

"You couldn't get FDA trials. The federal government knew your research was faked."

Gracie looked into the man's eyes. A realization took hold of her.

Not being able to get into the FDA trials, all those roadblocks she thought were just part of the tough path to success, they were more than that.

"Somebody framed me," she stated flatly. "Someone doesn't want me to cure cancer."

The man scoffed with a smile. "Come on, Enough."

Gracie shook her head. "No. There are six multibillion-dollar pharmaceutical companies that derive 50 percent or more of their revenue from their cancer drugs."

"Oh, I see. This is the Big Pharma conspiracy."

"You want to put it like that? Fine."

"And what's next? The lizard people from Neptune are pissing fluoride in the reservoirs?"

Gracie sat back and turned her head. "I'm not saying another word."

"You know, I misjudged you. I looked at you and thought, here was this girl who had to fight for everything in life. Had nothing but her brain. And she did get somewhere with that brain, but something went terribly wrong. But you know what, Gracie? I was mistaken. You know what I think? I don't think you have an ounce of brainpower working in your favor. I think you really are that cold-blooded terrorist—"

"No—"

"Anti-American. Someone who hates our country because she has to blame everyone but herself for her own shortcomings."

"The Constitution allows me due process."

"You're a cold-blooded terrorist."

"I'm entitled to my rights as a citizen."

"What was next on the agenda? A plane-load of passengers and a box cutter?"

Gracie leapt to her feet, causing Kessinger to jump back in his seat and the burly guard to rush to his defense, restraining Gracie.

"It's okay, Jim. I've got it from here," Agent Quinn said as he walked into the room.

Jim shot a death glare back at Gracie as he exited the room, muttering, "Feebs."

"I have nothing else to say," Gracie snapped.

Quinn smiled and held up his hands. "I come in peace." He sat down in Kessinger's chair. "I like you better without the dried blood and skull fragments in your hair."

His light blue eyes drew her in. "Yeah, they were nice enough to let me shower without shackles"

Quinn looked at the file of worthless patent applications on the table. "Gracie, I gotta level with you. This doesn't look good."

"Bic said they would frame me, but I didn't want to believe him."

"I read the report of the CIA agents first on the scene, and they killed two of the terrorists and said two escaped in the van, and you in a pickup truck, after two of their men were ambushed and killed. They said nothing about another man. From your description, this other man doesn't sound like the type that someone would forget easily."

"If that's what the CIA report said, then they're lying. I saw Bic shoot one of the terrorists right in the head just before they were going to execute me."

"Gracie, you have no proof. Even your uncle Bic—by the way if you're talking about your legal guardian, his name was Forrest Jenkins—he doesn't even exist. Everything you've said up until this point has been a lie and we both know that."

Gracie glared at Quinn, thinking that there must be something, before long it hit her. "If the CIA killed the two terrorists, then how in the world did I have the brains of one of them sprayed all up in my hair? You saw the nasty matter yourself. That *proves* they're lying."

"At 5:09, we received intel on your location, and we have the satellite images of a pickup truck and a white van leaving the farm after the CIA got there. You claim 'Bic'—which we know there is no Bic—left in the van. If so, the CIA operatives would have seen this other man, and so would the satellite."

"They are flat out lying," Gracie spat. "Quinn, people need me, all these suffering people with no hope—you have to believe me! *I have the cure.*"

"Where is this cure?"

Here Gracie paused, wanting to say something to Quinn, but not willing to show all her cards just yet.

Quinn leaned in and spoke with a soft sincerity as his eyes became moist with an awful pain. "Gracie, there's no one who wants to believe you more than me."

"Then try to prove me right."

"Okay, I'll bite. We're going to test the DNA on your clothes, but if this doesn't match, there are two terrorists on the loose. I need you to give me something in return. Fair?"

After a long stare, Gracie nodded. Quinn nodded back, then left the room.

24

From high above, the land plots in central Iowa look like a puzzle made of nothing but square and rectangular pieces of only a few varying sizes. Within each piece is a plot of farmland. If one were to descend upon one of them, one would see stalks of corn six feet high stretching out in a vast sea of wind-waving green. During September's cooling days, and the beginning of the corn harvesting season in Iowa, the ocean of stalks soon to be cut down waved in the gentle winds. The cutters will have a six-to-eight-week window in which to do it. Then their yellow gold will be sent all over the world.

Brad Thomson—the name he bought to start over—knew this as well as anyone. He crooned along to Hank Jr.'s *A Country Boy Can Survive* as he drove his John Deere combine with its eight-row corn header attached. Honey and a greenish floral smell filled the humid air, and he wiped at his neck with a do-rag.

He had bought the secondhand machine along with the modest farm six years ago. He liked the farming life, having grown up in it along with his brother, whom he called Kid, and he enjoyed the fourteen-hour days. He needed the long days to keep his mind occupied.

Brad sang decently in tune as the combine's header munched the massive rows of corn like some huge metal Pac-Man. To his left were the 200 acres he'd already mown down, and to his right were about 700 more waiting to be harvested. Short of any maintenance issues, he'd be done with the harvest in about two and a half weeks.

A disturbance in the stalks caught his eye. There was a straight line being cut through the field about 100 yards away—coming straight toward him. He'd heard stories of kids driving trucks through the fields for kicks, but this seemed unlikely considering it was early afternoon. Then the straight line broke into three lines. One was still coming right at him, the second going to his rear flank, and the third toward his front. From his past, he recognized this for what it was: a military tactic.

Brad downshifted the combine, placed it into park, and reached behind the seat. He kept an old camo backpack there, filled with goodies. He turned up the song and sang it loud and proud as he pulled the pin on a smoke grenade, opened the tractor door, and dropped the grenade to the ground. The white cloud continued to spew out of the grenade, quickly creating ample cover as one Humvee came to a stop with 15 yards of corn between them. Four men in Desert Storm fatigues jumped out of the vehicle with MP5 and laser sights turned on. The other two vehicles smashed out of the corn, then cut their wheels to a quick stop, one in front and one behind the combine.

Twelve men in total, flanked from three sides, pointed their lasers into the dense fog consuming the tractor and combine.

"Federal agents. We want to talk to you," yelled one of the men, cautiously standing behind his Humvee... As if anyone ever sent three heavily-armed assault squads "just to talk."

We'll talk then, thought Brad Thomson. And he grabbed his camo pack and leapt out onto the ground.

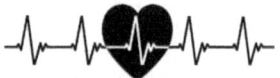

From 200 yards away, Jaco Ivanov watched his men through his sniper scope. The white cloud rolled towards them.

This wasn't going to be pretty.

Being the eyes of the operation, he spoke into his radio and into all his men's earpieces: "Roll back, you're losing visibility fast." Then muttered to himself, "Jesus. Dunces."

The difference between a killer and an agent is that an agent is trained to assess then react. It is at their core. Killers simply act, and with lethal intent.

Before his men could react, he saw three small black balls fly out of the cloud, one after another, right toward the vehicles. When they hit the ground, three explosions boomed out in near-unison.

Instantaneously the vehicles, and several of the men who'd occupied them, were engulfed in flames.

The few that survived the explosions opened fire at the smoke cloud. Bullets spattered in all directions. Some of it was friendly fire. He yelled into his radio to cease fire as he witnessed them picking each other off.

After several attempts to get the men to stop, finally things went silent.

Jaco barked out, "Get into the corn and form a perimeter!"

25

Brad quietly hummed to himself to keep his anger in check. He wasn't sure how they'd found him, but he sure didn't appreciate them coming onto his property to tie up their loose ends. He loved this farm, and now that they knew his location, he'd have to walk away. And so, though he could have fled into the 700-acre cornfield, he decided instead to send a little message for the next crew to think about before they decided it was a good idea to pay him a visit.

Brad crouched still as death, a silenced Beretta in each hand, nestled beneath his combine within the cover of the dense smoke. The song having ended, he now listened for movement in the corn, trying to gauge his surviving adversaries' numbers and positions.

By his count, there were five of the twelve men left—they had formed an arched perimeter within the corn, clearly trying to stop him from escaping into the field. Silently, still enshrouded by the dense smoke, Brad climbed back up into the cockpit and eased the door shut. Knowing each man's location like a bat with radar, he abruptly put the combine in drive and floored it toward the closest man, turning the corn header back on.

The combine lurched out of the white cloud of smoke like a serial killer from a dark corner. Stalks flew into the air as the diesel engine roared with a bestial sounding bloodlust. It drowned out the dying screams, which was a pity.

As they were eaten by the jaws of the combine, the men tried to fire shots at the machine. Brad let out a "Yee haw!" Outfitting the combine with bulletproof glass wasn't paranoid after all.

The final and fifth man ran out of the cover of the corn and into the open field.

"Get along, li'l doggie!" Brad laughed as he put the combine into street gear. He caught up to the man after about a hundred feet. Instead of running him over, though, he decided he deserved to have a little bit of fun, and bumped the man with one of the machine's large tires.

When the game was no longer fun, Brad opened his door, leaned out, and shot the man in the back. He then turned his tractor and ran the front tire over the man's torso, stopping with the tire on top of him. he jumped out of the machine, walked over to the man, and admired his work. The body was smashed in half. Brad bent down and grabbed the poor bastard's earpiece and radio.

He put the earpiece in, then spoke. "I just saw Herzer's head rolling around in my corn header, Jackoff."

"Hello Farmer," came Jaco Ivanov's cool voice.

"Name's Brad."

Jaco laughed at the notion.

Brad clenched his fist. "Tell me where you're at so I can kill you, Ivanov."

"I have something for you."

"You should've let me be," Brad said as he scanned the area. "I'm retired."

He saw the glare of a scope over a couple hundred yards away. In a fluid motion, he dropped to a knee and unloaded the magazine in his right-hand Beretta in that direction.

"Whoa there, big guy," came Jaco's voice. "If you don't start playing nice, I'm gonna have to put one in your chest."

"I'm not going back."

"I'm not asking you to."

Brad put his mouth directly to the radio. "I earned this farm, and now you bloodsuckers have taken even that away from me!"

"Farmer, when did you become such a drama queen? It's quite annoying. I'm here to bring you the one thing you crave more than anything."

"You've found him," Brad said, as something snapped, and he marched straight toward Jaco.

"I need you to put that gun in your left hand down," Jaco demanded.

The Farmer picked up his pace as he dropped the gun in his left hand to the ground.

94

When he got to Jaco, he kept on walking. Right past Jaco, who said, bewildered, "Where the hell are you going?"

The Farmer didn't look back. "To get a weapon, Jackoff."

"I meant what I said. I've got everything you could ever want."

The Farmer turned, his eyes a devil's glare. "I'm going to kill him with my brother's gun."

"Fair enough," Jaco said, as he watched the Farmer walk toward his house.

26

It had been well over 24 hours since Gracie had been moved to ADX. She ached to touch something on the outside, to smell a flower, or feel a breeze. To feel anything but the cold, unyielding concrete that surrounded her. Even the light in here seemed to scream "captive".

Perhaps the one saving grace, if she could call it that, was that confinement afforded her ample time to consider her circumstances. The effect wasn't pretty. With horror that grew by the minute, she realized that whoever had set her up to look like a terrorist had to have been very well connected indeed. If they could make her patents disappear, they could probably do just about anything. She had to figure something out, or she would be locked away in here for the rest of her life.

The outer steel door to her cell clicked open, and two guards let in Agent Quinn. Still between them were the steel bars that allowed the guards to enter the room and have access to the prisoner without being in danger. Gracie stood and went up to those bars.

"I don't have much time," he said in an urgent but soft voice.

"What's happening?"

Quinn looked back at the guards, then leaned in. "The blood on your clothes. It's Anna's."

Her stomach sank. "That's impossible! How could I have killed her if I had her grey matter and skull fragments splattered on clothes I *changed into* at the farmhouse?"

"I know," he said. "I took a small sample from evidence and had it retested." He lowered his voice to a hair above a whisper. "It's not her blood. Wrong type."

"So, you can prove my innocence." She reached through the bars and grabbed Quinn's hands.

"Hey!" the guard yelled.

She quickly withdrew her hands.

"It's alright. I'm fine," said Quinn. He leaned in again.

"This clinches it," said Gracie. "You can prove I'm—"

He closed his eyes and shook his head. "Gracie, I obtained the sample illegally. It's inadmissible. Worse, when I went back to get them with a request to retest, your clothes were... gone."

"What do you mean?"

"Gone. Disappeared."

"You can't be serious," she said, clutching the bars for support. She felt her knees weaken as the heaviness in her gut pulled her to the ground. She was on her knees, too oppressed even to tremble.

Quinn knelt to maintain level eye contact. "Listen, I want to help you. You understand that, right?"

Gracie looked at him. "Why?"

Quinn reached into his inside pocket, pulled out his phone, and showed her a picture. It was a little girl, about eight years old. She was in a hospital bed and surrounded by stuffed animals. She was emaciated, pale, and bald. Her eyes seemed oversized, as if pleading. She was smiling though, clutching a Harry Potter wand, apparently in mid-spellcasting.

"That's why," he said.

"Who is she?"

He looked at the phone, a moist-eyed smile on his face. "My goddaughter."

"What...?" She looked at him, unable to finish.

"Stage four. I don't need to tell you there's no stage five."

She shook her head.

"In my investigation, I spoke to Dr. Keith Vincent at Stanford. You can imagine he told me some pretty impressive things about you. Gracie, I need you to level with me. I'm already resigned to the idea of losing this girl. Maybe it's because I could no longer bear the idea of hopelessness. But I still remember feeling constant... *desperate* hope. It got to a point that I would have set myself on fire if I believed it would cure her." He leaned in again, grabbed the bars as if they were the source of his frustration. "Gracie, damn you, you'd better be who you say you are, and you'd better have what you say you have."

"I am... I do," she squeaked out through hot tears. Though scared, there was iron in her soul and her fists clenched with the outrage hiding behind her fear.

"If you want my help, I'll need proof of it."

"In my apartment, all of my formulas are on flash drives taped underneath my kitchen drawers."

Quinn nodded and stood. "Okay. I don't know who to trust at this point, so the rule is trust no one and let no one know that I'm helping you."

She looked into his eyes, nodded, then asked, "When will I see you again?"

"As soon as I get back from Chicago and clear this whole mess up," he said.

"I can save your goddaughter," she said with renewed strength.

Quinn pursed his lips and breathed deeply. "I meant what I said about needing God's help if you're not on the level. Because if you're not, I will make sure you pay for it. In the name of my goddaughter, I swear it."

27

Mack Maddox had struggled through Gracie Green's thesis paper, and read everything online he could find about her and her company. What was frustrating was the fact that the most cursory search for "Gracie Green" yielded a ton of stories repeating the terrorist narrative. He'd also discovered a developing narrative among conspiracy theorists that the cure she was claiming to have was actually a formula for some type of genetic chemical warfare. Not to mention the memes and nasty jokes blowing around the internet like so much toilet paper after Halloween night.

He heard Caroline cough from upstairs. The rattle in the cough made the muscles along his back clench.

"You okay?"

"I'm fine," Caroline replied in a hoarse voice. Before Mack could ask his next question, she followed up with, "She's fine, too."

"Let me know if you need me," he said, continuing to sift through the latest article he'd dug up. This one was about Gracie's coworkers. If any group deserved the description "ragtag," it was this one. They were three kids straight out of college with no real-world experience, assembled as if by lottery.

He had to be a good investigator and consider the possibility that they were nothing but dupes. It certainly looked that way. The memes and the media narrative and the conspiracy sites were getting to him, he thought. Time to change tack.

He found himself on the Facebook page of Diana Graham, Anna's mother. Anna had been Gracie's second-in-command at Greentech, and her mother was in the advanced stages of colorectal cancer. Bic had mentioned her. If there was anyone who'd have kept close tabs on Anna's progress at the company, it was Diana Graham. Anna was a sometime-poster in a support forum for people suffering from colorectal cancer. Field research, Mack had guessed. In more than one post, she'd mentioned her mother, who was suffering.

In fifteen minutes, he had Diana Graham's phone number.

"Hello?"

"Ms. Graham? My name is Mack Maddox. I'm with the FBI?"

"Oh God…"

"Um, ma'am, I'd like to ask you a few questions."

"Don't you have enough?"

"I'm sorry?"

"You people have been harassing me and I'd like it to stop. This can't be legal. My daughter is dead!"

"Ma'am," said Mack, stumbling over the word, "I'm terribly sorry for your loss."

"I'll bet you are," Diana snapped. "The only thing you get from my mouth is this: Gracie is not a terrorist." With this, she hung up.

Mack was about to call her right back when he heard a loud, hollow thud on the floor above him, followed by Sam wailing. He bolted up the stairs and found Caroline on the floor, unconscious with Sam next to her.

"God, please no," he said, rushing toward her. He went to his nightstand and fumbled through the drawer for a flashlight pen. Her pupils didn't respond to the light. He dialed 911, then scooped up little Sam. He cradled Sam in his arms as he paced in terror, waiting for the paramedics, mumbling prayers.

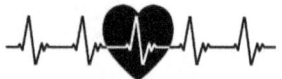

Three hours later, Mack sat in a hospital room next to Caroline, holding her hand and trying to ignore the symphony of beeps from the machines she was connected to. She hadn't regained consciousness since she'd collapsed at the house. Her vitals were stable for the moment, her body pumped full of steroids to reduce the swelling in her brain.

A few minutes before, the doctor had sat Mack down in that dreaded room, where she told him Caroline wasn't leaving the hospital this time. Her body was shutting down.

She had a week or two at best.

Caroline's hand twitched in his. Her eyes fluttered open. Mack smiled through his hopeless yearning. "You're back."

She managed a smile and said in a hoarse voice, "I love you."

Mack held her hand tighter. "Love you too. I'm sorry."

"I'm sorry you love me too." Even in this state, she could still snark at him.

Caroline drifted off, winced, before opening her eyes. "Promise me you'll stay safe for her."

He knew who she meant. "I promise," he said.

Caroline smirked. "That means don't forget your vest."

It had been a shared joke since their marriage. She'd even worked it into her vows. She never let him forget that it was she who'd saved his life, however indirectly, by being such a nag about wearing the Kevlar vest.

He understood what the return to this overused joke was meant to signify. She knew him, knew the only thing that he was truly afraid of was happening again. First his mother had left him and his father. Now Caroline was leaving him and Sam.

Only Caroline wasn't leaving for something she thought was better, like his mother had done. No, she was being murdered slowly right before his eyes.

But he knew that no matter what she said, he wasn't about to sit here and watch this terror play out without a fight.

He bent over and kissed his wife on the forehead, then whispered to her, "I know you'll be up when I get back," he said as he lingered a moment longer, staring at her still face. "You know how I know? Because you are the love of my life."

28

Mack pulled into a massive townhome complex located a block away from the Pacific Ocean in a town called Dana Point, two hours south of L.A. He had used the FBI database to look up Diana Graham's home address. It had been more difficult than he'd expected, as she had moved six months ago. His mind played the paranoid trick of supposing that she'd done this to keep one step ahead of *him*.

Ridiculous, he thought, as he stood in front of a well-manicured two-story building with a row of four units attached. Normally he would have noticed the warmth of the sun, the smell of the ocean... not today. He walked up the steps to one of the middle units and knocked on door 1109.

No answer. He knocked again.

Then again, louder.

Finally, the door opened slightly, the chain still on. A face appeared in the gap.

Mack flashed his FBI badge. "Diana Graham? Mack Maddox. We briefly spoke on the phone. It's urgent we talk."

"I have nothing to say."

Mack wedged his foot in the door before she could shut it. "I'm not asking." He took a moment to regain his composure. "I'm here to save my wife."

"What does that have to do with me?"

"You said Gracie was innocent." Mack withdrew his foot from the crack. "I need her to be, because my wife is dying of cancer."

The door shut and reopened a moment later, unchained. Diana Graham stepped aside to allow him entrance.

They sat at the kitchen table. Mack stared at Diana, confused by her appearance. She was in the final stages of cancer in the Facebook pictures he'd seen from four months ago. He knew all too well the frailty, the weak, beaten-down bloodshot eyes, the pale white skin, so thin you could see the veins through its papery surface. She had none of these signs now.

"If you don't mind me saying, you're looking well," Mack said.

She broke eye contact. "I'm hanging in there."

"The reason why I'm here is this: The man who raised Gracie has asked me to h—"

"Gracie's uncle?" Diana smiled. Even her teeth looked healthy, not all yellowed up by harsh chemo and radiation treatments.

"You know him?"

"No. Neither did Anna. She never met him, but he was known as the angel who found the investor for their company."

"Did Anna give you anything, or tell you where they backed up any of their research?"

"No." Diana replied. Mack could read the lie. It was all over her face.

"Diana, I need to know if there's a cure. If there's a chance to save my wife, I can't just sit there and let her die."

Diana rose from the table and walked over to the refrigerator. She paused with the door open, staring into it. "I'm sorry. I need something to drink? Can I get you anything?"

"She cured you, didn't she?"

The woman remained frozen, staring into the fridge.

Mack rose and walked to her side. "You're the proof. You're living proof that Gracie Green *did* cure cancer."

"Agent Maddox, I'm sorry if I gave you the impression that I'm cured. I'm... not."

"I just thought," he said, "I don't know what I thought... from looking at you..."

She smiled slightly. "God willing, I've got six more months."

Mack turned away, feeling his hope diminishing by the second.

"If you're looking for proof of their work," said Diana, "I can tell you Anna was quite OCD. There's no way she didn't back up their research somewhere, probably in a place no one but she would ever think to look for it. Here..." She went to a drawer and fumbled for a pen and paper. "Here's her address. Sorry I don't have more for you, but I'm feeling a little light-headed."

Mack took the piece of paper in a numb hand and followed Diana to the front door. Out of the corner of his eye, at the top of the stairs, he spotted a piece of luggage sitting on the stair landing.

Moments later, he was sitting in his car, wondering what the hell to do. The woman was hiding something. What's more, she was clearly preparing to bolt. If she disappeared, then the proof was gone, along with all hope of saving Caroline.

Proof.

She was proof, dammit. Why the hell would she lie to him?

Mack made a call to Tom Walton, a childhood friend who worked in cybersecurity at Langley.

He needed quick answers.

29

Diana Graham sat at her kitchen table, wondering if she was a terrible person as she stared at two bottles of pills—pills Anna had sent to her, unbeknownst to Gracie. She was going to be in the Phase I trials, or at least that was the plan. But when they couldn't secure FDA approval, Anna couldn't wait any longer.

The drug worked exactly as it had in the mice: Diana was cancer-free within two weeks. It was a true penicillin for cancer. Anna had explained how it worked, but it was too technical for Diana. Her understanding, in layman's terms, was that cancer cells liked sugar. The blue pill was a synthetic sugar that, when absorbed by a cancerous cell, created a marker. The red pill was the second half of the drug. When it interacted with a cancer cell containing the marker, a compound reaction occurred. This created a poison as lethal as cyanide, but only to the cancer cells, and killed them almost instantaneously.

Suddenly the back door opened, and a man stepped into the kitchen and pressed a silenced pistol at her head.

"Hello, Mrs. Graham," he said quietly, cocking the gun.

She didn't reply, didn't even move.

"What? Cat got your tongue?"

She shook her head. "So you're the man who's been threatening me?"

"Name's Jaco," he said with a smirk. "Pleased to meet you."

"I didn't say a word to anyone."

"Didn't say you did. Huh, what do we have here?" He reached over and picked up one of the bottles.

"It's not what you think."

He opened the bottle and saw about 20 blue pills. "Let me guess, the other contains red ones," he said, then opened the second bottle. "Look at that. I was right." He chuckled to himself as he walked over to the sink.

"Those are the only ones left," Diana said.

"I don't understand. Are you trying to initiate some sort of bargain?"

"You could save millions of people," she said. "You'd be a hero."

"And to whom would I take these? Assuming I wanted to be a *hero*."

"There's a scientist," she said desperately. "At M.D. Anderson—"

Jaco looked up. "Oh, yeah, that. You should probably be aware that situation's already been taken care of. Tragic car accident." He clucked his tongue. "Too bad. Got anything else?"

She was silent.

"I thought not," he said as he unscrewed the cap and began pouring the pills down the drain of the garbage disposal.

Diana bolted up from the table and Jaco pointed his revolver straight at her stomach.

"Not wise," he said sharply.

"What kind of monsters *are* you people?" Diana cried.

"The worst kind. Would you hand me those red pills please?"

Diana Graham stood erect, staring at him defiantly.

Jaco rolled his eyes. "Oh, c'mon," he said, and shot her in the stomach. Diana collapsed back into the seat, her hands clutching her belly.

"Ouch," said Jaco. "Bet that hurts worse than cancer." He picked up the second bottle of pills and poured them down into the disposal. Then he flipped the disposal switch on and conducted the grinding sound of the motor like a symphony. On the downbeat, he turned it off and turned on the tap, washing the remnants of the pills into oblivion.

He then turned and pointed the gun at Diana's head. "Sorry, lady. It's not like this is the first time we've uncured something."

She was gasping, and she looked up at him, pure, unfiltered hatred in her eyes. Her mouth trembled. And she squeaked out four words.

"You... go... to hell..."

"Hope so, I hear that's where all the cool people hang out."

30

In 10 minutes, Tom Walton had pulled Diana Graham's medical records.

Mack felt an awkward relief, one that only comes from being proved correct on a hunch that confirmed dire consequences for all involved.

On her last medical visit five months before, Diana Graham had weeks to live at best, could barely walk, and had lost all motor skills in her right arm. Since then, there was no record of her even stepping foot into a hospital or trying any experimental treatment. Either the reports were lying or she was.

Or perhaps not. He remembered what she'd said. *I'm not cured.* Perhaps the only word missing from that sentence was the word *yet.*

He shut the car and got out. If she hadn't been cured yet, but was on her way, then there was a good chance she had the drugs right here in her house—and he wasn't going to leave without them.

A flash of light lit up the front picture window. He knew that flash.

He kicked the door open.

A man in the kitchen pointed a gun at him. Mack dove for cover behind a couch in the living room as another shot rang out. Mack blindly returned fire.

The sound of a door.

Mack popped up ready to fire. The rear door was open.

He ran to Diana, who lay sprawled across the floor in a bloody mess. Her head lolled backwards by a bullet to the forehead. Her mouth gaped.

He went out into the tiny backyard, which butted up to a maze of similar four-unit townhouse buildings. There was no sign of anyone.

He reentered the townhome and locked the rear door.

His mind raced as he reentered the kitchen. On the counter next to the sink were two pill bottles with their caps removed that hadn't been there just minutes before when he chatted with Diana. He grabbed the empty bottles, then looked down the dark drain of the disposal, frowning. He took his phone and turned on the light to look down the drain.

"Dammit, Diana," he muttered sadly. "Why didn't you give these to me?"

He looked around the room, noticing a sticky note on the white refrigerator amongst the plethora of magnets there. The name *"Dr. Klein"* was written on the note, along with a phone number.

A search of Diana Graham's townhouse came up dry, save for a numbered key that looked like it came from a safe-deposit box, hidden within the lining of the single small suitcase on the landing.

After he left, he found a payphone and dialed 911.

31

At eight o'clock that night, the Farmer sat at the kitchen table in the darkness of a two-bedroom apartment in Cañon City, Colorado. Nestled between 3 penitentiaries, it was an idyllic and beautiful town with a thriving economy based on supporting the outlying correctional facilities. About two hours ago, disguised as a deliveryman with a crate-sized box, he'd walked into the small apartment complex undetected and easily picked the cheap lock on the front door. As he waited patiently, he continued to think about all the horrific ways he could kill Bic Green. Until a day ago, he hadn't even known that name. He'd only known of the assassin some called the Black Ghost. It was an appropriate name, considering that he'd spent three years trying to find the man and hadn't even unearthed so much as the man's initials.

Footsteps came from the hall, then a jingling of keys, and the door opened. A man entered and closed the door behind him. The kitchen light illuminated Jesse McNally, a full bearded man with brown shaggy hair. He was dressed in his work uniform.

"Hello, Jesse."

Jesse let out a startled sound and stared at the silenced Beretta in the Farmer's right hand.

"Relax," the Farmer said. He motioned with the pistol. "Sit down."

Shaking, Jesse followed his instructions.

"You'd think you'd be a little calmer, seeing as how you deal with the world's most dangerous people every day."

Jesse's eyes darted in utter confusion at the items arranged neatly on the small, round kitchen table. First was a bunch of strips of plaster gauze, cut into different-sized pieces. Next was a jar of Vaseline, a bag of craft plaster, an electric hair clipper, different sized paint brushes, wood glue, superglue, a piece of sandpaper, a can of air duster, and a roll of duct tape.

"What are you going to do to me?"

The Farmer grabbed the roll of tape and said, "Country boy's number one survival tool."

With his gun tucked in his blue jeans, the Farmer stood behind Jesse and ran a loop of tape across his chest and around the back of the chair, completing the circle back at his chest. He ran the circle two times.

"I'm a good person. I don't mistreat prisoners," Jesse said in a panicked voice.

"How tall are you?"

"What?"

"About five ten?" The Farmer made an X with the tape at the location of the man's heart. He then pulled out a map from his back pocket and unfolded it on the table. It was a diagram of the ADX Max Prison campus. "Tell me everything." He pointed to the map.

"What...?"

"Tell me everything."

Jesse shook his head slowly. "If it's smuggling you're looking at, I can tell you it's impossible for guards to sneak drugs into ADX. They even have sniffer dogs outside the bathroom stalls!"

"I'm not interested in drugs. I want to know your entire routine, especially in the D-Unit." The Farmer bent over, closing the distance. "Give me that, and I'll leave you in peace."

After about twenty minutes, Jesse had told the man everything about his routine, and had even confirmed Gracie Green's cell block and the interval of the guards.

"Now for your payment," the Farmer said, as he pulled out the note that Jaco had given him. It was the note Bic had left on the dead terrorist hanging from the ceiling fan at the farmhouse in South Dakota.

"Can you read this for me, Jesse?"

"Yeah, what does it mean?"

"What's it say?"

Confused, terrified, he said, "It's pork chop eatin' time..." Jesse looked up from the note to see the silenced pistol staring at him.

32

The Farmer grabbed some paper towels and wiped his face clean of Jesse McNally's blood, which had spattered from the wound directly in the center of the X on his chest. He then picked up a dry wash rag, tore it in half, and stuffed it down into Jesse's mouth. With the head tilted back, he applied the superglue to Jesse's teeth to bind his lower and upper jaw together permanently, then wrapped a swath of duct tape from below the lower jaw around to the top of the head and back again so it all could set.

He looked at his stash of materials and frowned. No hair dryer. Why was there always some mundane little detail to be dealt with? He went into the bathroom and rifled through the drawers until he found one.

Back in the kitchen, he taped Jesse's head to the broomstick to hold it up. He removed Jesse's eyebrows, beard and sideburns with the clippers, then applied a thin layer of Vaseline to the smooth face.

He stepped back to admire his work thus far. It was time for phase two.

He grabbed a mixing bowl from the kitchen cupboard and filled it with warm water. He picked up a piece of plaster gauze and dipped it into the water. After letting the excess water drip off, he applied the first strip of plaster to Jesse's face, then re-wet his index finger and smoothed out the surface of the plaster gauze. He methodically repeated the process until he had covered Jesse's entire face, then used the blow-dryer to speed up the drying time.

After the plaster mask had dried, he carefully peeled it off in one piece, then held the cast up to the kitchen light to make sure there were no holes. He smiled at his work. Satisfied, he put the mask nose-down into a small basket he'd stuffed with towels and cloth so it wouldn't crack.

Phase three.

He used a paintbrush to put a coat of Vaseline to the inside of the mask. Next, he mixed a bag of powdered craft plaster with water, then poured the liquid plaster into the mask until the face was full. Carefully he tapped the edges of the mask to rid the thing of air bubbles.

He looked at his watch, then walked into Jesse McNally's den and flicked on the TV.

There was a two-hour block of Judge Judy episodes on channel thirty-six. He grabbed a beer from Jesse's fridge and made himself comfortable in front of the TV.

Two hours later, the fast-drying plaster had solidified. He removed the inner mask from the plaster cast by inching it off piece by piece. Once the mask was removed, he took the cast and put it next to Jesse's face.

He smiled.

He picked up the clay-sculpting tool and fine-tuned some details around the eyes, nose and mouth. Next was a thorough—albeit delicate—buffing with a piece of sandpaper. He blew away the dust with a can of air duster, then painted wood glue onto the surface to seal it.

Phase four.

Still in the box was a quart bottle of Monster Mask Latex RD-07, the most important ingredient.

He tapped the layer of wood glue to test for dryness, then applied a very thin layer of Vaseline. Using a paintbrush, he applied the latex over the cast in perfect proportions.

When he was done, he looked at the mask, then at the corpse of Jesse McNally.

"You'll be doing the unthinkable tomorrow, my friend," he said, then pulled a couple dark colored strands of braided hair from his box to see which one color matched the best to Jesse's beard shavings on the floor.

33

Mack knelt next to Caroline's bed, holding her left hand in both of his. She hadn't regained consciousness since he'd gotten back. He knew he had promised Caroline he'd stay safe for Sam, but it was clear now that if he did what he wanted to do—needed to do—they could both end up dead by the end of the week, leaving Sam an orphan. He looked at the clock. It was midnight. He shook his head.

Mack leaned in, tears in his eyes. "You'll never guess what I got myself into," he whispered, holding her hand tight.

There was a sudden noise as the blood pressure cuff automatically tightened around Caroline's arm. Mack looked up at her vitals on the monitor. They were still strong, but this was also a reminder she was near the end.

"I can't go through this life without you," he said, then looked over at the two empty pill bottles he had taken from Diana's, which he had placed on her nightstand. "I know there's a cure now, but I… I really messed up, baby. You know what really sucks? If it was you visiting Diana instead of me? You would have gotten them right off. I just know you would have found a way." He fought back a break in his voice. "I need my partner back."

Mack closed his eyes in frustration. "I screwed the pooch another way, baby. I let her get killed. I know, I shouldn't do that to myself. In reality, if she would've just told me what was happening, if she'd just come with me, she would still be alive. But I did find this…" He pulled the safe deposit key from his pocket. "I found this in her luggage. What do you think? My gut tells me it's something important."

He gently ran his finger across her forehead and pushed her hair back. "Tell me what to do, Caroline. You know, the doctor said you probably won't regain consciousness, but he doesn't know how strong you are. Wake up... so you can tell me to get my head out of my ass..." His voice broke off.

He stayed by her side for the next couple of hours. He was just about to doze off, his chin about to hit his head, when something made him look up.

It couldn't be.

Her eyes were slits, and she was smiling.

"Hey," he said, taking her hand.

"Hey," she rasped weakly.

"How's it going?" His own voice was barely more than a whisper.

"Mack, remember our wedding night?"

"Of course."

"I never told you this, but that night, I knew we were creating a baby, I don't know how I knew it, I just did."

He smiled through his tears. "That was the most amazing night of my life."

"Mine too." She tried to laugh. "Actually, I think I got pregnant the month before."

"Yeah, the math didn't add up, but I wasn't gonna argue with you."

"Alright, I just wanted you to know I'll be here waiting for you."

"I love you."

She smiled as she closed her eyes.

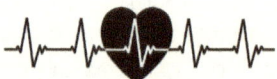

Twenty minutes later, Mack was startled by his phone. It was Tom Walton from Langley. Mack stepped out of the room to answer it.

"Find anything?"

"Couple of things," said Tom. "Diana Graham was flying to Chicago, then the next day to Houston. There's a Dr. Klein at M.D. Anderson hospital. I had a look at his calendar. She had an appointment with him at 2 PM. But Mack, Dr. Klein was killed in a hit and run accident yesterday."

"Jeez, that's convenient. Any idea why she was going to Chicago?"

"Not yet."

"Did she make any calls to Chicago?" Mack asked.

"Pulling up her records now. Yes, here's one, it's the number to the First National Bank of Chicago."

"Hmm, ok—wait a minute..." He reached into his pocket and pulled out the key. "Hey, quick question, does she have a safe deposit box there?"

"It'll take a second to get into the bank's records," Tom said as Mack heard the pounding of the keyboard through the phone. "Nope. Nothing."

"Crap."

"Hang on. Looks like her daughter does."

"Anna?"

"Yes sir. Box 1026."

Mack smiled as he verified the number on the key. "Nice work, Tom. I think I already have the key."

"It's a two-key box, so you'll need a second key to get in."

Mack's shoulders slumped. "If Anna had her key on her in the explosion, there's no way I'm going to find it."

"Well, if Diana was going there, she must have had it or at least knew where to find it."

"Good point. Thanks, Tom, I owe you big time."

"That's an understatement," the other man said cheerfully.

Mack hung up the phone, then crawled into the hospital bed with Caroline.

"Taking a little trip tomorrow, baby," he whispered, and kissed her head. "Wanna come with?"

His mind wouldn't allow him any thoughts of finality. He slept next to his wife.

34

"*Unacceptable*," Peter Rains growled as Jaco entered the private room at a Chinese restaurant in the RiNo district in Denver. The hipster wave of new residents avoided the old business like this one in favor of artisanal, locally sourced, hand crafted vegan restaurants, and the two men had the place to themselves. The staff were used to giving their patronage a lot of privacy, and getting overly large tips in return.

"Nice to see you too, Peter."

"Cut the crap, Jaco. First you blow up half of Chicago, then you turn Iowa into a war zone!" Rains slammed his fist on the table. "I've got 12 men buried in a cornfield in *pieces*! The only person you've managed *not* to kill is the one person you were *supposed to*!"

"You should have seen that hillbilly," Jaco said with a chuckle. "He killed five of your guys with a farm tractor."

Rains glared at him. "You're kidding me."

He glared back, "It's not good manners to change the terms of a contract."

"I can't believe it," said Rains, shaking his head at the table. "You sent those men after the Farmer to be killed so you didn't have to pay them, you sick, greedy devil?"

"Says the guy who's going to wipe the cure for cancer off the face of the earth. What's the old saying? Kill one man and you are a murderer. Kill millions and you're a conqueror. Just who are you conquering Rains? The feeble?"

Rains looked up, hatred in his eyes. "Listen here, you didn't deliver, you're not getting a red cent until the job is done."

"The million I asked for was for expenses."

"No money until the job is done, and it better be quick, I'm hearing from the intelligence community that China's caught wind of this. The only thing worse than her company finding a cure would be if the—" He looked around, then lowered his voice. "—if the *Chinese* get a hold of it."

"I'm going to need a chopper with a .50-cal."

Rains ground his teeth as he stared into Jaco's eyes. "What in the world do you need a chopper for?"

Jaco leaned forward. "The Farmer is going to break her out to the perimeter. Once he gets into the open with her, a chopper with a gunner will swoop in and grab them. Then the Farmer and the pilot will parachute out of the bloody thing just before it crashes into the side of a mountain." He brushed his hands together. "Oh, I'll need two parachutes too."

Rains stared at Jaco for a moment, then huffed and pulled out his phone.

The server came over.

"I hear you make a mean Mai-Tai," said Jaco.

"Best in Denver," she said with a smile.

"Uh huh. In that case, make it a vodka tonic. No lime."

Rains hung up his call and waited for the server to depart. "The chopper's on its way. Don't mess this up."

Jaco stood to leave. "Ok, I got work to do. Cancel my drink. Or have it yourself. I don't care. Oh, and I'm just warning you, within an hour after that chopper crashes, those fat, greasy asses you work for better send me the rest of my money or they're going to have a *big* problem."

Rains rolled his eyes. "Just kill her before she gets hold of someone she can get on her side."

Jaco cracked his neck to the right. "She'll be gone by the end of today— just make sure my money's there."

"Have you ever *not* gotten paid?" Rains called after him.

Jaco turned and thought for a moment. "No," he said finally. "Let's keep it that way."

35

Gracie lay asleep in her cell, until a man entered her room and hovered over her for a moment. Feeling his presence, Gracie opened her eyes.

"What are you doing here?" she said.

Agent Quinn motioned for her to be quiet as he knelt by her side. "Do you trust me?"

Gracie lost herself in his eyes. It felt right. She wrapped her hand around the back of his neck. He didn't resist, and she pulled him down to her.

Their lips locked together perfectly, as his warm hands pulled up her shirt...

The outer prison door loudly clicked open, waking her from the dream. She sat up, completely mortified when she saw Agent Quinn walk in. She couldn't even look him in the eyes.

Quinn picked up on it. "Everything okay?"

"Did you get my thumb drives?" she said blearily.

Quinn shook his head. "Chicago was a bust."

"What do you mean?"

"The drives were gone. Someone else found them first. We did find some traces of tape residue and damaged paint where you said they'd be."

She stared at him in disbelief. "Gone?"

"Is there anywhere else you might have kept any proof of your work?"

Deflated, Gracie said, "No. I don't think so." For the first time she started to feel like this was real, and there was no going back. No way out.

"Gracie, I need you to think." Quinn hesitated, but then said, "A lot's at stake here."

"You think I don't know that?" she responded, a bit too loudly. She passed her hands over her face and said, "Maybe one of my employees kept something. They weren't supposed to, but maybe."

"Who would be the most likely?" Quinn asked.

"Steve and Alice were rule-followers—it would be highly unlikely that they went against my wishes. But Anna thought I was being too paranoid about not keeping our data backed up on the cloud."

"So, ok, where do you think Anna would have kept it?"

"I don't know. She was kind of a pack rat. Maybe in her apartment? I'm not sure." Gracie looked down. "Her mother's been in the final stages of colorectal cancer for months, holding on, waiting to be the first to be in the human trials when the FDA approved the drugs. By the time I get this all straightened out, if I ever do, she'll probably be gone."

"Did Anna have any siblings, or a boyfriend?"

"She had one sister and they didn't get along at all. She never dated—she was too busy with her work."

"I'm going back to Chicago, Gracie. Make sure not to trust *anyone* until I can make sense of what's happening here."

Gracie nodded. Even though so much was at stake, she couldn't help but remember her dream. For all she knew, this would be the last time she would see Quinn.

"Hang in there," Quinn said, then stood.

As he walked toward the door of the cell, the guard opened the door to let him out.

"Thanks, guy," Quinn said, then stopped to take a second look at one of them. "You okay, pal?"

"Got a bit of a cold," the bearded guard replied, tilting his head down, shielding much of his face from Quinn's view. "Don't get too close."

"Feel better," Quinn looked at the man's badge, "McNally." He walked off without taking a second look.

The guard made eye contact with Gracie for the briefest of moments, then shut the cell door as a smile slowly spread across his face.

36

B ic looked at the ADX facility through binoculars from about a mile away, lying on his belly next to Hawk, tucked between some large bushes on the mountainous terrain. The prison campus was framed against a backdrop of pure blue and sunshine, which gleamed off the guard towers on the cloudless mid-morning. But then there were the guards themselves, armed men with high-powered rifles, and the fencing laced with razor-edged barbed wire. The living postcard held violence within its perimeter.

"What do you think, partner?" Hawk asked.

"We can't wait any longer. If Tony's right, they're coming for her—if they're already not in there right now."

"There's been some crazy plans, but this one—man, a lot of things got to go right, if you know what I mean."

Bic looked right at the entrance of the prison. "You cause enough commotion, no one's even going to notice me coming right through the front door." He turned and looked at Hawk, "You sure you can handle that chopper?"

"Now's a little late to ask. The answer's yes, by the way."

"Just making sure."

"Come on brother, that's the way we do it, money for nothin' and your chicks for free."

"Checks."

"What?"

"*Checks* for free."

Hawk looked at him. "You sure about that?"

"Maybe you're right, you are the 80's expert," Bic shook his head and pulled out a map with the schematics of the prison. "You send the rocket right here—"

"Man, we went over this a million times."

Bic shot him a glare. "Humor me. You take out these two guard towers—"

"Right, and by the time I finish that up, you'll be coming out this door from cell block D with Gracie. Then I snatch you up there in this area. Then we go play our guitars."

"I'll take my swat helmet off so you know it's me."

"You worried I'm gonna shoot ya by mistake?"

"Make sure to tell your gunner not to either."

"You're serious."

"We can't fail her."

"We won't, my brother."

The men stood and embraced.

"I don't deserve a friend like you," Bic said.

"Hold that sentiment until after the extraction and I don't shoot you."

Bic cracked a quick smile. "Will do."

Hawk handed Bic a duffle bag full of Swat gear. "Good luck, Bic. Catch you on the flip side." Then he grabbed one of the dirt bikes and left.

37

In the back seat of the Uber coming from the airport, Mack took a deep breath, mentally exhausted. He had texted his dad about 20 times over the last hour, asking if Caroline had woken up, but she had not.

He thought about texting his in-laws about how Sam was behaving, then thought better of it. The last thing he and Sam needed was passive-aggressive in-law action. Accusation had been the subtext of every conversation he'd had with them since Caroline had gotten sick. If he hadn't gotten her pregnant, then she would have been able to start the treatment when the cancer was discovered instead of having to wait almost seven months to begin, or so their narrative went. He knew without it being said that his mother-in-law would try to get full custody of Sam if Caroline died. And he was equally sure that his father-in-law, one of the highest-powered attorneys in LA, would use what Mack was doing right know as one of the reasons to deny him custody.

The thought of losing Caroline and Sam at virtually the same time terrified him.

As he cursed his in-laws in his head, the Prius came to a stop at a six-unit building in Wicker Park, Chicago. The neighborhood block was littered with mostly three and six-flat buildings, predominately red brick with some variances. Anna had lived on the third floor of a newer-looking three-flat, probably built in 2006 or 2007, right before the real estate crash.

Mack stepped out of the vehicle. He looked around, but didn't notice anything or anyone to be concerned about. He entered through the gated black wrought-iron fence and up to the common door. He cased his surroundings one last time before pulling out his lock-picking set and getting down to business on the front door.

After three flights of stairs, Mack opened Anna's door and ducked under the crime scene tape across it.

The apartment was neat and clean and looked like a page out of a Pottery Barn catalog—gray painted walls, furniture with clean lines, and all accessories in properly accented colors. The back-kitchen window showed a view of the downtown Chicago skyline.

Mack wasted no time as he went to all the obvious places someone might secret away a safe deposit key. In the kitchen, he rifled through the drawers and cabinets. He moved on to the work desk in the corner and looked through those drawers. Spotting a journal on top, he picked it up and rifled through it. A personal journal. He figured he'd save it for later and tossed it onto the kitchen counter.

He then went into the bedroom and looked through the jewelry box, the bedside drawer, and Anna's colorful underwear drawer. Lastly, he went into the bathroom and started rifling through the excess clutter of beauty supplies.

Mack looked at his phone. No text from his father. It had been a day since Caroline was conscious. This was his Super Bowl, and it was the final seconds of the game. He had to find that key. The obvious places had yielded nothing. It was time to dig deep.

In the bathroom, he went through everything, emptying the contents of every beauty item into the tub. After every container was emptied, he went into the bedroom. There was a picture of Anna and Diana on the nightstand. He grabbed it and pulled it out of the frame—nothing. About 20 books were on her dresser. No hollowed-out compartments. Nothing taped inside the covers. He checked all pictures on the wall—nothing. After searching through all the drawers, her clothes, pillows and mattresses and every container or shoe in her entire closet, he looked under all rugs. Next the trashcans for false bottoms.

Nothing.

He walked into the open living space with the kitchen and living room areas. He stared at a bamboo palm houseplant in the corner. How had he missed this? The four-foot-tall plant was in too large a pot relative to its size.

He rushed over and yanked the plant out. Dirt littered the floor. He stuck his hands in up to the wrists and dug around. When he was done, there was a pile of dirt on the floor and an empty pot.

It was just a plant.

Three hours later, as dusk began to darken the apartment, Mack flicked on the light, exhausted. His hands were just about frozen as he had unwrapped every single item in Anna's freezer. He looked at his phone. 7:27 PM Central.

He shot his dad a text. "Anything?"

His dad texted back, "Nothing. Sorry."

He grabbed Anna's journal from the kitchen counter and sat down on the couch to read it. From his quick glance, it appeared to be on Diana's cancer. He wanted to continue and flicked on the lamp that stood on the end table. It was dead. He tried it two more times. He unscrewed the bulb and shook it. Re-screwed it, then went over and flipped the light switch on the nearest wall. Nothing. He unplugged the lamp and took it to the kitchen. There was an outlet directly behind the coffee machine. He stuck the light plug into the outlet, and it didn't turn on. He then tried the bottom plug of the outlet, with the same result.

Hold on. Why was the coffee pot plugged into another outlet two feet away?

His nerves began to tingle.

He opened the kitchen junk drawer and fished out a screwdriver. He unscrewed the outlet cover. Once it had come loose, Mack felt the hair on the back of his neck raise up as he looked at the inside of a false wall outlet. Inside was a safe deposit key and a bottle of pills.

He laughed out loud and fished the items from their snug spot. He put the key in his pocket then opened the bottle of pills—a mixture of red and blue pills.

His eyes welled up as he stared at them.

That's when something smashed through the kitchen window and landed at his feet.

A moment later, the flash grenade exploded.

38

The pills had gone flying, scattering everywhere.

Mack dropped to the ground. His vision had collapsed into shattered webs of light with black dots of randomness, while his ears rung at a numbing pitch.

"No," he said as he scrambled on his hands and knees to grope for the pills.

He felt the vibrations of at least two men storming into the room. In desperation he pulled the key out of his pocket and put it in his mouth.

He took a breath, shut his eyes, and swallowed *hard*.

The thing grated miserably against his throat. His gag reflex fought it. He swallowed again, hard, and then again. He had almost no spit left. He got up and groped his way to the sink, blindly turned on the tap, and stuck his head under, lapping at a trickle of cool water. The key grated against his esophagus. He felt it enter his stomach.

Two men grabbed him. One reached inside Mack's jacket, snatching his gun and credentials.

"Hold on," the man said, his words muffled by a gas mask. "FBI."

"Call it in, see if we should still proceed as planned," said the other.

Blurrily, Mack could see the man emptying a large container all around them. The stink of gasoline was unmistakable. As his vision began to clear—he saw the pills were lying on the floor, soaked.

"Kill him," said one of the thugs, his finger on his earpiece.

Earpiece?

He finally was able to see these men. They were well dressed.

The other struck Mack in the stomach, sending him to his knees. He fought the urge to vomit.

The man with the gun pointed it at Mack's chest. "Sorry, Agent. Wrong place, wrong time,"

A spark and a glow. The other man had lit a small flare. "In the head," he said. "Guy's got a vest on."

The man raised his gun and took dead aim.

"I know where the formula is hidden," Mack rasped.

The man with the gun smiled. "So do we."

With only the speed of near-death adrenaline, Mack sprang from his knees as the man pulled the trigger. The bullet struck him in the vest, vicious as a punch from a heavyweight. He flew backwards onto the kitchen counter, spinning a half turn onto it. As if guided, his hand went to the knife rack. He grabbed a big one, spun around, and chucked it. It was just enough to jar the would-be killer and send the next bullet into the kitchen wall. Mack lunged forward and grabbed the man's wrist with one hand, driving his other fist square into the man's jaw.

The man dropped to the floor.

There was a gunshot and the second man's brains were splattered on the light gray wall behind him. The flare struck the ground and the floor burst into flames, Mack attempted to run, but the man who he'd been grappling with grabbed hold of his ankle. He clutched at Mack like a doomed man and began to scream as the lower half of his body was consumed by fire.

As Mack tried to shake free, he finally saw his guardian angel who took the shot off the fire escape deck. With dead aim, the angel shot the flaming devil holding onto Mack.

Freed, Mack outsprinted the spreading flames and made it out the sliding glass doors.

"This way," the angel said. Mack followed the young, suited man down the fire escape stairs and into his car, parked a couple of houses down.

As the driver put the car in gear he held out his hand, "Agent Quinn, FBI. Sorry, I'll show you my badge later."

Mack shook the hand. "Agent Maddox, FBI. Nice timing back there."

Quinn pulled out and accelerated quickly. "Hang on. I don't think it's a good idea to hang around here."

"I quite agree," said Mack. "Any idea who those two goons were?"

"Not yet, but they're probably way above our pay grade."

"So close," Mack said suddenly. His face in his hands.

Quinn looked over at Mack, saw the bullet holes in Mack's shirt. "You okay?"

"I had the pills! For a second time I had them and I—"

"What pills?" Quinn asked.

"Hang on. Who the hell are you?"

Quinn fumbled in his coat pocket. "Don't believe me?"

"Yeah, I know. FBI. But why are you here?"

"Following up on a lead."

"A lead from who?"

"Gracie Green."

"She's innocent, you know."

Quinn looked over at him. "How do you know that?"

"Anna's mom, Diana. Gracie cured her."

Quinn nodded slowly.

"You don't believe me."

"On the contrary. I knew Gracie wasn't lying." Quinn looked over at him again. "You know, my niece is sick."

"Cancer's the devil. My wife only has days."

"Agent Maddox, what do you say we find more of those pills?"

"Now you're speaking my language," said Mack.

39

A sharp metallic snap grabbed Gracie's attention, then the door of her cell ponderously swung open.

"Finally," she said as she popped up from her bed. She'd been promised some paper and a writing instrument. She had nothing but time here. If she could recreate a significant portion of her formulas, she could maybe get them to Quinn.

"Hurry up, our shift's ending in 10," the guard waiting outside the cell said as the other walked through the outer doorway into the isolated secure area in the cell.

The guard held a stack of printer paper and some type of clear rubber-looking crayon. Gracie reached through the bars for the handoff. The guard pulled the paper out of Gracie's reach.

The guard called out to the outer guard, "Entering inside main cell."

"Come on, McNally, let's hurry it up," the second guard said out of Gracie's view. "I'd like a warm dinner tonight for a change. You know my old lady doesn't like me to be late. She gets downright hateful with her cold food."

"Step back," the guard called McNally said to Gracie. He kept his head tilted at an awkward angle, downward, making it difficult for Gracie to see much of his face behind the bill of his hat and thick beard.

Gracie stepped to the back of the cell against the wall. McNally unlocked the door and slid it open to the right. He entered and placed the paper and writing instrument on the concrete desk slab sticking out of the wall.

Gracie looked anxiously at the guard, waiting for the okay to move. McNally stepped back and motioned with his hand. "It's all yours."

Gracie took a couple of cautious steps forward and sat on the immovable round concrete stool. She already knew exactly what formula she was going to write down first as she grabbed the weird writing instrument.

She put the rubber pen to the paper and attempted to write, but nothing was happening. She looked at it, shook it, tried it again.

She looked up at McNally. "This doesn't write."

"I'm here to break you out," the guard whispered.

"I'm sorry?"

"Bic sent me."

A flood of terrified relief went through her.

"Just relax and do as I say," McNally said, then turned toward the door. "Hey Garrison, you have another crayon on you?"

Garrison entered the cell. "These crap rubber pens—you just have to push down hard to get the ink started."

Both guards looked on as Gracie tried again. She wrote the capital letter A, but nothing was happening.

"Try again, push harder," Garrison said as he leaned in to take a closer look. "Hang on. McNally, you dunce, that's not the right pen."

There was a crack and a spatter of blood. Gracie gasped and jumped back as Garrison's body hit the table before spilling over onto the floor.

McNally stood poised with his nightstick. Then reached into his pocket and took out a packet of something, offering it to Gracie.

"Chew these," he said.

She turned the packet over in her hand. "Alka Seltzer?"

"You're gonna fake a seizure."

"I don't want to make things worse," she said, and looked at his face. *Really* looked at it now. There was something odd about it. Behind the beard was somewhat creepy and unreal.

"They're going to kill you," said McNally, who turned to heft Garrison's body off the floor by the shoulders. He grunted as he lifted the body onto the bed, took a breath, then covered the corpse with the bed sheet. He looked back at Gracie.

"You're on. Chew those. We're not playing here. They are going to *kill you*. Do you understand?"

Gracie chewed the two pills. Her mouth filled with white foam, so much that it started to spill out over her lips and run down her chin.

"Hide in the corner, I'll be right back," McNally said, then rushed out of her cell.

Gracie, with white foam oozing from her mouth, stayed still as she could, fighting the urge to spit the nasty things out. Her limbs were trembling uncontrollably. Still, there was something about that face. A mask? What the hell was Uncle Bic up to?

After a couple of long minutes of not hearing so much as a peep, the silence was broken with several buzzing sounds of cell doors opening. In the brief time she had been here she'd come to learn one thing—you never heard more than one of these sounds at a time. Prisoners here were let out of their cells with a two-guard escort, and never together.

Shouting and cheers followed.

"Freedom!"

The cheers grew in direct proportion to the increase in frequency of the door buzzes. Deep, aggressive voices. Screams. An alarm. This was a prison riot.

A prisoner entered her cell.

The man spotted Gracie. In his fifties, about six feet, narrow face with thinning gray hair he silently stared for a long moment.

Then a creepy smile swept across his face, flashing teeth like Chiclets. His shark eyes narrowed to slits.

"Daddy's home," he said, giggling.

Gracie hopped to her feet as quick as a cat, spitting out the remainder of the Alka Seltzer. She was going to fight to the death before she was going to let that man do whatever he was thinking.

"You come closer and it'll be the last thing you do," she said, her voice twittery.

"Good," said the slimeball, "I love fighters." He took a step forward. "It's more fun if we both bleed."

Gracie clenched her fist.

A sudden flash of black, then a quick snap of the man's neck with a wicked crack. He dropped, and there was McNally behind him, dressed in full riot gear, including a helmet and face shield.

He took out his radio. "Have assaulted female prisoner, unconscious and attacked by another inmate, need assistance to get her out." He put the radio to his side. "You okay?"

"I spit out the Alka Seltzer. I'm sorry."

"No, it's my fault. Took longer than I'd expected. I'll need you unconscious. Can you do that?"

Gracie nodded.

McNally wrapped his right arm around her back and his left underneath her knees and picked her up. "Just go completely limp."

She did so, and her neck ached terribly at the awkward angle. This wasn't going to be easy.

They were still unmoving when she heard McNally talking to someone, or was it two?

"What happened?" said a voice.

"She's unconscious," said McNally. "We need to get her to the medical unit quick!"

Another voice. "Is that Garrison? What happened to him?"

"Callum here," said McNally, probably referencing to the slimeball on the floor. "Must have hit him on the head with something."

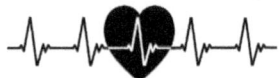

She poked an eye open and was horrified by the sight.

The cell block was in complete anarchy. About twenty violent prisoners were in an all-out brawl with at least a dozen guards. The guards had batons and shields, no guns. The hardened prisoners seemed more than happy to take a shot from a baton in order to get at a piece of the guards. Eyes were clawed.

She'd never felt so helpless in her life.

"Let me down," she said to McNally. "I can run with you. It'll be easier. There's too much chaos for anyone to notice."

"Can't take the chance. Do me a favor. At least keep your eyes closed. Try to stay limp."

She ignored the direction.

At least McNally was going in the opposite direction of all the fighting, which was somewhat comforting. He ran haphazardly down a series of hallways, jolting her at every turn, until finally he came to the steel door that led out of cell block D.

He paused at the door, entered a five-digit code, and the massive reinforced steel door opened.

"Home stretch," he said to her.

40

Dressed in full prison ADX swat gear, Bic slowly rolled his dirt bike down the steep mountain terrain. He had another hundred and fifty yards before he reached the flat land that led to the razor-wire-wrapped fence of the outer perimeter. This was taking longer than planned. The rock slope had a slickness to it he hadn't counted on, and even with the gear on he was a bit cold.

Completely focused on the task at hand—getting down this rock— he wondered what Gracie's reaction would be. In order to get her out, he was going to have to hurt a lot of people. Innocent guards who probably had families to feed. Would she even go with him, or would she shun him again like she had at the farmhouse, even running out on him again? If only she'd trusted him, she wouldn't be in jail right now, and he wouldn't have to attempt this crazy break out. If she decided to cut and run, she ran the risk of being gunned down by a tower guard.

The old rage began to surge within him, he lost his footing and ended up in a sideways slide that took him to the foot of the mountain. He cursed softly and stood. Here was a new glimpse of ADX, lit up bright by its perimeter lights. It had a simple compound shape, a single isosceles triangle with a rectangle for a base. The ninety-degree peak, the top of the triangle, pointed towards Bic and the mountains. Even though inside it was hell on earth, from out here, as he breathed in the fresh cool mountain air, it had an awkward calming effect.

Bic looked into the sky. Stars like glitter on black.

The air was cut by the distant whirring of a helicopter. The unmistakable noise increased in volume until the machine buzzed right over him.

What the hell?

This thing was way too low.

It hovered over him for a moment, then erupted in machine gun fire that spewed from its sides, the blinding white flashes lighting up the first guard tower like a tiki torch.

Bic pulled out his cell and called Hawk.

Before Hawk could answer, the second tower was consumed in a destructive fire. "Hawk, get here now, and be ready for a firefight. There's a chopper here laying waste to the place."

Bic jumped onto his dirt bike and kick started it. Within seconds, he opened the throttle up. As he closed the distance to the fence, the chopper made its way down the right side of the perimeter, going right down the line of guard towers and feeding each a steady diet of .50-cal gunfire—easily destroying the only two guard towers on the right side.

Twenty yards from the fence at the top of the triangle, Bic hit the perimeter gravel road, cut sharp to his left, and dropped the dirt bike. If only he had a sniper rifle instead of his MP5. Better than nothing, he thought, as he dropped to one knee and took aim.

He took aim at the window of the chopper just as it finished off the second-to-last guard tower in the lower corner of the perimeter. He did some quick calculations. The MP5 weapon system was zeroed in at 25 yards—really designed for close combat. The shot he was about to take was at least 200 yards. Then there was the upward trajectory making the compensation for gravity on the 9mm bullet even more difficult. Plus, there was the probability the bullet would start to tumble around the 200-yard marker.

The chopper swung around the angle of the perimeter where the triangle and rectangle met, and Bic took aim through his EOTECH sight.

The man holding the twin handles of the .50-cal came into focus. Bic aimed a foot high and six inches to the left. From there, his strategy was simple: if the first cluster of bullets didn't hit the target, he would walk the bullets toward it.

The .50-cal destroyed the final tower as Bic opened fire. Seeing sparks over the target, he walked the stream of fire down towards the gunner.

Before he hit the gunner, the chopper ascended back over the prison yard and lowered itself within the perimeter just opposite from

Bic's location. It was landing.

He sprinted down the perimeter road towards the corner, but his view was blocked by the prison cell block structures, not to mention the clouds of billowing black smoke that were rapidly obscuring everything. He pushed himself to sprint harder and came around the base corner of the rectangle. There he was blinded by the bright lights of a security pickup truck in his path.

He dove toward the fence to avoid getting shot, trying to clear his vision of the bright lights.

From the rumbling in his stomach, he knew the pickup truck was running, but did not sense any movement. A closer look revealed that the truck had bullet holes running up the hood and windshield.

Bic kept an appropriate angle with his weapon as he approached the vehicle. Inside was a dead driver, riddled with bullet holes. He pulled the dead driver out and onto the road and jumped into the driver's seat.

Speeding down the perimeter road, he spotted the chopper on the ground on the other side of the fence. Two men from the chopper were on one knee, aiming M-16s at the cell block structure. Rage and fear blotted out all other vision as he saw a guard carrying Gracie from one of the exterior cell block doors towards the chopper.

With the prison sirens blaring, two attack dogs sprinted towards the guard and Gracie, but the men with the M-16s opened fire and dropped the two canines before they got within ten feet of her.

Bic cut the wheel in the opposite direction of the fence and sped thirty yards away from the perimeter, then locked up the brakes and spun the truck back in the direction he'd just come from.

The guard had Gracie halfway to the chopper when Bic floored it back toward the twelve-foot-high chain-link fence, then smashed into it at 50 miles per hour.

He jolted to a stop about ten yards into the compound. With a sinking feeling he realized that while he was able to burst through the chain-link part of the fence, several strands of barbed wire were stretched like a net around him.

The truck was met with M-16 fire.

Bic ducked and then sprung up at the slightest pause to return fire with his Glock, then realized they'd retreated, and with Gracie in tow.

With the car wrapped in barbed wire, the door would not open. Bic leaned back, brought up his foot, and blasted the windshield off the pickup. He crawled out onto the hood and jumped to the ground, making a beeline for the chopper as the rotors picked up speed as the landing skids lifted from the ground. He grabbed onto the skid from the inside as it continued to rise. At about ten feet off the ground, M-16 fire erupted. Bic did a pull-up to keep his body underneath the chopper and stay out of the line of fire.

The barrel of the M-16 jetted down around the underbelly of the chopper. Bic grabbed the barrel with his right hand as shots were fired and yanked hard. The man holding the rifle fell headfirst out of the chopper.

The chopper did a slight swerve, changing course, headed toward one of the flaming towers. Bic pulled his chest up onto the skid as the underbelly of the chopper flew over the orange swirling flames reaching hungrily in the air.

Working to get a leg up to enter the cabin, Bic caught sight of something in his peripheral vision. A man had dropped out on the other side.

41

The guy, either a guard or someone dressed like a guard, had latched onto the skid opposite Bic like an Olympic gymnast grabbing onto a high bar. Using his momentum, he swung his feet toward Bic's back. He then launched himself forward, quickly closing the eight feet that separated them.

Bic spotted his assailant coming at him, and he tried to turn his upper body—leading with his Glock—but before he fully swung his arm around, the guard blasted Bic with both feet, knocking him off the skid.

Bic let go of his Glock to grab onto the skid, barely getting his fingertips wrapped around the metal rod.

Both men hung facing one another as the guard used his free hand to draw a shiny silver .357 from the front his pants.

Bic jabbed his left hand and caught the guard's wrist before he could fully draw the weapon. The other man's strength was unbelievable.

The guard kneed him in the ribs, then struggled like a crazy man to get a bead on Bic. Bic fought back with all of his might, the two bodies trembling with murderous effort.

Slowly, the guard managed to get his gun into the position to shoot.

The gun barrel was nearly at his temple.

The man's face...

...like a mask...

The strange notion threw some kind of switch inside Bic. It was a problem to be solved. There was a clarity born of detachment now. He was devoid of emotion, merely coldly calculating the physics of their struggle. Bic stopped resisting the guard and pulled his wrist as hard and fast as he could.

He propelled the guard's right arm through the kill zone, then with its continued upward trajectory, slammed his knuckles into the metal rod. The gun fell to the earth.

Both men quickly latched on to the bar with their second hands. The chopper was twenty feet off the ground and had cleared the prison by about two hundred yards on its way into the mountain range.

In a surreal moment, with the backdrop of the majestic mountain range, both men faced each other, silently glaring, each silently calculating the best way to kill the other.

Bic landed a right-handed haymaker across the man's masked face. A gash in the molded latex tore wide open.

The man swung his whole body at Bic, latching onto him, then let go of the bar.

Bic now held the weight of both men on the rail, defenseless as the guard wrapped his legs around his torso and volleyed short, vicious jabs.

With strength ebbing by the second, Bic struggled to pull himself up.

The man grabbed the skid with one hand, loosened his legs from around Bic's midsection, then pulled himself up, drawing back his right fist for the final blow.

At the high point of Bic's pull-up, he released his left hand and grabbed onto the back of the guard's neck and pinned his chin and throat on top of the bar, then did the same with his other hand clenching his fingers together behind his neck. He hung from the man, trapping him in an inescapable chokehold against the skid.

Bic watched the man's eyes bulge as he strangled. An unexpected life sprung into the man as the mask peeled and blew back, the face behind it a twisted caricature of animal fury and bloodlust. It was grainy, scarred and wooden. The face of his father in the guise of a Dan mask stared at him, through him.

The guard's face, a horrible, peeling mask, distorted even further as it went crimson, the eyes wide, the mouth agape with protruding tongue.

Bic's eyes suddenly went blurry, accompanied by a deep stabbing pain. Refusing to let go, he doubled down on his efforts as he tried to crush this man's windpipe. "Clarence Green, I'm coming for you," he yelled.

The pain felt like someone had just cut his chest wide open and dumped a shovel of burning coals into it.

He fought with all his might to stay conscious, but his body had reached its limit. His eyes rolled in the back of his head, his grip slackened, and he dropped into a dense canopy of evergreen trees.

42

The Farmer sucked in as much oxygen as he could before pulling himself up onto the skid. Then he stood and climbed back into the chopper, dropping himself into his seat like a drunken man.

Everything ached. What didn't ache, throbbed. What didn't throb was bleeding.

But none of that mattered, the first round of this fight felt amazing mentally and he wanted more. This was the sweet vengeance he'd been wishing for his brother for years. If his opponent was not worthy somehow, it would taint what he thought about his brother.

Gracie's mouth was moving. No words.

He put the headset on.

"Are you alright?" she said.

Still high on adrenaline. "Fine."

"What happened?"

"Don't worry about it. Hey, Swanson," he said addressing the pilot, "turn this bird around."

"No can do," he replied.

The Farmer popped out of his seat, walked up to the pilot, grabbed the M16 next to him, and pointed it at his head.

"Turn this bird around." He looked across the landscape, then pointed at the thick patch of tall evergreens, "Over there."

The Farmer went over to the opening and grabbed the handles to the .50-cal gun as he scanned the ground for Bic.

"Chief," said Swanson, the pilot, "we have a situation."

The Farmer looked up to see another helicopter approaching, and could barely react before .50-cal fire began streaming from it.

Swanson banked swiftly to avoid the stream, throwing the Farmer off his feet.

"Turn back!" he screamed.

"Shoot me if you want, chief. I'm getting us outta here."

The Farmer got to his feet and scrambled to the gun. The two birds were doing an air dance as the distance between them widened. Fire continued to spew from the unknown chopper's gun.

He took aim and fired for five seconds. Then ran out of ammo.

43

"Should we go after that bird?" the pilot asked.

"Let's go get Bic" Hawk replied. "Put us down where you can."

The chopper landed in an open area, and before the skids hit the ground, Hawk was out, running toward the thick area of Douglas fir trees. At least his buddy had only fallen about 10 feet. Chances were, he wasn't too messed up.

Leading with his MP5, he poked in and out of the maze of hundreds of Christmas trees.

After cutting through the middle, he ran diagonals, trying to cover as much ground as possible. Unsuccessful on his second and third diagonal crisscross, he stopped to catch his breath. He had a bead on where he thought Bic had fallen, but with dense trees in all directions, everything looked the same and his eye couldn't pierce the canopy.

Hawk took a deep, calming breath as he refocused his strategy. A pile of large boulders gave him an answer. He made his way to the top and was now a good fifteen feet above ground level. He looked in all directions. Nothing but a sea of green, the trees too thick to see down to the ground.

This ain't good, he thought.

Then, thirty yards away, he saw the top of a fir tree snapped.

"There you are," he muttered.

He dashed in the direction of the broken tree. A big black military boot poked out from behind it.

"Aw, brother," he said.

Bic lay motionless on his back.

Hawk checked him for a pulse. "Thank God," he said.

He then scanned Bic for serious wounds—gunshot wounds,

stabbing, or swelling on his head. Seemed he had only scrapes and bruises.

"I'm gonna get you to a hospital, brother." Hawk grabbed Bic from behind under both arms and began the laborious task of dragging him back to the chopper.

44

Gracie looked at the beaten and bruised McNally, the latex mask half-torn from his face.

"Who the hell are you, anyway?" she said.

McNally continued to pull off chunks of mask and beard from his face.

"Are you working with Agent Quinn?"

The name didn't even register a response. He continued to pull the rubber material from under his chin.

"Your name isn't McNally, is it?"

The bulk of his mask off, the man stood and glared at her, bits of latex still hanging off his face like leper's skin. "Not now, princess."

"Listen," she said, "I don't know who—"

The guard—if he was even a guard at all—held up a hand and placed his finger on his lips. His attention was drawn to Swanson at the controls.

He leapt toward the pilot. "What are you doing with that?"

"With what?" Swanson replied.

"The detonator you just turned on then slipped back in your pocket."

"You're crazy."

He reached into the Swanson's pocket and pulled out a device that looked exactly like the one the terrorists had used to blow up her lab.

"Does Jaco know about this?"

"Listen," said Swanson, "my orders were to destroy the chopper after we landed."

The guard looked at the detonator. "Take your chute off."

"Not happening," said Swanson.

"Take it off, Swanson. I'm not gonna say it again."

"Say it 87 times. You don't scare me, Farmer. You know how to fly this thing? Be my guest."

"If you insist." The Farmer drew his .357 and fired a round at Swanson's feet. Then put his gun to his temple, pressing the barrel against his head, hard. The hot barrel singed Swanson.

Swanson stole nervous looks as sweat began to drip from his temples. "Now, just a second…"

"One good old second. That's all you have before I blow your brains all over that there control panel. You wanna play around, city boy? Let's dance."

Swanson complied, his face twisted with worry and fear. He held the chute out.

"Good, now get us some altitude," he barked grabbing the chute.

Swanson did as he was told, muttering, "Psycho."

The helicopter ascended rapidly.

The Farmer walked back to Gracie.

"What the hell do you want from me?" she said.

"What do I want *with* you. Not from." He chuckled. "You're bait."

"What?" Gracie blinked in surprise.

He took off his headset and threw it on the floor. He motioned for her to do the same, then pointed to the detonator in his other hand. Scrambling to comply, it took her a second to understand, then she replied frantically, throwing the headset away from her. He put the chute on. Then he took aim at Swanson's head.

The hand cannon flashed. Swanson's body chucked forward, brains and blood spattering the windshield.

Gracie screamed. Before she could react further, the twisted Farmer guy grabbed her.

"Grab on tight," he screamed, wrapping his arms around her. She threw her arms around him, a numbing fear taking hold of her body.

The chopper jerked to the right, and the man spilled himself and Gracie out into the sky.

Everything spun into a hysterical blur.

Solid colors turned into streaks of lights and shadows.

The wind slammed into her face, her eyeballs pushed back into their sockets.

And seconds into their tandem fall, she saw the detonator in his hand, and the movement of his thumb…

The chopper exploded in a horrendous ball of flames. Its flaming carnage dropped to the ground like a meteor.

The Farmer yelled out, "Yeah! A country boy can survive," as he pulled the ripcord and the chute blossomed above them.

45

Hawk slouched in the chair of Bic's hospital room, watching the news with the volume turned down as Bic lay still beside him. He didn't know how he was going to tell him that Gracie's chopper had crashed. What was worse, according to the news, three bodies had been found, one of them alleged to be Gracie's.

Anthony Parelli, in a three-piece suit, walked into the room.

Hawk jumped up from his chair and hugged the man. "Hey. It's been a long time, brother."

"Easy," said Parelli. "The back's been giving me trouble. Damned sciatica. How is he?"

"They're not sure."

"Look at that bruiser. He can't be taken out just like that."

"Thanks for getting him in here."

"The least I can do. Bic will be treated like a king here, no questions asked."

"How'd you manage it?"

Parelli looked over his shoulder, then back at Hawk. "The president of this joint owes me a favor. I told him to put his absolute best on this, around the clock."

"They have been."

"I'm telling you," said Parelli, a forehead vein bulging, "if some intern's working on him—"

"The docs have been top notch." Hawk looked away for a second. "They have no idea what's wrong."

Parelli raised an eyebrow. "He took a fall. It's not a concussion?"

Hawk bit his lip.

"What is it?" said Parelli. "You look like you know something."

"Man, you're not gonna believe it."

"Try me."

Hawk hesitated for a moment. "It's just that… well, Bic was under the impression that maybe his dad had something to do with it. Like, you know, that voodoo stuff? And, I mean, that *would* explain why none of these docs can find anything wrong."

Parelli put his head in his hand. "Jesus. I'll talk to the doctors myself. There's no such thing as a curse. Where I come from, there was all these Sicilians constantly putting curses on each other. Trust me, if any of them stuck, I wouldn't be here."

"I'm more afraid if he wakes up. What with Gracie…"

Parelli shook his head, "There's going to be some heads rolling for sure." He clenched his fists and said, "I've got to get some air. I'm gonna go talk to the docs."

46

With the rising sun to her right, Gracie figured they'd been trekking north. They'd be going nonstop for at least eight hours. In the distance, she saw a small town.

She had tried to talk to this man to figure out what he wanted. By what she'd witnessed, she knew how lethal he was and that he was keeping her alive for a reason. But so far, every attempt had gotten her nothing but silence.

Now, fed up with eight hours of cluelessness, she cut in front of him and spoke, walking backwards. "Enough of the silent treatment. I want you to tell me who you are and what's happening."

"Can't hurt, I suppose. They call me the Farmer."

"So you're a farmer."

"Yeah, I am. But it's Farmer with a capital F. The Farmer. That's my name."

"Mr. The Farmer."

"Is that all?"

"No. Tell me what's happening. And I want the truth."

"I don't lie."

"Oh, a virtuous vicious killer."

"Yeah. I got no reason to lie. I'll answer a question, but first you gotta answer one for me."

Gracie nodded.

"What's with Bic and the pork chops?"

This floored her. "Bic? *My* Bic? What's he got to do with this?"

The Farmer smiled. "Well, girl, who the hell did you think I was fighting with underneath that damn machine? The Tooth Fairy?"

Her pace slowed as her heart sank in her chest.

"Did you kill him?"

"Nah." The Farmer walked past her. "He didn't fall far."

"But did you kill him?"

The Farmer stopped and turned. "No. He fell. That was that. Come on." He resumed walking and she kept up with him.

"So," he said, "you gonna answer my question?"

"What was it? Something about a pork chop?"

"Yeah, a pork chop. What's the deal with that?"

"I have no idea what you're talking about."

He stared straight ahead. "Then we don't have nothin' else to talk about."

There was so much turmoil within her now, roiling like the base of a waterfall, with all that she'd learned about her uncle. She didn't know whether she could trust this strange man who called himself the Farmer, but she was sure as hell she couldn't trust Bic. Her memories of the man he used to be threatened to drown her. She couldn't bear it.

A pork chop?

A thought came to her. "Wait a second. When my mom had just passed away, Bic had told me he lost his mother too, when he was a kid."

"Okay."

"He never spoke of it, but I remember finding a police blotter in the newspaper about it. His father had beaten his mother to death right in front of him with an iron skillet. He then tried to choke him to death by stuffing a pork chop in his mouth."

The Farmer looked at her, his attention obviously piqued. "Really...? That's pretty messed up."

"Yeah," she said. "It is. That's why it stuck with me. Now, I answered your question. My turn, why did you break me out?"

"I was supposed to break you out of prison, then kill you. Simple as that. But I'm guessing Jaco knew that I wasn't going to kill you until I took care of some unfinished business. He's a smart dude. He was going to blow us both up on that chopper."

"And what's this unfinished business that's keeping me alive?"

He looked at her. "I'm going to kill Bic, Princess."

Gracie concealed the twisting emotions inside her. "So," she said, wearily, "where does that leave us now?"

"You're going to help me kill him."

"Why would I do that?"

The Farmer stopped and turned. "Because if you do, I will make sure your cure gets out there."

Anger and skepticism burned inside her. "You would do that?"

"To pay back the men who tried to kill me? You bet. Ain't nobody friends with nobody in this business. I reckon I can do my job *and* get double payback, and get you what you need too."

Gracie cocked her head to the side. So many questions...

The Farmer handed Gracie his phone and a piece of paper with an address on it. "Call him, tell him I have you here."

Gracie hesitated.

"I give you my word. I will clear your name after I take care of my business."

"I'm not going to take your word."

He shook his head in frustration. "Think of it this way. Bic wants to come save you. If he kills me, then he *will* save you. If I kill him, I clear your name. Now, if we don't have a deal, fine. I'll just save us both a lot of time and heartache and snap your neck right here."

He held out his phone.

She took it.

47

Hawk sat in Bic's room alone. About ten minutes ago they had taken him for a full body MRI, thanks to Tony Parelli ruffling more than a few medical feathers.

Bic's phone rang on the bedside table. Hawk stared at it. Only a few people had his number. Important people. He picked it up.

"Yeah?"

"Bic? It's me, Gracie!"

Before Hawk could respond, there was a rustling sound on the other end, and then a man's voice said, "You have twenty-four hours to save her." The line went dead. A moment later, a text appeared. It was an address.

Hawk sat back down and began to think.

Forty-five minutes later, the nurse rolled Bic back into the room.

"Any changes?" Hawk asked.

"Unfortunately, no," the nurse replied. "The doctor will be in shortly to discuss."

After she exited, Hawk stared at Bic for several minutes, then finally said, "Hey. We got a little problem here and I can't solve it myself. Now, we been friends for a long time, me and you. One thing I know is, Bic Green ain't a quitter. So what do you say you kick this thing and wake up, my brother?"

He stared at his friend, the massive chest heaving with every breath.

"Hey, 'member that time we were in Kennesaw? Or better yet, how about that girl I met in Tampa?" He laughed at the memory. "You thought she had a face like twelve nightmares. Then you looked at her again and said she was a cop that was about to raid the joint for allowing underage drinkers. I swore you were full of it. Well, you were right, my man. She got up in the middle of me trying to pick her up. Said she was going to the ladies' room. Then out comes the badge." He threw his head back and laughed again. "Dammit, Bic, you got like six senses about that stuff. I never understood it."

Hawk watched his friend, and his smile faded along with the memories. He bent down and spoke into Bic's ear. "They say nothing's wrong with you, so wake up, you SOB."

He fought back tears as a strange anger came into him. "You know what? I read online that a good crack across the face can wake you up from the deepest of sleeps. So you better wake up, cuz I'm fixin' to lay my five spot across your face... you don't think I'll do it, do you?"

Hawk started at Bic for a long moment. He took off his two heavy metal rings and dropped them onto the food table, making sure they made as much noise as possible. "That's it, I'm going to count down from three..." He held his hand up high. He couldn't stop it from trembling. "Three... two... one!" He slapped his friend hard across the face.

Bic showed zero response.

"Sorry, brother," said Hawk, tears now flowing freely. "I had to try." He replaced his rings, then grabbed a piece of paper and wrote a note:

The girl is alive!
Tried to wake you, but you wouldn't.
Went to save her.
Won't let you down brother.

Hawk.

He folded the note and placed it on his bedside table, then put his hand on Bic's shoulder and said, "I won't let you down, brother. I'm gonna go get the girl."

He grabbed Bic's phone and left the room.

48

It was just after midnight when Mack bit into his third bean burrito for the evening and washed it down with his fifth beer.

"You really like burritos, huh," said Agent Quinn.

"You don't know the half of it," he said.

They sat on a picnic bench outside a taco truck called Fooditos, located in the parking lot of a dive bar by the name of Shawshanks.

"My wife and I are nuts about Mexican food."

"I don't trust anyone who isn't," said Quinn.

Mack sucked his teeth and stared at the tiny Mexican flag on the top of the truck, blowing in the sweet night air. "There's this little joint around the block from us that keeps changing its name. We used to go there every Wednesday night when we first got married. Drinks and apps were half price on Wednesdays. We'd start with margaritas. Best damn margaritas on the planet. They muddled jalapenos into them. I never heard of that before. We'd drink three of those and get totally buzzed."

"Sounds like a night," said Quinn. "I'm getting another Corona. Want another?"

"You read my mind."

Quinn left and returned with two bottles. He handed one to Mack and clinked it with his.

"Yeah, it was really great back then," said Mack, noticing he was starting to slur his words. "We'd play the *Would You Rather* game, drunk. Ever play the *Would You Rather* game drunk?"

"No, but I once played with a Ouija board while on acid."

Mack stared at him. "That must've been... weird."

"You don't know the half of it," he said, winking.

Mack twirled his bottle. "One time, she asked me, 'Would you rather live in a world where burritos existed or a world where they didn't exist but there was no paperwork on case files."

Quinn chuckled. "Man, that's an easy one."

"I tell ya, I hate paperwork like anthrax, but I don't think I'd make it a month without a burrito. I told her so. Then I asked her a serious one. 'Would you rather die in five years with no regrets or die in sixty with many regrets?' You know what she said? She said, 'Five years with no regrets.' I just remembered that."

He raised his beer to Caroline and took a swig, then stuffed another bite of the *#5 Barbacoa y Carnitas* into his mouth.

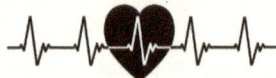

Quinn had dropped him off at home just in time. It was three o'clock in the morning when the plan kicked in.

After three bean burritos and one with meat, an entire six pack of Coronas plus one Corona Light, and three trips to the bathroom since late last night, Mack finally recovered the key he'd swallowed. With the second key, now all he had to do was figure out how to get into the bank's vault and get access to Anna's safe deposit box without getting a subpoena and losing the probable contents to evidence.

A knock at his door. "Mack, it's Quinn."

Quinn entered his hotel room.

"I got the key," he said, holding the triple-washed thing up for Quinn to see. Best not to tell him.

Quinn stared at it for a moment, lost in thought, then said, "Mack, I have some bad news."

He cleared his throat. "Gracie died last night in an attempted prison escape."

"What?"

"They just confirmed it."

"This can't be."

"I know, partner. Listen, if you want to go be with Caroline, I understand."

Mack looked to Quinn. "Yeah. Yeah, maybe that's a good idea."

"I can go check the box, let you know if I find anything."

Mack stared at the key in his palm, thinking about Caroline and what she'd do, then said, "No. I'm going to see this through."

"You sure?"

"I'm sure."

Quinn shook his head once. "Your call, partner. I'd hate for you to... you know."

"Yeah, I know. But there's too much riding on what might be inside that box."

Quinn put his hand on Mack's shoulder.

"I got an idea," said Mack.

49

The address Hawk got from the text on Bic's phone was a Nebraska one. The sun had slunk behind the horizon and night peppered the sky with stars by the time he got there. He decided to park his car a mile away and walk, hopefully to gain the element of surprise. Lying in the tall, unkempt grass, he looked through the scope on his sniper rifle. The moon hung smoky and grayish in an otherwise inky sky behind the small house sitting on its acreage.

Peering through the scope, his heart raced when he saw Gracie sitting at the kitchen table, tied, with her mouth duct-taped. The Farmer was nowhere in sight.

After an hour, Hawk's patience began to wear thin. He'd yet to see the Farmer enter the only lit room in the house. He knew he was using Gracie as bait, he just didn't know how. To Hawk's left was a large tree. He had eyed it a couple of times now. If he climbed about ten feet, he'd be able to see the corner of the room in which he suspected the Farmer might be hiding. One problem, climbing that tree meant exposure, wherever the Farmer was.

He stared into the darkness, waiting for any indication of the Farmer's presence—a glare, a light from a cell phone, anything. Concealing the light from his phone under some heavy grass, he called Gracie's phone as he peered into the dark window on the second floor—Straight to voicemail, no light on the second floor. *Shoot,* Hawk thought.

Finally, he gave in to the need to see that corner of the kitchen. On the other side of the tree trunk, facing the house, Hawk ascended.

You're gonna get your dumb ass shot, he thought.

About eight feet in the air, Hawk sat in between a large Y of two massive branches. He situated his rifle and peered into that corner. Hawk smiled.

"There you are, you hillbilly bastard."

The Farmer sat in the corner of the room with a MP5 resting beside him. He had on a green John Deere hat, but Hawk wasn't going for a headshot. He triangulated his chest and aimed for the SOB's heart instead.

Hawk slowed his breath as he planted the crosshairs on the Farmer's chest, then took the shot. The bullet tore through the Farmer's chest, a direct hit. Blood streamed out of the man's body.

Hawk snaked down to the ground and quickly slung his rifle across his back. Sprinting quickly forward, he entered the front door of the house, his nine-millimeter drawn. He swept the front room—all clear—then entered the kitchen.

Gracie saw him and screamed frantically through her gag.

He saw the Farmer slouched over. His hands were resting on his lap with his sweater over them.

Was he seeing this right?

The Farmer's hands were cuffed and tied down to the wood chair.

Gracie erupted in a spasm of muffled howls.

A violent puff of air, and there was a dart stuck into Hawk's chest.

Darkness from the pantry closet reached out to him, and everything went black.

50

Quinn and Mack stood at the massive steps of the First National Bank of Chicago. The stone columns supported the front of the building like some type of heavenly gateway as the building elevated higher than most others nearby.

Mack breathed in the cool October morning air, then spoke into his invisible earpiece, "Tom, walking into the bank, wait for our signal."

"Ten-four," Tom replied.

"Let's do this," Quinn said.

They shared a glance of determination, then the two men walked into the bank.

Mack approached the woman at the desk. "Hi, who can help us take out a safe deposit box?"

"Across the hall there, just sign in."

"Thank you," said Mack, then walked across the lobby.

Quinn followed and whispered out of the side of his mouth, "You sure your guy can take out those cameras?"

"This is a piece of cake for him," Mack said as he spied the nameplate on the man's desk. "Henry Kingston."

The man looked up from his computer screen at Mack and Quinn. "How may I help you?"

"We'd like to take out a safe deposit box today."

Quinn mustered up an awkward smile.

"Ah, sure thing." Henry motioned for them to sit down then reach into his desk and pulled two signature cards. "I'd be glad to help you with that."

"Great," Mack said. "Can I make a special request?"

"I'll try my best."

"Numbers are very important to us—can we pick our number?" Mack asked.

"Usually it's the next box up for rent, but I should be able to pull up a list of some boxes available."

"You're amazing." Mack looked to Quinn.

Quinn smiled and nodded.

After some paperwork, they followed Henry into the vault. The vault was massive, with thousands of tiny steel doors tagged with a black number plate outlined in gold trim and three keyholes the same color as the trim around the number plates. Mack knew Anna's box was 1026, and he also knew that the box they were renting was 1073, which was in the stack just to the right of Anna's. Now all he had to do was get into her box.

"Here's your new box." Henry pointed to number 1073.

"How about those Cubbies?" Mack asked.

"They might win it again," Henry said as he pulled out the bank master key and inserted it into the first keyhole of three, before pulling out two additional keys. "These are your keys," he said and inserted them as well. He then turned the keys and opened the box.

"Vault cameras will go dark in ten seconds," Tom said into their earpieces.

Henry pulled a metal box from inside the box halfway. "This is where you will keep any of your valuables." He glanced at both of them quizzically, then commented, "It doesn't look like you have anything today?"

"Cameras are dark for 60 seconds," Tom said.

Henry started to slide the box back in, but Mack stopped him. "Wait," he said as he pulled a folded piece of paper out of his front pocket. "Our vows."

Henry looked at Mack for a moment, then he looked at Quinn. "Right."

Mack reached for the box from Henry, then said in surprise, "Your nose, it's bleeding."

"What are you talking about?" Henry said, touching his nose with the back of his hand.

Out of Henry's line of sight, Quinn pulled out a handkerchief from a Ziploc bag, already covered in fake blood and doused in chloroform.

"Let me help you," Quinn said as he quickly covered Henry's nose,

"I always carry one of these around," then he immediately pulled it away from him so he could see the handkerchief."

"Jesus, that's a lot of blood," Henry said, sounding woozy.

"Relax, I'm a nurse," said Quinn. "Put your head back." He placed the handkerchief back over Henry's nose and mouth. "We'll stop the bleeding in no time."

"I don't know," said Henry. "I'm feeling really light-headed."

"It is a lot of blood," Quinn said as he guided Henry, so his back was to the vault.

Mack pulled the bank master key from the other deposit box and two keys from his pocket and inserted them into box 1026. He opened the door, pulled the box out, and reinserted the box from his vault. He then locked the box and pulled the keys out.

"There, I think it stopped," Quinn said.

"I think I need to go sit down, I feel... like I'm drunk."

"That's probably a good idea," Mack handed Henry his bank key.

"Thanks."

"Take your time, we'll be in the privacy room."

"Of course." Henry suddenly dropped down and sat, "I think I'll just wait for you guys here."

Inside the privacy room, Mack placed the box on the table. He looked to Quinn for a brief moment before opening it.

Inside the box were some papers in plain view and an envelope addressed to Gracie.

Mack opened the letter. He and Quinn huddled and read over it together.

First, I want to apologize for going behind your back, but after the second denial by the FDA, Steve's constant paranoia and conspiracy theories, along with my mother running out of time while we sat there with the cure, got the best of me.

If you do not know already: I've been treating my mother. Again, I am so sorry! But the cure works. It's amazing and we did it! Secondly, something totally crazy might happen and Steve's doomsday scenario might become true that he kept scaring the crap out of me with "Skynet is trying to terminate our formulas." He thought, in that case it would be prudent to have copies of the formulas hidden off the grid. The only clue he would give me was, "My favorite book at my favorite place to read." I'm assuming you know.

He also wanted me to tell you not to worry, all formulas will be posted in the event all else fails.

Love you always and hope you never read this letter.

Anna

"His favorite book, favorite place. Too bad he's gone." Mack shook his head as he reached deeper into the box and pulled out two pill bottles.

"Is that what I think it is?" said Quinn.

"Touchdown," Mack said and high-fived Quinn.

"I can't believe I doubted you. Good work, Mack."

Mack opened one pill bottle, then quickly the second. His smile left his face.

"What, no pills?" Quinn asked.

"There are pills."

"You had me worried there for a second."

Mack glared at Quinn. "Just enough to save one."

"You sure?"

"Ten red and ten blue. Why the hell would she only keep one dose?" Mack wondered.

"What do we do now?"

"Save your niece." Mack said.

"I can't take them." Quinn became emotional.

"There's no way Caroline would forgive me, I know it—here, take them," Mack said as he handed the pills to Quinn.

Quinn reluctantly accepted. "I don't know what to say."

"You saved my life at Anna's apartment; my daughter would be fatherless without you. It's the least I can do."

"I'll never forget this."

The men embraced one another.

51

Parelli stared at the unconscious Bic, lost in thought. Over his shoulder he heard a nurse admonishing someone.

"Sir, per special instruction, we can't have any other visit—oh…"

The sudden break in her voice made Parelli look up.

"*I'm* not allowed up here?" The man was smiling genially.

"I'm so sorry, Dr. Goodwin, sir, please—"

"It's fine," said the president of Lodestone Memorial Hospital. "May I have a word with Mr. Parelli?"

"Of course," said the nurse, ushering him in with a gesture.

Parelli chuckled softly at the command this guy had over the masses. Tall and well-dressed, salt and pepper hair—not one out of place, and a killer crooked smile. He could swear the nurse literally had a twinkle in her eye.

Parelli stood from his bedside chair.

"Mr. Parelli," Goodwin said.

"They're not fixing him," he said curtly.

Goodwin's face went stone. "I'm doing fine. Yes, the wife and kids are fine too. And so's the dog."

"Don't gimme that smug attitude. We talked about this. You need to send in someone better, smarter, and it needs to happen now!"

"I assure you I am doing everything in my power to help here."

"You need to do more."

Goodwin whispered in a firm voice as he jabbed his index finger at Bic. "I've run a quarter of a million dollars in tests on a guy who doesn't exist. I'd say I'm trying pretty hard."

"Then what the hell's wrong with him?"

"I don't know."

Parelli threw up his hands.

"Now look," said Goodwin, "you know as well as I do that diagnosis is largely a process of elimination. So far, we can't find anything, but that doesn't mean there's nothing. He's unresponsive, that's for sure, but there is no damage to his cerebral cortex or his RAS. Both are functioning fine. No drugs in his system, no metabolic abnormalities."

Parelli stroked his chin. "How 'bout you give him a jolt and wake his ass up?"

"A *jolt?*"

"Yeah, you know… a jolt."

"I'm not trained in *jolting*."

"You know what I mean."

"No, I don't."

"Listen," said Parelli, "when your girlfriend OD'd on pills—"

Goodwin's face went taut as he held up his hands. "For Christ's sake, keep your filthy voice down."

Parelli raised his voice. "Pills that *you* gave her, sonny Jim—"

"Enough!" Goodwin rasped.

Parelli stepped in closer. "I fixed it for you. No one but me. So now you listen closely, you worm, this man's niece is gonna die. They're gonna do some epic nasty things to her, and possibly take out other innocents, if we don't wake this guy up."

Goodwin's attention suddenly was drawn to the rising heart rate on the monitor. "Something's happening."

Goodwin squinted at the monitor, then grabbed Bic's wrist. "His heartbeat is rising." He looked at his watch. "It's rising dangerously fast."

Bic's hand came to life and grabbed Goodwin's wrist in a catlike reflex as the huge form sat up in the bed. He turned his head slowly. The eyes were milky white. He looked like a zombie coming back to life on the slab.

"Where is she?" Bic growled, staring through Goodwin.

Parelli savored the look of terror on Goodwin's face for a moment before deciding to intervene. He pulled Goodwin out of Bic's grasp. "Take it easy, big guy. You've been unconscious for a couple of days."

Bic noticed the sensors stuck to his head and chest and began peeling them off one by one.

"They have her," said Parelli, and handed Bic the note. "Hawk left this for you."

"This is incredible," Goodwin said breathlessly as Bic read the note from his friend.

Bic looked up. "You heard from him?"

"Hawk? Not since last night."

"How do you feel?" said Goodwin.

Bic stared at him for a moment, then back at Parelli. "He didn't leave an address?"

"I have the address," said Parelli.

"Let's go then," said Bic, swinging his legs off the bed.

"Whoa, hang on," said Parelli. "We still need to figure out what's wrong with you."

Bic took an aggressive step toward Parelli. "I'm fine."

Goodwin inched towards the door. "I'll leave you guys to it."

"You're not going anywhere," Parelli said to Goodwin, then turned to Bic. "It doesn't do anyone any good, especially Gracie, if you have another attack."

"Give me the address now," said Bic.

"It ain't gonna happen. The last attack you had, you fell from a chopper."

"Gentlemen," said Goodwin, "if I may? Bic, can you tell me in your own words what happened to you?"

Bic looked from Parelli to the doctor. "Everything is fine, then in an instant I feel like hot molten lava is burning me from my insides out. Sometimes I spit up blood—lots of blood—before I black out. Last couple of times, it seemed to be triggered by a really intense moment." Bic looked away.

"Is there something else?" Goodwin asked.

Bic hesitated, then said, "Before I blackout, I feel the presence of my father. I even... see some things."

Parelli turned to Goodwin. "His dad did a number on him, killed his mom right in front of him when he was just a boy."

"Where's the pain originate, Bic?" Goodwin asked.

"Usually in my side."

"We didn't find anything there," said Goodwin.

"Listen," said Parelli, "we just need your best medical guess. His veins catch fire, he's burning from the inside. Then he blacks out. So what can he do?"

"See a psychiatrist?"

"Are you punkin' me Doctor?" Parelli snapped. "Where's a damn scalpel."

"Okay, fine. Sounds like panic attacks. If it's a life or death situation—"

"What do you think we're talking about?"

"I would use an adrenaline shot." Goodwin finished.

"So that'll work?" Parelli calmed down.

"Maybe, or maybe it kills him."

"Okay, good," said Parelli. "Get us some adrenaline, then."

"You want me to get you some adrenaline now?"

Parelli spread his arms. "We're in a hospital, aren't we?"

Goodwin paused for a deep breath. "Listen, if I do this, no more favors. We're even."

"Make sure it can take effect instantly," Parelli added.

"An EpiPen delivery system into the muscle will take effect in two to three minutes."

"That's not fast enough, doc, it needs to be instant."

"Impossible."

"Like if he's driving a car and ready to run off the side of a cliff, or in a gunfight or something like that."

"EpiPen into the muscle. That's as fast as you get. Sorry to disappoint. Now, if you'll excuse me..." Goodwin left quickly.

Bic went into the tall closet cabinet and retrieved his clothes. "Okay, now that that's settled, give me the address."

"Old friend, wait another couple of minutes until you have the shots, then I'll give you the address."

"Fair enough."

"Thought you'd be interested in another patient here at the hospital."

Bic looked back to Parelli, curious.

"That FBI agent's wife."

Bic thought for a moment. "Caroline?"

"Yeah, her cancer got worse. Rumor has it he's been going all over the country trying to clear Gracie's name and track down some of those pills in order to save her. She's on hospice, not gonna make it."

Bic sorted through his clothes, then said, "I need a favor."

"You just heard me call in my last favor here."

"I want you to handle this personally for me."

Parelli nodded to Bic's request as Goodwin entered the room and handed Bic two capsules that looked like Tylenol gel caps

"Pills?" said Parelli.

"The best delivery system for the quickest results, barring jamming it into your heart or directly into a vein, is intranasal. Normal dose in an EpiPen is 0.3 milligrams epinephrine per 1 milliliter. I put 1 milligram in each capsule to get you an instant boost. You put one into each nostril and squeeze until they break and release the drug."

"He's a big guy—you sure the dose is enough?"

"It's enough for a horse."

"Thank you, doc," Bic said, then turned to Parelli. "Now, the address."

52

Mack walked up to the ticket desk at Chicago O'Hare airport with a scowl that matched the drab airport's intensity on his face. A call to Dr. Klein's assistant at MD Anderson had come up dry. No one there had any idea of a meeting Gracie was to have with the man, let alone her cure.

He approached the girl at the counter. "Can I get the next flight back to LA?"

"Sure, just one moment." She typed at her computer and stole a glance at him, a smirk appearing on her face. "Why the long face? LA's not so bad."

"No, it's just—" his phone was ringing. It was his dad. "Hang on…" He answered. "Is everything okay, how is she?"

"*Mack*! There's a man in Caroline's room and he won't let anyone in."

"What? What are you talking about?"

"We just went to visit her and this guy barred us from the room."

"Did you tell the staff?"

"We did. They said he's authorized to do so."

"Ok," said Mack. "Um, is he a doctor?"

"I don't think so. He looks more like a," his father's voice went low, "a *Mafioso*."

"What?" Mack said incredulously.

"He's in a suit and he's, you know, intimidating. Should I call the police?"

"Let me talk to him."

There was a jostling of the phone.

"Hello," said a voice.

"Yeah, who is this?"

"Agent Maddox, I'm a friend of Bic Green, and he asked me as a favor to watch over Caroline until you get back. So that's what I'm doing."

"And who exactly are you again?"

"A friend of Bic Green."

"You'll need to narrow that down a bit. Got a name?"

"I'm watching over Caroline. That's all you need to know. And I'm not letting anyone come near her. Not family, not no one. *Capisce?*"

"Why are you watching her? Is she in danger?"

The man chuckled, a gravelly sound. "Not with me here, she's not."

"So why are you there?"

"Eh, I guess Bic felt he owed you something, you know, for clearing Gracie's name."

"Yeah, but I failed," said Mack.

"It's still early, Maddox."

"She's dead."

The same, gravelly chuckle. "Yeah, and I'm a Chinese fighter jet pilot."

"What are you saying?"

"I'm saying they got her and Bic's going to get her."

"She's alive?"

"Jeez, you're slow. Yeah, she's alive."

"Where?"

"Small farming town on the Nebraska-Colorado border."

"I found a letter from Anna in her safe deposit box. You have to let Gracie know the formulas are hidden in Steve's favorite book at his favorite place to read."

"Bada bing! Now I see why Bic likes you."

"You can protect Caroline, right?"

"You got nothing to worry about, my friend. You have my word. I'll personally take great care of her."

He hung up.

Mack looked up to see the woman at the ticketing counter staring at him with a thinly patient smile. "Oh, man, I'm so sorry."

"Man?"

"Listen, I'm gonna cancel the LA thing right now. So sorry."

The woman shrugged and tapped two keys on the computer.

Mack stepped away, hitting Quinn's number. He tapped his foot impatiently.

"C'mon, Quinn…"

"Yeah?" Answered Quinn.

"It's me. Gracie's still alive."

"What?"

"I got a tip."

"That's amazing—where's she at?"

Mack paused, realizing the implausibility of it all. "Yeah, listen, Quinn, this is just a tip."

"Okay?"

"I'm going on some weird second-hand info here."

"Okay."

"She may be at a small farm town on the Nebraska-Colorado border."

"Do you have an address?"

"That's all I got."

There was a pause, then, "Uh huh. So, you're looking to, what? Drive up and down the Nebraska-Colorado border checking in at all the small farms?"

"I honestly don't know."

"Okay, you understand you're not giving us much to go on here."

"I thought maybe we could put our heads together or something," Mack said hopefully.

"That's fine. I'm, uh, a little involved here though at the moment. My niece was just given the first dose."

"Anything?"

"We'll see."

"Okay, listen, Quinn, I'm going to sit tight in Chicago for a bit until I can sort this thing out."

He hung up the call.

Suddenly it hit him there, in the middle of the Chicago airport: I just gave up the cure to cancer to a guy I don't really know.

He took a seat in the ticketing area, thinking nasty, pessimistic thoughts.

53

The last 50 miles were a blur, with Bic going well over 100 mph on his motorcycle, carefully zipping around the occasional car he shared the roadway with. Between the flight and drive time, he'd had a lot of thinking time. Mostly about Gracie and how he could possibly regain her trust. She was the sweetest, most kindhearted, all-around good person he had ever known. The last couple decades, she had been his mission—to raise her to become the woman she had become.

It was his life's legacy. More than that, it was his redemption.

Without her, all he had contributed to this world was a bunch of murders.

At dusk, Bic pulled up to the address of the house Hawk had left him. The rumbling of the bike eliminated any chance of surprise, but he wasn't in the mood for games. This man wanted to kill him, so here he was, out in the open.

The kitchen light was the only light on in the house. Classical music was playing out the open kitchen window. Bic pulled a Glock from his underarm holster, the only weapon he had, as he walked up to the house.

Through the front door, he cleared the front room with his gun, to the eerily calm piano strokes of the classical piece. He couldn't help but walk toward the source of the music coming from the kitchen.

Bic stared at the closed kitchen door as he listened one last time to the beautiful run of perfect piano notes, but this time he was also focusing past the music to see if there was anything else he could sense. The house, except for the music, was still—no movements, no creaks, no additional sounds.

Rage and impatience got the best of him, and he kicked the door open.

His eyes darted in every direction—on the old kitchen table sat a wireless speaker, and in the chair a man sat with a massive bullet hole in his chest. A white plate with only a bloody pork chop resting in its center and a full place setting, with napkin, silverware and all, were on the table in front of the man.

What a strange loop of evil here before him.

Bic's father created him, the monster that he is. Bic is forever locked into the fetishized version of his father's violence—a tiny, innocuous piece of meat.

And now here, someone has laid this iconography before him, the spawn of a new evil—a byproduct of his actions.

Bic stared at it, outside himself, and yet fully aware of the person he could be at his worst. The sight of the bloody chop made him want to puke.

He closed the flower-patterned curtains to obstruct any further sniper's shots. The music played on. Bic snatched the speaker off the table and smashed it on the floor. The room snapped into silence. He went over to the man in the chair—he was ice cold. He had to have been dead for several hours at least.

A Facetime ringtone came from the man. The front shirt pocket lit up.

Bic grabbed the phone and answered the incoming call.

The Farmer appeared on the screen, his face covered in a scruffy blanket of whiskers. The men instantly locked eyes, volleying stony, murderous glares in protracted silence.

The Farmer twisted his face for a moment. "Do you remember John Stomen?"

Bic continued to glare at the man.

The Farmer couldn't contain his anger. "Answer me!"

Bic did not answer.

"You're gonna remember him, I promise you."

The screen view flipped, and there was Hawk, both of his hands duct-taped to his face, his palms covering his eyes, with one finger wiggling freely above. He was sitting in an old metal chair, his body tied securely to it.

"John was my brother, and you killed him," the Farmer said off-screen.

"Don't you worry about me, brother," Hawk said.

There was another sound off-screen, the mechanical revving of a power drill…*RIZZZZZZ.*

"That's right," said the Farmer, "don't you worry about Hawk, your lifelong best friend, who you fought side by side with in 'Nam. Not like losing a brother, but it's a start."

The camera screen flipped back to the Farmer, his rigid, cold, hard eyes glaring at Bic. "Wanna see my toys?"

The screen flipped again, and there was a table with several different-sized screws, ranging from three-fourths of an inch to two inches.

Bic scrutinized the scene, desperate for any clue that might give away their location, but the camera angles were too tight.

"The skull is about a quarter of an inch thick," the Farmer said as he snatched the smallest of the screws from the table.

The camera stayed on the remaining screws.

The drill went *RIZZZZZZ…*

Gracie screamed at the top of her lungs.

Rage flooded Bic's entire body.

Then Hawk screamed. And it was different.

Bic had heard this scream many times. It was a scream of anguish, of excruciating pain…

"Always wanted to do that," said the Farmer.

The camera turned to Hawk. The top of his hand by the knuckle had a screw through it and into his forehead. Blood was pouring out over the duct tape. Hawk was whimpering like a child.

The camera turned back to the screws.

"That was a three-quarter incher," the Farmer said, camera still on the screws. Hawk groaned pitifully in the background. "Shut up, I'm trying to talk! Where was I? So, let's see now, with the skull being a quarter inch, and our buddy Hawk's finger being a half-inch thick or so, I'm guessing an inch-long screw will start to scramble some brain."

A hand snatched a screw from the table.

The sound of the drill… Gracie's protests… Hawk's screams of agony…

The miserable cries clashed hellishly with the whirring of the drill. Then the gear tripped, and the drill made a sickening, ratcheting sound. It tore through Bic, as if the drill was boring into his soul. An unmistakable sound.

Anyone who's ever drilled into a stud knows it.

The camera went to Hawk. There was a screw through the other hand. Blood ran freely.

Hawk was moaning. It sounded like some twisted Gregorian chant. The camera was placed on the table. All Bic could see was the ceiling.

The drill started again. Hawk's and Gracie's screams of hysteria and terror swirled over one another's. The primal sounds of wild panic made the adrenaline surge through Bic's veins.

Bic joined his friend in a scream of his own. Rage colored his mind red.

The ceiling.

His breathing was in hitches.

The ceiling.

He wanted to run somewhere and cover his ears. There was the jungle, and the ambush in the night, and Charlie coming at you with hellfire...

The ceiling.

He wasn't there. He was here. And the horror was just as real.

The ceiling was high. Industrial, like a plant.

The drilling stopped.

"Let's see if that shuts him up," the Farmer said.

The camera tore away from the ceiling and went back to Hawk. Blood was everywhere.

Hawk had gone limp.

The Farmer turned the camera back to himself. Blood spattered his face, his beard. "One down, one to go."

Bic growled, foam filling his mouth.

"There's the old rage! I missed you, Bic."

The screen then flipped to Gracie. She was standing on a stool, a thick rope around her neck attached to a massive meat hook hanging from the rafters. Standing on her tiptoes, she was one sudden slip from being hanged.

"See," said the Farmer, "me and the girl had a deal. She hates you so much, she agreed to help me lure you out and kill you if I cleared her name. Too bad there's gonna be a hangin' tonight, cuz. See ya 'round."

The picture disappeared as the call disconnected.

Bic roared in anger as he ran outside the house.

In the moonlit night, he looked in both directions, frantically trying to decide which way to go. He felt like a terrified animal.

The ceilings were high, real high.

There was a part of his mind that was nagging him now. The only rational part of his brain was trying to tell him something.

It had to be a large plant of some sort.

That hook, he thought, then focused on what he saw and realized she was attached to some type of rail system. It was a setup used in a meat processing plant.

He searched the internet for meatpacking plants in the town. There was an abandoned slaughterhouse three miles away. The only disused plant in the whole state.

He hopped on his bike and took off, ready to lay waste to the whole world.

54

The complex was comprised of two large main buildings about 25 yards apart and attached by curved, tunnel-like tubes. Having worked in a meat plant for a short while as one of the many jobs he'd had after the war, Bic was familiar with the structure. The building with the lower roof, not fully enclosed, probably held the livestock holding pens. At night, the whole place was a sinister maze of Machiavellian shadows and imagined tortures. The tubes fed the live cattle from the holding pens into the slaughterhouse, an enclosed two-story building of faded white brick.

Bic had a good idea where he would find Gracie. In the video, she was hanging from some type of overhead rail line system. In a slaughterhouse, this system would run through much of the main plant, where the carcass, hung on a meat hook, could be easily transported from one station to another. The highest ceilings with the largest open area of the rail system usually were in the hanging room. This was the spot where the cattle, after being bled out, skinned, trimmed, and cleaned, would hang to chill while waiting to be processed and packaged.

He entered the building with the livestock holding pens first. The place still contained many of the remnants of its time in full operation. The smell was pungent, a mixture of animal rot and mildew.

From there he proceeded through the stunning room and on into the bleeding room. It was there he saw the start of the overhead rail system about eight feet off the ground. Visibility was low and virtually all the equipment was left behind, a lot of it stainless steel with its still-shiny surface refracting what little moonlight was coming through the broken-out windows above.

Keeping tight to the wall, he slid in and out of rooms until he made it into the washing room. By the rails above, he expected Gracie to be in the next room, unless the Farmer had moved her. He went to the entranceway and peeked in.

What he saw there made his heart drop.

Gracie hung in the middle of a room the size of a basketball court. The ceiling had row after row of metal rails, and hundreds of old meat hooks still attached to them. Her face full of anguish, Gracie stood on her tiptoes, legs trembling. At any moment, she could lose her balance, fall off the wooden stool, and hang herself.

He saw Hawk next, covered in blood with his hands screwed into his head.

He tried to get his bearings, to uncloud his mind for just a moment.

He looked and saw a rope tied to one of the legs of the stool Gracie stood on. The long rope ran across the floor of the entire room and through a door, which appeared to lead to a small room—a utility closet, perhaps, or a small office. Every now and again, the rope tightened, then slackened, tightened, then slackened.

It was a simple trap, but brilliant. The Farmer was obviously leading him toward rescuing Gracie, toward the center of the room, where he'd be a sitting duck.

Bic looked for possible ways to go through the room and get to the other side unseen.

There were support pillars down the center of the room, but they were far too skinny to provide cover.

Gracie yelped as she lost her balance, struggling she regained her balance .

Bic saw the rope on the floor tighten, slacken, tighten…

Bic eyes went to the small room. It was dark, but there was a darker form filling its threshold.

There was the Farmer, rope in hand.

He emerged into the light, smiled, then yanked the stool out from underneath Gracie.

Gracie jerked and twisted in the air, her eyes wide, her mouth gaping, a horrible mask of agony. Her hands went to her neck as she dangled there.

Bic retreated to the room behind him and grabbed one of the stainless-steel tables. He lifted the thing upright, then charged into the room table-first.

Flashes of light lashed out from within the dark doorway. Shots clanked into the table as Bic went to Gracie.

He stopped when he was between Gracie and the small room. There he put down the table on its side so that it still served its purpose as a shield. He drew his Glock with his right hand and fired a volley into the doorway. While he did so, he grabbed Gracie with his free arm and lifted her into the air.

Fully elevated, she was able to reach high enough to unhook the rope. Bic dropped her behind him. He then grabbed the table and marched backwards, exchanging gunfire with the Farmer.

Backing around the corner into the washing room, Bic took aim, waiting for the Farmer to come out of the room.

"Go," he said over his shoulder. "My keys are under the bike."

"Come with me," she pleaded.

"I'm not leaving Hawk behind."

"He's dead, Bic."

"I'm not leaving him. Steve hid the formulas in his favorite book at his favorite place to read."

Another series of shots riveted the table.

"Dammit, Bic! Come with me!"

"Get out, now."

"I can take the truck out back," she said. "The key's in the ignition."

"Fine."

"Meet me at Harold Washington library," said Gracie. "That's where Steve must have hidden them."

"We need a plan first. Tomorrow, we meet at your momma's grave. Then we'll go get them."

He looked back at her, fear blanketing over her as she looked into his eyes.

"Go," Bic said. "You may not trust me, but trust that this is what I do best."

Two more shots cracked into the table, each one ratcheted up her adrenaline until she took Bic's advice and ran in the other direction.

55

The gunshots stopped, and a cacophony of silence descended.

A moment had gone by. Bic was confident Gracie was well on her way to safety when a sudden noise shattered the preternatural stillness, and a thumping sound rushed through his ears, scrambling his thoughts into a chaotic mess.

The sound was as unmistakable as the voice of ghosts. Someone was thumping a bare hand on a cast iron frying pan.

"Hear that Bic?" the Farmer yelled from within the small room. "I'm playing your momma's favorite tune!"

The stainless steel reflected the inhuman glow in Bic's eyes piercing out of him like rays of death. His veins swelled to the point of explosion.

Thump...

Thump...

Thump...

"After I kill you, I'm going to go have a celebratory drink with your daddy. I think he can teach me a lot. We'll exchange frying pan tips."

One hollow thud after another beat into Bic's skull, rendering logic to a spot of violent red. "It's pork chop eatin' time," he muttered through the gathering foam in his mouth.

Bic charged across the room, using the steel table as a shield.

Bullets clanked into the metal.

Ten feet away, the shooting stopped and the door slammed shut.

With a guttural yell and a full head of steam, Bic crashed the table into the door. It blasted off the frame, shattering everywhere. Bic torpedoed into the small room, smashing the heavy table into the

Farmer, pinning him against the wall. He blasted the Farmer with a right hook. The head snapped back hard.

On the floor was the frying pan along with the Farmer's gun. He kicked the gun into the corner of the room. He then grabbed the Farmer by the neck and pulled him out from between the wall and steel table.

He brought him into the hanging room and threw him out onto the concrete floor. He then retrieved the black iron pan and walked toward the Farmer lying on the floor.

Bic swung the pan at the Farmer's head putting every ounce of his strength behind it. It smashed the concrete floor as the Farmer rolled to the side. He gave Bic a kick in the wrist. The kicked hand fell away. No matter. There was too much rage now.

Bic maintained a backhand grip on the pan and he wound up again. Sudden, swirled visions of his dad intertwined with the image of the Farmer before him.

The Farmer nailed him in his kneecap, then again in his chest.

The pan slipped, catching only a swipe at the Farmer's face. Taking advantage of the momentary incapacitation, Bic mounted the Farmer's chest, wrapped one of his massive hands around his throat, then raised the pan high up in the air.

There was a sharp, stabbing pain in his side, like a burning spear was being slowly driven into him. Bic howled as he let go of the pan and fell from his perch atop the Farmer's body. The pain magnified, clouding his vision as he struggled to retrieve the pan.

He felt as though his internal organs were shutting down.

The Farmer picked up the pan and smacked him across the face with it. It was a weak blow, but effective enough. Bic felt the blood in his throat. He fought for consciousness.

He reached into his pocket and pulled out the adrenaline capsules. With what energy he had left, he jammed a capsule into each nostril.

Before he could break them, the Farmer took another swing with the pan, catching him in the head.

The world went black.

56

The Farmer stood over a motionless Bic. His need for revenge had served as a slow acting poison in his soul—and absolute payback was the only antidote.

The Farmer dragged a four-by-four folding table out of the room Bic had pulled him from. He took a quick inventory of the rooms contents:

Skew back handsaw—check.

Car tire, P205-55R-16—check

Can of Zippo brand lighter fluid, 12 fl. oz.—check

Mini butane torch—check

Pork chop, 10 oz. center cut rib—check

Grunting, he pulled Bic up against the wall. He stood up, caught his breath, then grabbed the can of lighter fluid. Methodically, carefully, he filled the inside of the tire as best he could with the fluid. Satisfied, he carefully lowered the tire over Bic's head and dropped it around his neck. The fluid ran down his chest.

He smiled triumphantly as he stuffed the pork chop as far as he could inside Bic's mouth.

He grabbed the blow torch next. It fit snug in his grip, the size of a spray paint can. He clicked the ignition button and a bright blue flame shot out from the shiny metal flame guard.

Perfect.

He bent down, his face inches from Bic's. "Wake up, you sonofabitch."

Bic was unresponsive.

The Farmer backhanded him.

Nothing.

He clenched his fist. "Open those disgusting eyes, you ugly

mother. I wanna watch them melt."

He punched Bic in the face.

Nothing.

He punched him again, right in the nose. The eyes flickered open, glassy, tearing.

The Farmer smiled. "There we go," he said as he relit the torch. He held the spike of flame in front of Bic's face like a glowing blue stiletto. "Can you hear me, Bic? I wanna make sure you hear me. Listen up. On the day I saw my brother's head sitting there on that table detached from his body, a pork chop stuffed in his mouth, I've thought of a thousand different ways to kill you."

Bic's jaw moved around the chop. *Not time yet*, the Farmer thought. *I want him fully conscious.*

"I promised my brother when I did, it would be like nothing ever done before. But you got my little bro pretty good. I had to think about how it was gonna go down for you, Bic. So, here's what's I'm fixin' to do."

The eyes set on him. Bic's muscles strained, but he was eerily motionless, understanding that movement equaled death.

"That's right, baby. You stare at me. I want you to know who's responsible when you light up like a pit barbecue. When it's done, when you're charred like a three-hundred-pound pig, I'm going to saw your big ugly head off your body and put it in that frying pan."

Bic's eyes cleared. The eyebrows lowered.

The Farmer brought the torch up close, inches away from the tire.

"Then," he said, "I'm going to find that niece of yours and treat her like a Thai whore. How 'bout that?"

The eyes went wide. The nostrils flared. And a gush of air blew something out. Smashed gel caps?

Bic's hand sprung to life, grabbing his wrist holding the blow torch.

The men's arms were in gridlock.

The Farmer groaned as he heard and felt his wrist bones cracking.

Bic raised the tire up from around his neck as he stood, ignoring the fluid that splashed over both of them. The Farmer used his free hand to stop Bic from putting the tire over his own head.

As Bic's eyes widened, the veins on his neck and temples throbbed. Whereas before the Farmer had been overcoming Bic on pure strength, whatever this surge was, there was newfound strength in Bic. The Farmer's desperation of vengeance fought Bic's will to protect Gracie. The two killers were deadlocked.

The tire lit up. Flames shot out as both men now held the flaming mass of melting rubber between them.

Bic kicked the Farmer's gut. The brawny self-styled country boy flew backwards as his breath was knocked out of him. The next thing he felt was his back hitting the floor.

And he saw the tire come down around his neck.

He jerked and rolled, throwing the flaming tire off, then popped back onto his feet and grabbed the saw.

Both men ignored the small fires burning on their clothing.

Bic stood, his eyes stained with an inhuman glow, far more intense than the reflection of the tire behind the Farmer.

With a bellowed roar of challenge, the Farmer charged.

He swung the saw at Bic's throat. Bic lunged into the arc of the swing, deflecting the Farmer's hurt hand with his forearm. Then, using the Farmer's momentum, he spun in place and threw him into the wall.

A jolt of hellish pain shot through the Farmer's shoulder as he crashed into the brick. His head had hit as well. Oddly, he felt nothing. But the world was slurring before him. His eyesight was blurred. He stumbled away from Bic realizing his right shoulder was completely out of joint.

He saw Bic walking toward him, the flaming tire in his hands.

The Farmer, clutching his dead shoulder, ran from the chiller room.

57

It would have been nice to kill him.

Bic wanted nothing more. He could have done it. He could have gone after the Farmer like a lion after a wounded zebra. But instead, he found himself running towards his best friend. Hawk lay in a semi-fetal position, a bloody mess on the floor, hands bolted to his head.

Bic reached down and checked for a pulse. Weak, but still there.

"Hang in there, partner," Bic said. He lifted Hawk from the floor and hurried toward the exit as best he could, kicking the old door open.

Outside, his motorcycle sat in front of the livestock building. He flopped Hawk on the bike in a sitting position. Bloody spit flung from the slack jaws. The weight from his hands attached to his head pulled the body forward.

Bic sat behind Hawk, then started the bike.

A shot fired from the exit door. The bullet tore into Hawk's leg.

Bic wrapped one arm around Hawk and hit the gas with the other. The engine roared and the back tire kicked up dirt as more shots came, ricocheting off the chrome. The bike's back end flared out hard right. Bic stopped it from tipping with his foot while letting off the gas. After gaining balance, he reaccelerated.

The bike picked up speed. And the moment the wheels went from gravel to the street pavement, Bic opened it up.

Twenty miles down the road, he pulled over and called Tony to arrange care for Hawk.

58

Blue and red lights flashed in the distance on an otherwise dark road. Gracie didn't think anything of them at first, but suddenly realized that could be a checkpoint waiting for her. Even if it wasn't, she didn't have a driver's license, or insurance for that matter. Pulling over to the side of the road, she cut the lights. The truck was about out of gas anyway. About seven hours still to Chicago—she'd have to figure out another way.

The flashing lights turned off. It wasn't a checkpoint after all, just someone being pulled over. She looked at the gas gauge—it was hovering on E. She started the engine and prayed to the patron saint of fuel tanks.

Twenty minutes later, running on fumes, she rolled into the gas station in the middle of nowhere off I-80, breathing a sigh of blessed relief.

The pumps were ancient. She needed only to flip the lever on the side and start pumping. A little old man stood watching her from within the station. That was it. She was seen. Now what?

She sauntered into the station. "Howdy," the man said. Then his face changed. "Hey, you alright?"

She only just realized that she must have looked half on her way to death.

"I'm... okay."

"Ya look like you been in some kinda accident."

No, just spent the last however many hours hanging from a meat hook, screaming my bloody brains out. That's all.

"I was," she said. "I got out of my car to change a tire, and I didn't realize in the darkness how close I was to a drop on the side of the road. I took a pretty bad tumble."

"You... want me to call someone?"

"No, I'm fine. Really. But I need to ask you a huge favor."

"Sure."

"It's... been an awful, awful day," she said, and the tears came. It wasn't hard. She didn't need to act. She continued through high-pitched sobs. "I'm sorry, I thought I had my wallet in the truck... but I must have left it at the house..."

"Hey, hey," the man said, stepping out from behind the counter. "It's okay. It's gonna be just fine. Sshhh." He put a hand on her back.

"I'm so sorry..."

"Ssshhh, nonsense. You live far?"

She shook her head.

"Alrighty. Just go home, get your wallet, and come on back. That is, if you want. If you don't, I'm sure I'll survive without your money. But uh, just don't let it get around." He gave her a wink.

Gracie threw her arms around him. "Oh my! Thank you!"

"Oh, ho, ho, don't worry about it." He withdrew from her hug. "It's a kindness. I want you to pass it along. Deal?"

"Deal," Gracie said as she ran out of the station. "I won't forget you!"

59

The late-afternoon sky was mostly deep steel blue-grays, save for a band of brilliant pink along the horizon. Across a busy two-lane street from St. Michael's Cemetery, Gracie sat in a red vinyl booth at a hole-in-the-wall diner, looking out the window, watching Bic at her mother's grave. The comforting smell of homestyle biscuits and gravy and pot roast wafted out from the kitchen filling her nostrils, as well as the rest of the diner.

He stood, statuesque and motionless. Subtle gusts blew red and yellow leaves off the trees, showering him. The gentleness of the scene represented what she once knew Bic to be—her loving caretaker. She had not so much as heard Bic even raise his voice at another person. As for the sunglasses that he wore all the time, he'd told her he was embarrassed by the uniqueness of his eyes. It especially hurt his feelings when little kids cried and hid from him like he was some sort of monster. She had always told him they were beautiful, one of the great wonders of nature.

Should she go to him? Men were after her. Other men, like the Farmer, were after Bic. Did it make sense for her to go to him? The bell on the entrance door jingled.

Quinn entered the diner.

She got up, ran to Quinn, and hugged him.

Their bodies tangled nicely as Quinn said, his mouth nuzzling her ear, "I thought I lost you."

Gracie didn't want to let go. She finally felt safe.

They separated, and sat down in Gracie's booth.

"I didn't know who to call," Gracie said.

"You did the right thing."

"You're not going to arrest me, are you?"

Quinn smiled. "Arrest you? How? You're dead, remember?"

She looked into his blue eyes. "That means a lot."

"You mean a lot to me."

She looked away.

"What is it?" He reached across the table and rested his fingertips on top of her hands.

Gracie looked away. "There's something you ought to know." She dropped back into his eyes. "There is one last copy of all my formulas at the Harold Washington library."

"That's fantastic," Quinn said. "Let me guess, hidden in Steve's favorite book."

Her mouth went agape. "Now how could you possibly know that?"

Quinn unfolded Anna's letter for Gracie to see. "Mack and I found it in Anna's safe deposit box."

Gracie read the letter through tear-filled eyes. "I miss her so much."

He touched her arm. "What is his favorite book? I can have someone get them for us."

"I don't trust anyone else. I need it to be us."

Quinn looked at her for a moment. "Let's get you somewhere safe. Tomorrow we'll go get the book and set about clearing your name."

Walking out of the diner, as she was getting ready to enter Quinn's car, Gracie hesitated as she saw Bic in the distance.

"Everything okay?" Quinn asked.

She entered the car. "Yes, now it is."

60

Bic's heart sank with the sun's slow departure over Chicago's skyline. Even though he'd known Gracie might not show up, he was counting on her to forgive him for his deception and his sins, to listen to how it had all happened, to understand him and who he was. They were family. That strength had to prevail.

"Hey big sis," he said to the grave, "getting a little chilly out. First snow is right around the corner." He tucked his hands into his jean pockets. "I thought Gracie was coming to see you today, but she's not too happy with me right now. I kind of earned it, but it still hurts."

He stared at Chandra's small grave marker as if waiting for a reply.

The long moment gave way to a series of horrific flashes, first his mom beaten to death, then Chandra withering away to nothing, then Hawk as he left him a bloody mess at an emergency room in a hospital in Iowa, barely breathing.

He reached down to the marker and scratched some dirt off her name with his thumb. "I'm not sure how it got so out of control, sis. I *thought* I was doing the right thing for Gracie." He shook his head in disgust. "But I know now that I was using it as a selfish excuse. I was so wrong for what I did. I... I messed up." He continued to clean the header, obsessively scratching at it. "She has to know how much I love her."

He and Gracie had stood in this very same spot over twenty years ago and made their pact. He pictured her back then, big brown eyes so determined and full of passion. She would find a cure, she said, and in turn, he would make sure nothing got in her way—not their poverty, the color of their skin, or anything else.

He could feel the heat in his body rising. Thoughts swirled in his mind about what they were going to do to her. Stone cold killers just like him wanted her dead, and he couldn't help but wonder how many people he, Bic, had brought into existence. How many twisted psychopaths like the Farmer did his own evil beget? He thought he could just walk away, but now he knew what he had done, all the killing wasn't something you can just walk away from.

His phone rang.

"Tony. How is he?"

"That tough S.O.B. is gonna make it. They're not sure if his egg is scrambled yet. Doc said we won't know until the swelling goes down."

"Gracie didn't show up."

"What the hell is she thinking?" said Parelli. "If they get their hands—"

"I betrayed her."

"What? Stop it. You did what you had to do."

"I didn't *have* to kill anyone, Tony."

"You're a survivor. Don't overthink it, it will cloud your judgement."

"You and I have a nice way of rationalizing things, Tony. But intelligent, decent people like Gracie would call it murder."

"There's one thing you have to remember, my friend, and that is without you, Gracie would be dead right now. Those pricks would have pinned her as a terrorist and wiped her and her cure off the face of the earth. She needed a Black Ghost by her side to see this thing through."

Bic fought the sob that threatened to catch in his throat. "I hope you're right."

"Sam Hill, I'm right! And partner, it's for real. You just need to keep that girl safe."

"I need to find her first." Bic hung up the phone, and looked back to Chandra's grave. "Sis, I swear, I'll find your baby girl before they do."

61

Quinn and Gracie entered the motel room at dusk. Quinn immediately locked the door and closed the curtains, then twitched the synthetic plastic-cloth back to peek outside.

After a long scan of the parking lot, he said, "No one's followed us, we'll be safe here until morning."

Gracie sat on the bed, then pulled up her knees and wrapped her arms around her legs.

"Sorry about the single bed, that's the only setup they have in places like this. I'll take the floor."

"It's fine," Gracie said looking away as a thought crossed her mind about what usually goes on in places like this. She blushed.

Quinn handed her his backpack.

"After the last couple of days, I figured you'd need a change of clothes."

Gracie pulled out the clothes, "These are all the right sizes." She became embarrassed as she quickly scanned the bra size, 34C. "Are you Clark Kent?"

"Three sisters," Quinn replied.

"Older?"

"Yep."

"I bet there are some great stories."

Quinn smiled. "No, they didn't dress me up like a doll and put makeup on me every other day."

They both laughed.

"Thanks for this." Gracie stood with her pile of clothes in hand, but one piece fell to the floor.

"Thanks for trusting me." He picked up the white cotton underwear from her feet and stood very close to her. "By the way, my sisters tell me these are the most comfortable."

"You have smart sisters," Gracie said, staring at Quinn for a moment, noticing the full contour of his lips—lips that if kissed, she sensed, would be warm and soft. "I'm going to take a shower."

"Okay, I'll keep a watch out."

The hot shower had been a taste of heaven. She came out of the bathroom, still drippy, her towel wrapped around her.

"Everything okay?" said Quinn, who was sitting on the bed.

"That shower was pretty much the greatest thing in the world. At least since the invention of the donut."

He laughed, exposing smile lines by his eyes. "Glad to hear it."

She went over and sat down beside him, her leg touching his.

After a long silence, Quinn spoke. "Something wrong with the clothes?"

She looked into his eyes. "When you face death, you suddenly realize there's so much you haven't experienced."

She took a breath. She felt a weird tingling inside, and wanted to explore what this subtle sweet spasm could turn into. She could be dead by the end of the week. She needed to let her guard down, experience this moment to the fullest.

She leaned over and kissed him.

When the kiss ended, she threw her head back, offering up her throat. As his tongue darted out, accepting the invitation, the towel slid off her and fell to the floor.

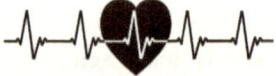

She had no idea how long it'd been since they finished, but their warm bodies were still tangled.

Gracie was spent physically, but not mentally. The closeness she now felt to Quinn gave her the excitement that he would help her see this through.

62

With bloodshot eyes, and on his third coffee of the morning, from inside a corner cafe at the base of a nineteen-story high-rise just south of the Loop, Mack cased the arched entrance of the red brick Harold Washington library. He had been fighting the morning sun reflecting off the three five-story arched windows covering the face of the building and couldn't stop himself from glancing at the glass construction roof.

Parelli had sent him a text at three AM with three words—Harold Washington Library.

All he wanted was to be with Caroline. Making things worse, no one was returning his calls or texts. Parelli, Quinn, not even his father.

He called directly to Caroline's room. No answer.

He called the switchboard at the hospital and was transferred to the nurses' station on Caroline's floor.

"Hi, this is Mack Maddox, my wife Caroline is in room 1909. Was I transferred to the right floor?"

"Yes."

"Can I ask how she's doing?"

"I just started my shift. Would you like me to go check on her?"

"Yes, that would be amazing, thank you."

Mack waited for a couple of minutes.

"Hi, Mr. Maddox?"

"Yes?"

"You said room 1909, correct?"

"That's right."

"1909 is empty."

A feeling of nauseous terror came over him and he stumbled over his word a moment. "Did she...?" He couldn't bear to finish the sentence.

"Well, the thing is, I'm checking the records right now, and... yeah, there doesn't seem to be anything in the system. Are you absolutely sure it was room 1909?"

"Absolutely."

"What was the last name of the patient again?"

"Maddox, M-A-D..." He felt like he was in the middle of some bizarre prank.

"Huh," said the nurse. "Um, I'm so sorry, please bear with me."

How can this be happening? he thought as he saw Quinn walk up the steps of the library with Gracie.

"Snake."

"Sir?"

"No, not you."

"Just bear with me, please. I'm contacting everyone."

The minutes slogged by as he waited.

Moments later, a black Suburban pulled up in front of the library. Four men exited the vehicle, their movements tactical.

Mack's adrenaline flooded his system like nitrous gas in an engine.

The pride had just shown up to hunt.

63

Gracie and Quinn strode across the black-and-white marble floor of the grand two-story lobby, her new sneakers quietly squeaking. Gracie was surprised the library already had this much traffic right at open, but the place was as silent as snow. Somehow, the silence made it worse, like an audio spotlight shining on her. It felt like every eye was on her.

Quinn glanced suspiciously behind them.

"Something wrong?" Gracie asked.

"No, not really. But let's just get these books and get out of here."

"It might take a while."

"You don't know where they are?"

"Not exactly."

They came to a directory. "This place is a maze. Nine floors, dozens of rooms. This might take days."

Gracie walked up to the computer card catalog. "Steve hid it for me."

"Who's Steve?"

Gracie stopped typing, her fingers still resting on the keyboard as she stared at the screen blankly, and said, "Steve gave his life for me."

"Sorry."

"Yeah, so am I."

"So, you really have no idea?"

"No, my only instruction was to make sure no one could find it."

Quinn paused with a look of confusion.

"No one, that is, except me." Gracie said as she pulled up Steve's favorite book in the catalog. Gracie grabbed a scratch piece of paper and wrote down the book's location as Quinn peeked over her shoulder.

Le Morte d'Arthur.

Gracie's eyes teared up a little, "I didn't pay him much, but our deal was that once we found a cure for cancer, I was going to take him and his renaissance cronies to England and he and his friends were going to get to reenact their favorite scenes from *Excalibur* in front of the Queen of England."

Quinn gave a quizzical look. "He didn't just want to be paid more?"

Gracie smiled. "You just had to know Steve. He figured if we found a cure, the Queen would grant us this one request. I humored him, what can I say?"

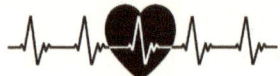

Jaco Ivanov watched from the opposite end of the lobby as Quinn followed Gracie to the east side of the building. He and three additional men had made themselves invisible in the two-story lobby. One of them was the Farmer. He loved libraries. They were so quiet you could practically hear the secrets people tried to hide from you.

Jaco's trust for the Farmer was on thin ice, but Peter Rains confirmed through satellite clips that there was indeed another chopper that day. Either way, he knew he had to keep a close eye on him. Considering the possibility of Bic showing up, he was willing to risk having the Farmer there.

Patrons continued to enter and exit the lobby at a steady pace. With a circulation desk and a separate information desk on opposite sides of the room, the incoming traffic split evenly. He wasn't sure who else knew about this location, about the cure and where it was hidden. He didn't want to let his and his team's presence be known until he was sure the final copy of the cure was destroyed.

Jaco spoke softly into the tiny microphone concealed by his hand and connected to his men's earpieces. "Make sure not to engage until I have confirmed we have the second target located." Staring at the Farmer, Jaco asked, "Is that clear?"

The Farmer nodded. "Clear as a virgin's tears."

64

The stacks were nothing if not bewildering. Gracie turned down the row marked FICTION—M. About halfway into the aisle, at eye level, she began tracing her finger along the spines of the books.

"Malory… Malory… Ah…"

She pulled out the classic book and stared at the majestic-looking king on the cover. "This is the same exact book. He kept a copy on his desk."

"Modern Library edition," said Quinn.

"Hmm?"

"Nothing. I have the 1962 New American Library edition, that's all. From what you've told me about Steve, he probably would have preferred it."

She smiled at the picture on the cover. How often had she seen photos of Steve dressed exactly like this? People like him were what was good in this world. People like him were the reason she needed to keep fighting for the cure.

She settled in at a table anxious to get what she needed to turn this bad story back into a good one. She opened the book with confidence, but diligently. With Steve, she needed to be ready for anything.

She thumbed through the book with trembling fingers. Twice. Nothing. No clues, no markings within the book.

"There's nothing here," she said defeatedly.

"Mind if I take a look?"

She handed it to him. "I don't understand."

As Quinn thumbed through, he asked, "Did he say this specific book?"

"He said his favorite book at the Harold Washington Library."

"Are you sure you have the right book?"

"Yeah. Like I said, he kept it on his desk."

"I don't see anything here," Quinn said, frustrated. "I wish we had a specific title."

"I know his favorite book, I'm sure of it." Gracie paused, deep in thought, then got up and walked back into the row.

She paused before the row, then looked at Quinn.

"What is it?"

"You mentioned another edition before. I'll bet there's another book in this library somewhere."

"We need to go back to the circulation desk," said Quinn

Gracie and Quinn walked through the corridor and entered the lobby. Gracie looked up at a man standing on the second-floor walkway, which spanned the entirety of the room. He was bent over the railing, looking down at the main lobby.

Quinn sneezed, very loudly.

"God bless you."

"Thanks. Let's find this book. I think I'm allergic to this place."

Gracie looked into his eyes. "Hopefully you're not allergic to girls who are bookworms."

He smirked at her. "You can learn a lot of useful things from books."

Quick flashbacks of last night sent a warm twinge through Gracie's core as she walked up to the front desk.

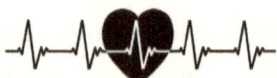

The Farmer sat on the bench counting dead sheep in his head, eyes locked on Gracie but concealed beneath the brim of his Cubs hat. The only thing holding him back from attack was an invisible cage.

"Hold your position," Jaco said into his earpiece. "I repeat, do not engage. We don't have it yet."

The Farmer looked up to see Jaco across the room, glaring at him over the top of an open magazine.

The Farmer gave a subtle nod.

Oh, I'll hold my position, you back stabbing bastard, until it's time for you to pay the price for trying to mess with the devil.

65

"Hi," Gracie smiled. "I was wondering if you could see if you have a book on hand?"

"Sure," the librarian said. "Which book?"

"*Le Morte d'Arthur.*"

The librarian punched away at her keyboard. "It's showing two here. One's checked out. We should have another one."

"Hm," said Gracie, "I just looked and couldn't find it."

"If you don't mind," said the librarian, "I'll ask a page to see if they can find it for you."

"Can I ask you a question?" said Quinn. "Where did you get that pendant?" He pointed to the sapphire book pendant around the librarian's neck and squinted, leaning forward. Taking his body language cue, she rose from her seat and leaned in.

She took it in her hands and held it out. "My husband got it for me for our anniversary last year."

"It's beautiful," said Quinn, leaning in further, squinting. "Have you ever been to the Pierpont Morgan Library in New York? Because they have something similar."

She smiled. "That's where he got it."

"I've been looking all over the place for one just like it for my mother…"

It didn't take Gracie long to realize that this was her moment. She leaned over the counter to get a look at the librarian's computer screen.

Quinn turned slightly, as if to get a better view of the pendant. The librarian turned with him.

It was a stretch, but just enough so that she could read the name there. She grabbed her phone and jotted down the name, "Benjamin

Surewood" and his address.

"Got it," she said as they turned away from the desk. "Do you have that power over all women?"

"Gotta know all the tricks," said Quinn with a sly grin.

Gracie showed him the address in excitement. "Let's take a trip."

She suddenly felt a coldness in her gut. Someone was watching her. Nervously, she glanced around the room and locked in on a man wearing a Cubs hat.

"Quinn," she said, her voice a rasp. "It's *him*. Three o'clock. Cubs hat."

The Farmer reached for his gun.

Quinn grabbed Gracie's hand and led her over the solid marble U-shaped counter. Bullets pounded into the white stone as they did.

Screams reverberated throughout the building. Patrons in the lobby scattered like minnows.

"You're bleeding!" Gracie said as they both hunched under the front desk.

Quinn reached for his ear, "I'm okay."

With the U-shaped desk attached to the wall on both sides, the only way out for them was over the countertop or by opening the gate attached to the wall. Quinn, with his gun pointed to the open space, waited for the Farmer to attempt entry.

From the reflection in the mirror on the wall Quinn could make out something in The Farmer's other hand that was not a gun. "Oh no, he's got a grenade!"

Gracie stifled a scream.

The Farmer stepped up to the counter. "The preacher man says it's the end of the line," he said, pulling the pin.

A burst of blood exploded from his right shoulder.

66

Bic cursed to himself. The angle he had from the second-story walkway sucked, otherwise he'd have hit the Farmer right in the back of the head. As it was, he now had to reposition himself for the kill shot. It was then he realized that the Farmer had dropped the grenade onto the counter directly above Gracie. He had to do something. The grenade was about to roll over the edge of the counter. He'd only moved a few steps when Jaco and the other men opened fire at him from flanked positions on the other side of the lobby.

From a new position behind a six-by-four bookcase loaded with children's books, Bic watched the Farmer scatter to the right with his firearm, aiming to pick off anyone who attempted to escape from behind the desk. He was about twenty feet away from Gracie, up against the same wall the counter was attached to, behind a marble column that jutted out from it.

Bic used the massive case full of books as a shield to advance his position directly above the Farmer's location. He growled as he heaved the bookshelf from the second story.

The massive object smashed down onto the Farmer.

At the desk, the grenade dropped to the floor.

Quinn scrambled out, grabbed the grenade, and chucked it into the middle of the room. The thing exploded midair. Glass from the shattered ceiling rained down like falling daggers.

It was at this point that Bic noticed Mack had just entered through the main doors. Apparently, he was the only one who'd noticed.

One of Jaco's men made a run for the escalator to the second-floor walkway. Mack squared up his shot, fired, and dropped him.

Mack opened fire in Jaco's direction. Jaco, covered in glass and weaponless, bolted toward the arched corridor leading back into the library. Bullets pockmarked the walls around him.

Bic repositioned as he saw Jaco's other man firing at Mack. The stone wall above Mack's head, weakened by the grenade blast, crumbled, leaving Mack in a fine mist of concrete dust.

The man charged towards Mack, firing at him, forcing him to retreat.

"Hang tight, Mack," Bic muttered as he lined up to shoot the man in the back of the head.

The side of the guy's head exploded before he had a chance to fire. Bic looked over and saw Quinn standing from behind the counter, his gun extended.

Quinn pulled Gracie up, then they both hopped over the desk.

The Farmer covered in shards of glass, blood puddling around him from his broken back, raised his gun slowly at Gracie.

Bic took aim. Fired.

The gun clicked on an empty chamber.

He looked around frantically. A bullet-ridden flag on a four-foot pole stuck out of the wall above him. He pulled the pole from the wall and leapt from the second floor onto a reading table. He tucked and rolled and landed on the floor.

He sprang up, ran ten feet, and plunged the pole into the Farmer's chest, driving it through to the other side. Blood sprayed from his gaped mouth.

Quinn led Gracie out the main doors.

Bic reached down and grabbed the gun from the Farmer's dead hands. When he stood, he locked eyes with Mack.

Both looked toward the door Jaco had just fled through.

67

They'd cleared the stacks and a couple of learning rooms. With no sign of Jaco, they stood in the center of the room next to a colorful display of African art.

Mack gestured toward the opposite side of the room. "He must have gone into the stairwell."

Bic nodded and walked toward the door. Mack followed. There were two sets of stairs.

"He could have gone up or down," Mack said.

Bic pointed at a shard of glass on one of the steps and followed the clue as he headed down the stairwell leading to the basement.

"Maybe we should go after Gracie," Mack said with his gun drawn over Bic's shoulder.

"The guy, is he one of your guys?"

"Quinn? He's FBI. Not my guy though."

Bic shot him a look.

"Don't worry. He saved my life. She's in good hands."

Bic continued down. As they rounded a staircase, Mack cleared his throat. "You recognize this guy we're chasing?"

"His name's Jaco Ivanov."

"Former associate of yours?"

"No," said Bic.

"Right," said Mack. "But someone hired this guy to kill Gracie, so he's, uh, sort of like you, then, isn't he?"

"Nothing like me," Bic frowned.

"How so?"

"I never enjoyed it," Bic said.

Bic opened the door at the bottom of the stairwell and both men entered at the ready. Mack scooted to his right, taking aim at the mechanical room entrance.

Bic then looked into the mechanical room through the door's large wire-glass window, then opened the door.

On the left side of the massive room, two large boilers at least ten feet in height hummed monotonously. The rest of the walls were lined with workbenches, carts, and shelves filled with every kind of tool imaginable. There was a potent smell permeating throughout.

Mack pointed to the large boilers, two 25-foot-long steel cylindrical tubes on their sides. It was a perfect spot to hide. Mack and Bic approached from opposite sides.

As he did, he was trying to place the smell that was now beginning to make him feel lightheaded.

He regained focus and popped around the corner on one knee, staying low, he aimed.

In the shadows of the boiler, there was nothing except Bic on the other end.

Suddenly, the smell got stronger, and another sense kicked in from a slight hissing sound. He reached down and felt the floor. It was wet. He brought up his hand and took a whiff.

"Paint thinner."

He walked to some shelves along the back wall of the boilers. Here everything was wet. He took a closer look. Several cans and containers were capless and upended. On closer inspection, he noticed all were flammable liquids.

He took another whiff at the air. Rotten eggs.

"Oh, no," he said. It was mercaptan, the chemical added to gas for easy detection.

He yelled to Bic, "We need to get out of here."

Mack and Bic started toward the exit when they were stopped by a pool of liquid pouring in from underneath the door.

In the wire glass window on the other side of the door, Jaco appeared with a flare in hand and a red plastic gas can.

Mack took aim to shoot.

"Don't shoot," Bic growled, staying his hand. "The gas."

With a wickedly triumphant glow, Jaco ignited the flare.

He then waved goodbye and disappeared from the window.

Instantly the exterior of the door burst into flames. A blanket of fire rolled into the room. Mack turned to see Bic removing a manhole cover from the storm drain flood protection system and tossing it aside like a Frisbee. Bic descended and Mack followed, diving head first into the drain and crashing down into two feet of water.

He stayed underwater for as long as he could, worried the gases inside the sewer might ignite.

Finally, unable to hold his breath any longer, he came up for air. The basin was illuminated by the flames above.

From the smell, or lack thereof, he realized he was in a storm drain, not a sewer. They were in a well about eight feet deep. At the water line were two 10-inch pipes attached to the basin.

Mack looked at Bic in amazement, knowing he'd saved his life again. Bic didn't say a word as he looked at the flames in the maintenance room above through the opening they'd both just dove through.

The room above filled with rancid smoke, pushing the poisonous fumes downward.

Mack coughed. "I don't think we are going to be able to ride it out down here."

Bic tore off one of the sleeves of his shirt and dunked it in the water, then wrapped the sleeve around his face. "Get ready to follow me."

Mack hurried as he pulled his sleeve off and wrapped his face.

Bic submerged his whole body underwater, then erupted upward. His massive frame sprung out of the hole with the power of an Olympic gymnast.

With all his might, Mack jumped upward. He grabbed on to the outer edge of the manhole frame. It was hot, very hot, and as he pulled his body upward Bic grabbed him by the back of his shirt, pulling him up into a room that was now alive and raging with hellfire.

68

Gracie and Quinn entered the elevator of a high-rise on LaSalle street just blocks from the Harold Washington Library. After staking out the place for a moment, Quinn walked in and talked with a security guard. Gracie watched as he shook hands with the man, and clasped his shoulder warmly, laughing. He headed back out.

"Give it a moment…" The guard walked away.

"Did you just," Gracie started.

"Hold that thought. Follow me, exactly. I'm going to keep us out of view of the cameras."

They easily avoided what little security the building had. They boarded the elevator and once Quinn pressed the badge he had lifted from the guard, they headed toward the twenty-ninth floor.

"You okay?" said Quinn.

"Nothing about this is okay. Do they really teach you how to be all James Bondy in FBI school?"

"Funny. No. I took extra credit courses. Don't worry Gracie, we'll get you through this."

They walked down the long hall to apartment number 2957. Quinn knocked solidly on the door.

No answer. Quinn knocked again. This time louder.

"Mr. Surewood?"

After a second's long wait, Quinn reached into his pocket and pulled out a couple of tools.

Gracie looked left, then right, then spoke softly. "Are you doing what I think you're doing."

Quinn stuck the thin rectangular piece of metal with a serrated L at the end into the keyhole. "All you have to do," he whispered, "is apply just the right amount of tension in the direction the key should turn."

Next, he put a thin paperclip-like piece of metal with a L hook upward into the keyhole above the tension wrench. "A typical lock has five pins, so all we have to do is push all of the pins up while keeping the right amount of tension and…" The lock clicked. "*Voila.* After me."

"I can't believe it," said Gracie. "Well, I'm a terrorist. Why shouldn't I pick a few locks while I'm at it?"

"Let's start with the obvious," said Quinn. "Desk, nightstand, coffee table."

The apartment was a typical bachelor pad, with no trace of a woman's touch anywhere. Eighty percent of the furniture budget in the living room was spent on an Alienware computer system and a massive flat screen. A gamer's chair even still had a warm can of soda in the cup holder.

"I'll take the bedroom," Gracie said.

In the bedroom were a platform bed, a nightstand, and a great view of just north of Chicago's skyline. On the nightstand was some pocket change and a sales receipt. No book. She peeked in the closet. It was a smelly mess. Dirty clothes piled on the floor in front and about twenty Air Jordan boxes stacked up in the back.

"A girl's got to do what a girl's got to do," Gracie mumbled to herself as she began digging into the pile of dirty clothes.

"Found it," Quinn yelled.

"Thank God," she muttered.

She went out into the kitchen where Quinn was sitting at the table thumbing through the book.

"Did you find anything?"

"There's a message on the inside cover."

She leaned over. "That's Steve's handwriting," she said excitedly. "To all the hard-working men, the man eaters are coming for you… SavoTay xoxoxo."

"Do you know what it means?"

She smiled. "No idea. One of Steve's riddles."

"Glad it makes you smile." Quinn said, unamused. "I might know someone at Langley who could take a stab at cracking it."

"Can't risk it," said Gracie. "I'll figure it out. I just need time."

She hugged the book to her chest and closed her eyes. "C'mon, Steve, speak to me," she whispered.

69

The room was engulfed in flames. Both men were on one knee, trying to stay just below the fat clouds of rolling smoke. The challenge of escaping a fire was not the heat, but rather making sure the smoke doesn't overcome you.

"No matter what, do not stop," Bic instructed as he pointed to the door.

Bic hunched low in a starting block position. Mack did the same, as if Bic was the fullback and he was the tailback following him through the hole.

Bic took off, and Mack followed. A couple steps in and they were running through fire. The heat was unbearable.

At the door, which was glowing hot and licked by flames, Bic dove shoulder first. Mack plowed into Bic's body with everything he had. The door blew off the hinges, their bodies tumbling into the hallway.

A maintenance man covered them with foam from a fire extinguisher, putting out any flames on them.

Bic stood, his body smoking and covered in white foam. "Thank you," he said, and walked off.

"Appreciate it," said Mack, flashing his FBI badge. "Now, any discreet exits you mind pointing us to?"

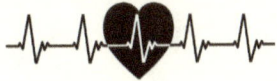

Once outside, they were picked up by a man in a town car who didn't ask any questions, and didn't care that they were wet with sewage and smelled like a cocktail of smoke, moldy water, and chemicals.

"Why do you do it, Bic?" Mack said after a couple of minutes of silence in the back of the car.

"What are you talking about?"

Mack looked at him. "Your job. Why?"

Bic took a long pause as he gazed out the side window, then turned back to Mack.

"I don't do it anymore."

"Ok, fair enough. Why *did* you do it then?"

Another long pause. "It's complicated."

"Give it your best."

"You're starting to bug me, Mack."

Mack chuckled. "And you almost cost me my life once. Granted, you saved it, but I still think I'm entitled to an answer to my question."

"It has to do with what happened with my father when I was a kid." He looked at Mack. "You know the story. But like I told you at Tidwell's that day, I'm done. And I've kept my word. I'm no longer for hire."

Mack nodded. "Okay."

"You don't believe me?"

He looked at Bic. "I said, okay."

Bic called up to the driver. "Stop right up here."

"Where are we?" said Mack.

"Where I'm staying. I need a change of clothes."

Mack watched him exit. "You wouldn't happen to have anything in a 42 medium, would you?"

70

They stopped at Mack's hotel after Bic's, for a clothing change, and then took a different town car to a storage unit facility on the South Side. The place had been abandoned, and was a broken-down shell of small buildings. The perimeter was surrounded by a run-down chain link fence on grass littered with fast food wrappers, broken beer bottles, and cigarette butts.

"That's odd," said Mack.

"What?"

"The razor wire on top of the fence."

"What about it?"

"You don't notice?"

"I ain't got all day, Mack." Regardless, Bic studied it, trying to see what the other man saw.

"It's brand new. It's obviously been installed well after this place was abandoned."

Bic stared at it for a moment, looked back at Mack, then got out of the car. After retrieving a duffle bag from the trunk, he gave the roof a tap and the car drove off.

He grabbed a key from within the bag, opened the padlock on the gate, and they entered. Mack followed Bic down the center road, where weeds of all sorts sprung up through the cracks in the pavement. Mack continued to play with his phone, making several attempts to turn it on. Waterlogged, it appeared to be broken.

Deep inside the facility was a seemingly endless row of storage units with rusted out garages, door after door. No locks on the doors. Some of the units were open, with deserted, picked-over junk tumbling forth, the vomit of past lives staining their mouths.

"Nice place," said Mack. "I'm thinking of wintering here."

Bic turned to a closed metal door with a mixture of rust and peeling orange paint on its surface, just like the others. With no lock, it didn't appear to be anything special, until Bic pulled one of the bricks away and punched a code into a keypad hidden behind it. The gears of a motor kicked in and the door began to rise.

"Hang on," said Mack. "You own this place?"

"I do."

"And you let it fall by the wayside just to hide this one unit?"

"I didn't let anything happen. It was already abandoned. I actually did some repairs to stop it from being condemned."

Mack followed Bic into the unit. The door closed behind them, and fluorescent lights illuminated a large room full of composite sketches of a black man covering the walls. They appeared to be all the same man at different phases of his life. In the center of the back wall over a desk was a map of the US, with notes and dates written all over it.

Mack stood next to a well-used punching bag hanging in the middle of the room. Bic took a seat at the desk and raised the cover of a laptop.

"You've been after this guy for quite a while," Mack said.

Bic continued typing on his keyboard.

"Who is he?"

"Someone I've been looking for. It doesn't matter."

"Your father?" Mack made one of his intuitive leaps that made him, in part, such a great agent.

Bic studied the other man for a moment, then nodded. Twice in ten minutes Mack had surprised him—which meant he bore closer watching.

"These pictures span quite a few years. How long has it been?"

"Long enough. I found a message from Tony."

"What's it say?" Mack lunged forward to look over Bic's shoulder.

"As of last night, Caroline was still hanging in there."

Mack let out a breath. "Thank Jesus. Where the hell is she?"

"Doesn't say. Just says that she's safe... no... *no... no!*"

"What's wrong?"

"The Chinese have a large bid on the black market for Gracie and her formulas."

"Maybe no one will accept the bid," Mack said.

"It's too big. Someone will."

Bic stood and pushed the desk to the side several feet. There was an old piece of plywood beneath it and he moved that as well, revealing a large safe securely hidden within the cement floor.

Bic got on his knees and opened the safe. It was filled with tactical weapons. He handed Mack two silenced Berettas then handed him the duffel bag.

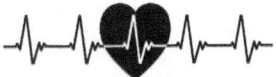

They checked all their weapons, then concealed what they could within their clothing. What they couldn't conceal, they shoved into the duffel bag.

Bic handed Mack one of two EpiPens.

"What are these?"

"Adrenaline shot. If I pass out or lose consciousness, you need to hit me with the shot. Got it?"

"Got a peanut allergy or something?"

Bic didn't answer.

Mack sighed and put the pen in his pocket. He then chambered a bullet in each of his Berettas. "Loaded. What's next?"

"A visit to the butcher shop," Bic said as he put on a pair of IT-style glasses.

A wave of nausea came over Mack. "Are you sure this is a good idea?" Even though he couldn't see Bic's eyes, he could feel them. "I'm still an FBI agent. I can't be part of some serial killer ritual." Mack hesitated, watching Bic's face for some tinge of a reaction. "Yeah, that's right, Bic. The FBI has you profiled as a serial killer. Freelancer or not. That's what you are."

"That's nice. You don't understand, and their profile doesn't really mean anything to me."

"You say you don't do it anymore. Fine. Let's skip the butcher. This isn't about your father. This is about saving Gracie and Caroline."

Behind his *Terminator* glasses, Bic continued to stare ahead. A thousand different things could have been going through his mind. Mack wanted to know exactly what.

"Talk to me, Bic," Mack said softly.

Bic removed his sunglasses and stared at his feet. "When I was seven, my drugged-out father beat my mother to death with a cast iron skillet. Right in front of me. When I tried to stop him, he shoved a pork chop in my mouth and choked me half to death with it. I guess when I went unconscious he thought I was dead and left me."

"You don't need this anymore," Mack said.

"I still got a fear of choking."

"This isn't you, Bic."

Bic put his glasses back on. "Let's go."

71

"Mr. Ivanov," said Mr. Zhou genially as he entered the dining room.

Jaco had been taken by surprise. The man's steps made no sound and there'd been no warning that he had been coming. He rose from the Chicago penthouse's twelve-foot dining room table.

"Mr. Zhou, pleasure."

Mr. Zhou kept a distance of at least ten feet at all times. Probably something he learned as one of China's top spies for the Ministry for State Security, thought Jaco. The lighting in this place, a penthouse that consumed the entire 83rd floor of a building on Michigan Avenue, was as dim as a bowling alley. But the lighting was adequate enough for Jaco to notice two things about Mr. Zhou.

1) He was tall, and thin as a pipe cleaner.

2) The tip of his left pinky finger was missing.

Mr. Zhou took a seat at the other end of the table and folded his hands neatly on the glossy high-end wood. "A cure for cancer as effective as penicillin is to an infection has been found... China wants it."

"America wants it gone."

Mr. Zhou smirked, "Yes, I know. Their supposed free market isn't so free, is it?"

"I have no comment on the free market," Jaco shrugged. "It's kept me employed."

"Nevertheless," said Zhou, "your people are eager for some

restraints, are they not? With a cure for cancer, the US will agree to all our trade terms, and this cure will become the world's ultimate bargaining chip. If your country wants the cure, you must agree to China's terms."

"Listen, Mr. Zhou," said Jaco, "with all due respect, I don't care a rat's fluffy ass about your Bond villain plans for world domination. What's the world's ultimate bargaining chip worth to you? That's all I want to know."

Zhou stared coldly at him. "We will pay you ten billion dollars. Five billion for the formulas and five billion for the scientist, Gracie Green."

"What makes you think she can be bought?"

Zhou smiled. "I'm surprised at you, Mr. Ivanov. You, more than any other man, should know the power of a sum. At any rate, in case the formulas are incomplete, a key step in the process is still in her mind."

"How about you can the balloon juice, Zhou. Let's face it, this woman cured cancer. What else is she capable of? What's it gonna be, huh? Mind control drugs? Bioweapons that alter DNA? That little girl's mind is worth a lot more to you than what you're offering."

There was something terrible in Zhou's smile, like a piranha, but Jaco barely let it register. Zhou may think he's the predator, but it was Jaco who controlled this room.

"Twenty billion, the girl and the formula," Jaco confirmed.

"You are like a pufferfish, Mr. Ivanov," said Zhou. He held up a placating hand as Jaco's face went red. "It is a compliment. The pufferfish is one of the deadliest animals on the planet. In its tiny body it contains enough neurotoxin to kill thirty humans. But the most interesting thing is that there is a single animal, just one, that pufferfish toxin has no effect on. The shark can eat the deadliest fish in the ocean with no consequence. They even enjoy them as a snack. Do not tempt the shark that is China, Mr. Ivanov."

Jaco tapped a fingertip on the table for a moment. The gentle warning was getting under his skin, but he could tell that it was a promise, not a threat. "Fine. Eleven."

Zhou smiled and bowed his head once. "We have a deal, then."

Jaco stood and placed a piece of paper on the table. "Wire me ten million today as an advance, *then* we have a deal. Oh, and balance is due *immediately* upon delivery, I don't do accounts receivable."

Zhou nodded to the man standing. He retrieved the piece of paper and brought it to Zhou.

"The money will be in your account within the hour. We will prepare the rest in a numbered account which we will allow you to take possession of upon delivery."

"Fantastic. In that case, you'll have to excuse me, boss. I have some work to do. I like to be thorough."

Zhou watched him walk away. "And I like professionalism. I'm sure your sister in Bulgaria and her four kids would appreciate it."

Jaco paused at the door, clenched his fists, then showed himself out. A shark indeed.

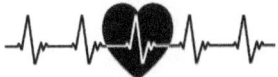

Outside the Chicago high-rise, the skyscraper's windows reflected the warm glow of the afternoon sun. The street was packed with cars and people walking in all directions. Jaco, in the middle of them, read a text he'd received from Peter Rains while he was in the meeting with Zhou.

"Status?"

Jaco texted back, "Everything should be completed within 24 hours."

This was ludicrous. Handing Gracie and the formulas to Zhou could ruin Peter's career or get him killed. He hoped the latter. Peter needed to be taught the ultimate lesson of respect. Maybe he would show up at his door after he screwed him over and break the news to him—right before he put a bullet in him.

"What now," Jaco said as his phone pinged again. He looked at the incoming text, presuming it was a follow up jab from Peter Rains. He smiled. It was a deposit confirmation. Ten million dollars had already been deposited into his off-shore account.

He headed into the Rolex store with the intention of upgrading his nine-year-old Submariner to a GMT Master II.

The shiny watches glimmered under the glass like sun diamonds in the sea.

Now, he thought, what do you suppose would look good around my wrist when I hand Gracie over to the Chinese?

72

Quinn paced back and forth between the kitchen area and the modest living room of the FBI safehouse on lower Wacker Drive, while Gracie sat at the round kitchen table littered with half-eaten Chinese takeout boxes. They surrounded the book like towers of Camelot. Steve would have appreciated that.

As much as this had Steve written all over it, she couldn't help but think of her college days. This would be the scene on several occasions before a test. Her and Anna would order Chinese from Jing-Jing's and stay up half the night quizzing each other.

"This brings back so many memories," Gracie said, still reminiscing. "How'd you know I'd like Chinese?"

Quinn was in the middle of a text in the living room. He stopped. "Everyone likes Chinese. Anyway, how could over a billion people be wrong?"

"I don't think Chinese takeout over here is actually common over there..." Gracie teased, then looked at his phone. "Everything okay?"

"Keeping my boss at bay. I think he's onto me."

"Can you trust him? Maybe we should go meet with him."

"Not sure we can." Quinn came to the table. "You want me to clear the table?"

Gracie shook her head no. She liked feeling her best friend all around her. She took a deep breath and refocused on the words Steve had written on the inside cover.

To all the hard-working men, the man eaters are coming for you.

SavoTay xoxoxo

She mumbled to herself, "What were you trying to say to me?"

Quinn went behind Gracie and started massaging her shoulders.

She rolled her head from side to side. "That feels good."

"You've been looking at that for hours now. It's almost eight. Maybe we should send it to Langley."

"Maybe you should rub a little deeper," she said.

He obliged, and Gracie fell into deep relaxation.

"Did he ever use any codes or anything like that?" said Quinn. "Maybe it's certain letters from each word? He seems like the type that would be familiar with old rail ciphers or things like that."

"Steve was complicated. That's all I can say."

Quinn continued to massage her. His hands kneading down her back. "Was SavoTay a nickname he used for something or someone, like maybe a friend of his?"

"No, SavoTay? I don't think... wait..."

She tore the lid of a Chinese food container and scratched the word on it. SavoTay. "I remember when we first met, he would often speak in Pig Latin. Silly things like referring to countries." She stared at the word as she spoke. "Tsavo."

"Is that a country?" Quinn asked.

She did a quick Google search. "It's a river in Kenya." Gracie looked back at the book and read out loud, "To all the hard-working men, the man eaters are coming for you. Hard working men on the East Africa railroad." Her body tensed. "The Halloween party." She gasped, then stood as if she'd seen a ghost on the page.

"What is it?"

"I cracked it." Gracie looked at him. "Tsavo man eaters... *The Ghost and the Darkness.*"

"The lions?" Quinn's face was quizzical.

"It was Steve's favorite movie, he even dressed up one year as Charles Remington."

"Okay, where does that lead us?"

"The Ghost and the Darkness are stuffed here at the Chicago Field Museum. They've been on display for decades. Steve went there all the time to see them. He loved that place."

"Perfect, we'll head there tonight. I can't believe he left a scavenger hunt across the institutions of Chicago."

"They're closed," Gracie said.

"You saw my lock picking skills. Plus, it's better to be in there without a bunch of people—no one can hide in plain sight from us like they did at the library."

"Maybe we should get my uncle to help us?"

Quinn placed his hand on the outside of Gracie's arms with a caring touch as he spoke in a soft voice, "That man was the most notorious assassin on the FBI's most wanted list in history—his file says he's dead, and I'd have to arrest him if I saw him again. I'm sorry, but he's a stone-cold killer. Your uncle is no different than the guy trying to kill you. He comes after innocent people and kills them for money. There are 22 cases that we know of."

Gracie's nostrils flared. Her once fond memories of Bic now jaded with the knowledge of something truly horrific.

She suddenly felt as if she was going to vomit.

Quinn tried to comfort her. She turned to him for a hug.

With her face buried in his chest, she mumbled, "He raised me, cared for me all my life—I've never felt so betrayed, my company was funded with blood money."

"Not your fault. The best thing we can do is get your research back and clear your name." Quinn pulled away slightly. Still holding her shoulders, he looked her in the eyes, "I promise you I will make this right. All of it."

He kissed her gently.

They didn't stop.

73

"I can't see a thing," said Gracie. "Can't we turn the flashlights on?"

"Not yet." Though he had somehow picked the locks and disarmed the museum's security, he was sticking on this point.

Moonlight shone through the glass ceiling of the thirty-foot-high main entrance hall that stretched from the north to the south of the Field Museum. The place seemed more alive than she'd remembered during her last daytime visit. Lingering over the top of their heads, casting a 40-foot-long shadow, was a T-Rex skeleton named Sue with a mouth full of railroad spikes for teeth.

"This is way creepy," Gracie said, grabbing onto Quinn's arm.

"Is it just me, or do you kind of feel like a snack in this place?" Quinn said, staring up at the grin of the most notorious carnivore in history.

Once they exited the main hall, they turned their flashlights on and followed the map towards the lions.

On the west end of the museum they reached the display case. On the glass, written in gold lettering, were the words, "THE LIONS OF TSAVO." One was standing, the other lying on its belly on some rocks with thorn bushes behind them, no doubt taken from the Tsavo region for authenticity. Outside the glass, about waist high, was a plate with some facts about the cats and the region of Tsavo.

Quinn shone the light on the lions. "These guys look like kitty cats."

Gracie lit up a photograph within the case on a tall piece of smoked gray glass. It was of one of the lions, with the man who'd killed it sitting next to it on display. "If you really want to see what these lions looked like."

Quinn stepped right up to the glass, took a close look, and read the caption at the bottom of the picture. "His length from tip of nose to tip of tail was nine feet, eight inches. Okay, that's no kitty cat, that's a certified beast." Quinn continued to read the story etched in the smoked glass and shook his head. "They just don't look right."

"They're maneless. It makes them almost look like females," she said, inspecting every inch of the display case. She looked to Quinn. "Are you going to help or keep asking questions?"

Quinn got on his knees, shining his light underneath the front of the display case. After a thorough inspection, he poked his head out and said, "Just some gum stuck underneath. That's all."

"What flavor?"

Quinn stood. "Steve must have left you a clue. Maybe you should taste it."

Gracie appreciated the snarky comment with a smirk.

"Nothing's jumping out at me," he said.

Gracie paced back and forth, looking at every inch of every item in the display case from different angles. Every time she got to the far-left side of the display, she reread every word on the gray smoked glass, which was six paragraphs highlighting the story of the Tsavo lions, plus two photographs.

"Anything?" Quinn asked.

"I'm just so confused." Gracie shone the light at the lion lying on the rocks.

Quinn came up over her shoulder. "Did Steve know anyone who worked here?"

Gracie squinted. "Not that I'm aware of, but it wouldn't surprise me. He came here probably once or twice a month to decompress." She smiled at him. "We're thinking the same thing, aren't we?"

"That we should get a look under that lion's belly? Yep."

74

Quinn had worked his magic on the lock of the glass case.

Within, carefully, Gracie reached underneath the standing lion, patting and feeling where she could, trying not to disturb too much.

She looked back, and Quinn was frowning at his phone.

"Who's texting you at three AM?" she said, still digging around.

"My boss, wondering why I used a safehouse."

"Did you tell him?"

"No. If I did, he'd demand I arrest you."

Quinn walked over and squatted down on the other side of the lion. "Find anything?"

She sat back on her knees and sighed. "Maybe we have to come back in the daytime. There might be something I'm missing. A clue in another display or something like that."

"We're running out of time," Quinn said.

He stared at the cat lying down. "Did you check this guy yet?"

"I did."

"Hang on," he said, and flipped it over on its side in a fluid motion.

To Gracie's surprise, the lion's belly was a hollow cavity.

"Now I know why they had this thing on its stomach," Quinn said as he started digging into its underbelly.

"Quinn," Gracie finally said.

"We need to find the flash drive."

"Yeah, but destroying the exhibit isn't going to help."

He sat back, exasperated. "Dammit. Nothing."

Quinn took a deep breath, then sat back and hugged his knees next to the gray smoked glass.

"You're looking a bit intense at the moment," she said.

"I'm sorry," he said. "My boss texting me at three AM is not a good sign. For all I know he's got agents tracking me down right now—if he triangulates my phone, he'll see I've broken into a damn museum in the middle of the night. There's no explaining that. We have twelve hours max, if not less."

Gracie stared at Quinn and an idea came to her. "John Henry Patterson."

"Who?"

"That's got to be it," she said.

Quinn looked at the photo next to him of the man sitting, just as he was, next to the killed lion. "This dude?"

"Yeah. Oh, Steve. The Halloween party! Of course!"

"Halloween. Not following."

She bent down to his level. "Steve came as Charles Remington to the party a couple years back, and his best friend, Shay, came as John Henry Patterson."

Quinn's eyes lit up. "You think Shay has the damn flash drive?"

"I think we cracked it." Grace looked up. "Thank you, Steve, you will always be awesome."

They began to exit the display case when Gracie said, "I just realized something. I don't know Shay's last name. I have no idea how to find him."

"You know where Steve's house is?"

"I do."

Quinn smiled. "Well then, it's a good thing you just happen to have an FBI agent lying around."

75

At four AM, Quinn and Gracie rolled into Oak Lawn near the Chicago South Side. They pulled up to one of a row of several similar well-kept bungalows on the long block. Barricade tape surrounded the house.

Once inside the house, Quinn headed to the computer desk located in a second bedroom that had been transformed into a man cave. On the desk was an open bag of Doritos and a square outline of dust.

"Crap, they confiscated his computer," he said, and moved past Gracie toward the outer rooms.

After about 30 minutes of rifling through drawers, Quinn pulled out his phone and went back into the room with the empty computer desk.

"I didn't want to have to do this," he said, his phone to his ear. "Do you know if he spoke with Shay often?"

"I don't think so. Steve didn't talk on his phone much, at least not at work."

"Hey, this is Quinn," he said into the phone. "I need you to see if you have anyone with the first name Shay in Steve Cotwell's phone records. I need an address... It's for the Gracie Green case."

After a moment, "I'm here... Okay, thanks anyway." Quinn put down his phone. "Nothing."

"That's crazy. I can't believe he never called him. I know he'd drag in some mornings from playing video games with Shay all night."

"Video games, huh?"

Gracie looked over at the Xbox console.

"What game is in it?" Quinn asked.

Gracie checked, "*Fortnite.*"

"Turn it on."

She did.

Quinn grabbed one of the controllers and navigated to see if he had been playing with any friends. Only one name came up.

"WilliamWallace10:26," he said.

Quinn redialed his contact. "Me again. This might be a tall order, but can you check to see who is registered with Microsoft Xbox for the Fortnite game under the name 'William Wallace-10-colon- 26?"

"Who is this magic man on the other end?" Gracie whispered.

Quinn put his hand over the phone and whispered back. "Owes me about a hundred favors. I found his lost dog for him."

"Look at you, hero."

He uncovered the phone. "Yeah? Alright. Thanks again, dude." He lowered the phone and blew out a sigh of relief. "Not even sunrise yet and we've got our man."

76

After a two-mile drive, Quinn and Gracie walked up to the three-story flat. Early morning sunlight glowed softly on the horizon, throwing an eerie hue over the dew-stained lawn in front and reflecting off the facing windows.

Quinn hit the buzzer for Apartment 1B. The old brick building showed signs of wear, but the solid triple brick construction would hold up structurally for another hundred years.

They buzzed again.

A tired voice came over the intercom. "Who is it?"

"Shay?"

No response.

"It's Gracie Green. Steve—"

The door buzzed and Quinn and Gracie entered. They walked up a flight of stairs and entered the landing area of the middle unit.

Before she could knock on the door, it opened.

A head poked out. It was obvious from his matted curly brown bed head that he'd just woken up. But his eyes, hazel, set back in a thick skull with chubby cheeks, were open wide and alert. He had on a well-worn t-shirt with an old-school graphic from *The Incredible Hulk* hanging over blue and white striped pajama bottoms.

"Don't be alarmed," she said.

"I've been expecting you."

She took a breath. "I'm so glad. May we come in?"

Quinn flashed his badge. "It's OK."

Shay stepped aside to allow them entrance.

Gracie turned to Quinn. "Would you mind? I'd like a moment alone."

"Sure. I'll be right out here."

She entered the apartment and Shay shut the door.

She told him everything. From the details of Steve's valiant death to the involvement of her Uncle Bic. When she was done, Shay came forward and hugged her.

"I still can't believe he's gone," said Shay. "I thought he was just a paranoid maniac. I guess he wasn't."

"I'm afraid not."

Shay went from somber to frustrated. "You know, I never believed this terrorist BS. Steve was a patriot. And you were always on the up and up."

"I know. Seeing myself on TV, what they said about us... I'm so sorry for what happened."

"Don't be. I think you know how Steve felt about you."

Gracie smiled. "We were, we *are*, family."

Shay pulled open a drawer in his kitchen, then reached underneath it and retrieved a flash drive.

"Here you go," he said.

"Just one?"

"That's the HyperX Predator, one terabyte of data."

The second Gracie had the data back in her hand, she felt as if she'd just pulled Excalibur from the rock and now had what she needed to win this uphill battle.

"Password is Guinevere, 'at' symbol, then one digit greater than every digit of your phone number, underscore, nineteen."

"Got it."

"I want you to know I got your back like Steve did. I have an additional copy offline. Just know, if something happens to you, I will not give up until I clear your names. Steve will not be remembered as a terrorist."

Gracie hugged him, saying with determination, "When I take these guys down and clear our names, can you do me a favor?"

"Anything."

They separated, and Gracie grabbed onto Shay's hands.

Gracie teared up. "I want you to take Steve's place as King Arthur when we go in front of the Queen of England."

"I'd be honored."

Shay stood a little taller. "One day a king will come, and the Sword will rise again." He opened the door and ushered her out with a flourish. "Go thou forth, milady."

Gracie exited, and Shay reached for her. As he spoke, he glared at Quinn, affronted that a handsome man was keeping her company rather than Steve. "Remember, there's always something cleverer than yourself."

Gracie reached out for a final goodbye. "You are everything that is right with this world."

Shay stood in awe as he fell under the same Arthurian magic spell that had had Steve so mesmerized.

The second they were in the stairwell and the door had closed behind them, Quinn asked, "Did you get it?"

"All of it," Gracie said, her voice trembling with excitement.

"Great, I've got a plan." Quinn said reaching out for the drive.

Gracie put it in her pocket. "Nuh uh. I'm never letting go of my formulas again."

"Smart girl," he said.

Outside, Quinn scanned down the street, frowning.

"Everything okay?"

"Uh," he said, still preoccupied. "Yeah… no…"

"What is it?"

"I just saw a dark Suburban pull around the corner."

"Okay."

He turned back to Shay's building, then back to the street.

"Quinn, you're scaring me."

"It's alright," he said. "Probably just a—"

Shay's building exploded with a hell-storm of brick and fire. The supersonic blast threw Quinn and Gracie to the ground.

77

She tried to pull herself up. Her ears were dead and ringing and her vision was blurred. She felt something wet on her lips. She touched her face and her hand came away coated with blood.

The building was all but gone. Whatever was left of it was in flames.

She looked to Quinn who was on the ground, unmoving.

She crawled towards their car. The driver's side had been facing the explosion. Fragments of brick and wood jutted out of the sheet metal as if it had sprouted like weeds from within the car.

Still on her hands and knees, a buzzing ring in her ears, she noticed a pair of large combat boots to her right. A hand snatched her up by her hair.

The pain was excruciating, but she didn't give Jaco the satisfaction of a scream.

The men surrounded Quinn on the ground. He was moving now, and was awkwardly reaching for his gun.

One of the three men reached down, took the gun as if it had been offered, and placed it in his own pocket. The largest of the military-looking men then kicked Quinn hard in the side.

Within 20 seconds, Gracie and Quinn were zip tied and thrown into the back seat of one of the two Suburbans that had pulled up behind their car.

The convoy quickly headed north down the street.

Gracie found it weird they'd buckled her seatbelt. She also noticed they did not for Quinn, who was still recovering. Gracie wasn't sure if it was the explosion or the kick to the ribs that got the worst of him.

"You okay?" she rasped.

"I'll make it," he replied, wincing and short of breath. He opened his eyes and looked at her, blood trickling from his busted lip. "Sorry I couldn't protect you."

Quinn coughed, a rough, grating sound. He shook his head in defeat. Hunched over staring at the floor he mumbled, "I should have known calling the Bureau for the address was a bad idea."

"What?"

"They must have someone on the inside. It's the only way, given that I all but announced where to find us."

From the passenger front seat, Jaco turned back to Gracie. The sun beamed into the vehicle, illuminating Jaco's deep blue eyes. He held the flash drive up. "You don't have any nude selfies on here as well, do you? I mean, I'm not judging. I'll delete them if you do." His eyes wandered up and down her form. "Or maybe I won't."

"Go to hell, you murderer!"

Jaco glared at her. "You know, if you'd cooperated just a little, so many people wouldn't have to die, like your uncle." He smirked. "Oh yeah, I forgot to tell you. Bic's a little extra crispy at the moment. Along with that FBI agent buddy of his."

"You might as well kill me now," she said. "Because whatever it is you want, I'm not giving it to you."

Like a striking snake, Jaco lurched into the back seat, grabbing Quinn by the throat and clamping his thumb and index finger on his windpipe.

He waited until Quinn started to gasp for air, then spoke in a calm, vicious snarl.

"I've been killing for longer than you've been alive, you little nit. I've never failed, and I have the resources of the most powerful people in the world."

Quinn's body gyrated spastically, fighting for breath.

Jaco gripped even harder, then continued. "Option A, you cooperate. I'm going to sell you and your formulas to the Chinese. You'll go with them to the land of eggrolls. They'll give you the best facilities and all the money in the world to continue your research."

"Let him go!" she screamed, watching Quinn's face go crimson.

"Let me finish. Option B, you don't cooperate. In that case, I kill your cock buddy right here and now and then cut off your toes one by one until you do agree to cooperate."

Gracie looked at Quinn, then at Jaco. "Let him go, you animal!"

"That wasn't a no or a yes." Jaco put a hand to his ear. "Hear that?

That's his brain cells dying."

"Let him go!"

"Option B it is," Jaco said, his face hardening to pure evil.

Without warning, a white SUV traveling fast blew through a stop sign at an intersection and struck the Suburban on the passenger side front end. The vehicle's sheet metal crumpled like tin foil. The glass shattered as the passenger side airbags deployed.

Jaco's body smacked into the side airbags as they burst open.

The Suburban spun around twice as the white SUV's momentum took it across the intersection and up onto the curb, taking out a postal drop box on the street corner.

Silence fell on the scene. Both vehicles, front ends at about three car lengths apart, faced each other, hissing softly. The strong smell of burnt chemicals from the airbags permeated the air.

Quinn was stuffed down on the floorboard, moaning. He was definitely breathing.

The vehicle that struck them, a white Ford Bronco, now displayed a hood that was buckled so badly you could barely see the windshield. The Suburban sat in the middle of the intersection. Everything seemed to be caught in slow motion.

"It can't be," Jaco said as Bic, like a ghost materializing from across the veil, stepped out of the Bronco, a Beretta in hand.

In the blink of an eye, Jaco had a shiny .357 magnum drawn. He reached out the already shattered window and unloaded the magazine at Bic.

Bic retreated to the rear as bullets riddled the front of the Bronco.

The driver of the Suburban hopped out of the vehicle with an MP5. Hiding behind the front fender of the Suburban, he popped up periodically, spraying clusters of rounds.

"He's afraid to hit the girl," Jaco said to the driver. "Stay close to the car."

The driver nodded, taking aim at the Bronco, waiting for anything to move.

Jaco turned back to Gracie. "If you or the cock move an inch, I'll execute you on the spot."

78

Mack crawled out the rear hatch of the Bronco. "Damn door was jammed." He crouched next to Bic, weapon in hand. "What now, Kemosabe?"

"Just make sure you don't shoot Gracie."

"Wasn't planning to, but okay." He darted out and fired a shot off to the side, keeping their targets pinned, then ducked back beside Bic again.

Bic looked at a large tree across the street, flanked to the right of the Suburban, "If one of us can get behind that tree, we'll have position."

"One of us meaning me."

"You're quick, so yeah." Bic nodded. "I'll cover you."

Mack got in a sprint ready position, then shot out from behind the Bronco like a rocket.

Bic reached around from behind the Bronco, leaving most of his body covered. He fired, into the front end of the Suburban making enough noise to keep both men pinned down.

The man with the MP5 popped up and opened fire at Mack.

Mack dashed across the street, bullets ricocheting off of the pavement inches away from him. Bic opened up on the shooter.

Mack dove head first in the grass baseball-style, stopping behind the tree as if it was a base.

Bic, already reloaded, had the shooter pinned down.

The driver fired at Bic. Mack rolled out from the tree, took aim, and hit the man, first in the shoulder, then in the head.

Bic stepped out from behind the Bronco and took dead aim at Jaco. Jaco ducked down under the dashboard.

Bic waved for Gracie to get out of the line of fire, but Gracie, pinned down in her seat, didn't move.

Bic walked slowly across the street toward the Bronco, arm extended, staring down the sights and ready to fire if Jaco popped his head up. Mack took aim as well.

"*Unc!*" Gracie yelled as the other Suburban came screaming out from the side street. No time to dive out of the way, Bic jumped and rolled onto the hood to lessen the force of the strike. His back smashed into the windshield, the shatterproof glass caught him like a basket.

The Suburban cut sharply sending Bic flying into the air. He landed in the grass and rolled, stopping next to the mailbox lying on its side.

The car continued to cut the wheel right, pulling up on the driver's side of the wrecked Suburban.

Two men hopped out. One, an MP5 in hand, walked into the middle of the intersection. Gunshots cracked into the air as he shot at Mack to his left, pinning him down behind the tree. On the other side of the street, to his right, the other turned his attention to Bic. Bic dove behind the mailbox. Bullets pelted the solid steel box.

The second man retrieved Jaco, Gracie, and Quinn, and loaded them into the surviving vehicle.

Bic, lying down, no weapon, stood. He grabbed the wrecked mailbox and pulled it up from its bolts in the ground. He then charged the man, using the thing as a shield.

The man in the street shot at Bic. Multiple bullets pounded into the box. The fire then ceased.

Bic lowered the mailbox. The man lay on the ground in a pool of blood, Mack to his right.

Bic nodded toward Mack.

"It was literally nothing," said Mack. "The dumbass was too busy with you to notice me standing next to him."

The Suburban's wheels squealed, the burning rubber smoked, lurching the vehicle forward.

Bic dropped the mailbox and sprinted towards the vehicle.

Mack fired shots at the tires. Sparks flew beneath the car.

Both were too late. The vehicle was gone within seconds.

79

Bic retreated back to the smashed Bronco to recover his phone. Mack ran up, still jacked up from the gun fight. "I thought we had them."

Bic called Parelli and put the call on speaker, unconcerned with the people starting to look out windows now that the action seemed to have died down. This was not a nice part of Chicago, and he had at least 10 more minutes before police would arrive.

"Did you get Gracie?" Parelli asked.

"No."

"Not good, my friend. Word on the street is she is being sold to the Chinese. Good news is they want her alive, bad news..." Parelli hesitated.

"What is it?" Bic asked.

"If they get her out of the country, they'll keep her locked up as a work slave for the rest of her life. It will be somewhere none of us could find in a thousand lifetimes."

Bic could tell Mack was holding his tongue, and Bic nodded to him.

"How's Caroline?" Mack asked.

"She's hanging in there. One tough lady you got there."

"How's she look?"

"She looks surprisingly well, considering."

"Okay, so what's our next move?" asked Mack.

"Rumor has it," said Parelli, "Zhou is making the deal for China. If so, he likes to do things by boat. And when I say boat I mean *big* boat."

"We're gonna need a Ouija board to find him," said Mack. "There're tons of marinas on Lake Michigan."

"Just look for a big ol' yacht, something big enough to go across the ocean," said Parelli. "He always names it something flashy and Japany sounding, like teeth of the dragon."

A loud noise came through the phone.

"Was that a car horn?" said Mack. "I thought you were with Caroline."

"I am. It's a medical bus of sorts. Don't worry, kid, this is a hospital on wheels."

"A medical bus?"

"We're coming to Chicago," Parelli said. "I've kept my word, kept her safe, but now you need to save Gracie so she can do her thing."

About the time Parelli finished speaking, a black car pulled up. It was just like the one that had picked them up from the library, except a different driver.

"Your ride has arrived," Parelli said. "Make sure you don't underestimate Zhou—he's a dangerous man." The call disconnected.

Bic retrieved his bag from the Bronco, making one more call to Mack didn't know who, though he heard him talking about finding a boat as the two men entered the back of the limo.

"Your buddy Tony there is pretty amazing," said Mack.

"He is, but just know that when the time comes, he expects you to be just as amazing back."

"Listen, if that's the price to save Caroline's life, it's worth it."

80

"**P**ut a bullet in this John's head then throw his FBI corpse into the dumpster," Jaco said.

Gracie looked around. No one was in sight in the dark, narrow alley down behind the shadows of a couple of tall buildings where they were parked. She had the awful sense that this was one of those types of places where bad things could happen and no one would be coming to your rescue, no matter how loud you screamed.

She looked over at Quinn. They had duct-taped his mouth. He breathed heavily through his nose. Her eyes welled up at the sight of him.

The driver of the vehicle slowly twisted a silencer onto his gun. With each turn, the sound of metal against metal made what was about to happen seem more and more real.

The man hopped out of the car, then pulled Quinn out. Placing the dark piece of steel on the hood of the Suburban, he lifted Quinn up and rolled his body into the dumpster.

Gracie watched Quinn, laying there in a sea of garbage, in the mouth of a green metal monster, tied up and gagged with his head perfectly poised to receive the bullet this evil man was about to put into his skull. Then, with the shuffle of one trash bag, Quinn would disappear from the earth. The only music at his funeral would be the hydraulics of a dump truck spilling him into a landfill under thousands of pounds of garbage.

She turned away, not wanting to watch. When she turned back the man had his arm extended, the silencer tip not more than twelve inches away from Quinn's head.

"No," Gracie screamed. "Some of the formula is in my head, I'll write it down if he lives! Please, don't...!"

Jaco grinned, then said, "Deal."

They hauled Quinn out and placed him back into the car.

"Put his window down, will you, he smells like a rhinoceros!" Jaco barked.

"I couldn't let them kill you. I hope being trapped somewhere in a prison in China with me is a better fate," Gracie whispered to Quinn.

There was a smile of appreciation in his eyes.

"Congratulations," said Jaco. "You're the proud winner of a first-class ticket on a cruise to China… you're welcome!"

ack and Bic entered the Chicago Yacht Club harbor off Monroe Street. Walking along the concrete sidewalk built as a pier, it ran hundreds of yards on the edge of Lake Michigan. Most of the boats were sailboats and they were not parked against the pier, but attached to a buoy anchor system in the harbor, neatly stacked in rows as if they were in some type of invisible parking lot in the water.

"If I didn't know any better, I'd think we were at the ocean," Mack said staring into the deep blue vastness that was Lake Michigan.

"When I was a kid," said Bic, "my mom would take me to 57th Street beach every Saturday after she got home from her shift. She and I used to pretend we were on some type of expensive vacation. It was an awesome escape that both of us needed from reality." Bic pointed out to all the boats. "I remember whenever a boat sailed or cruised by we would get into the water and act like our yacht had finally arrived to pick us up to take us off to the Bahamas or Europe."

"Sounds great," Mack said.

"It was, until the bus ride home. I hated the look in my mother's eyes, the disappointment she had knowing where she was taking me back to—the jungle, our building was called."

"Your mom sounds like she was a great lady."

"I wish those trips to the beach would have never stopped. If Mom hadn't been taken... killed... things would have definitely turned out different. It's no excuse for what I've done, but things would have been different." Bic's scan stopped on a boat that was larger than all the rest. "There." He pointed to an 80-foot yacht, an ocean cruiser with multiple levels and decks. "That, as Tony would say, is a big boat."

"It definitely sticks out from the others. Should we stake it out?"

"No time. If we're wrong, they'll be gone before we know it." Bic pulled out a pair of binoculars and took a look. "There are several harbors here on the lake, and they could be in any one of these. But, I figured the ones closest to downtown will have the water depth deep enough for the bigger yachts. Yeah. She matches the info I got. The Jade Katana."

"Anyone aboard?" Mack wondered again who the mysterious short call after Tony had been to.

"Not sure. The decks are empty, so no one's been at this boat recently or they are intentionally making it look that way."

Mack and Bic walked down the dock sidewalk. The boat was parked next to a floating dock off on its own, in a special area to accommodate its size.

"Do we need to get wet?" Mack asked as he stared at the thirty yards of water between them and the boat.

Bic looked at Mack, but didn't answer.

"I'll take that as a no."

A couple strode toward them. The man held a bottle of champagne in one hand and a picnic basket in the other.

Mack approached them. "Excuse me."

"Yes?" said the man.

Mack pointed. "That beautiful boat over there. You don't know if it's for rent by any chance, do you?"

The man chuckled derisively. "God no. That's Winston Biesterfield's boat. He doesn't even use it but twice a year. The rest of the season it just sits there empty like a big eye sore to remind everyone who's got the biggest boat in the club."

"That's a shame."

"Mm," The man said, nodding in agreement. And having had enough of the small talk, the couple started walking away.

Mack watched them for a moment, then called out, "You a religious man?"

The man turned back with a raised eyebrow. "Pardon me?"

"Are you religious?"

"Yes."

"I was given something a couple of months ago when I got some really bad news about my wife, a friend of ours said that the secret to having it all is knowing the Lord has already given it to you. Just thought I'd pass it on. Hope you both have a great day."

"We will." The man raised his bottle of wine and the couple walked off.

"Nice work," Bic said.

"Thanks, I thought they could use a little perspective. That guy really seemed to be worried about the bigger boat when he should be proud that he actually has a boat of his own in the harbor."

"I meant finding out that yacht isn't the one we are looking for."

82

aving ditched the Suburban, Gracie and Quinn were transferred into the cubed cargo box of a 12-foot U-Haul moving truck. Jaco had joined them as well. He sat on a wooden, rectangular crate with a small camping lantern at his feet, leering at Gracie. A crowbar steadily grasped in his right hand.

Quinn, still tied up, lay on the floor facing the wall. Jaco had instructed his driver to anchor him in a way so he wouldn't have to see Quinn's face. Gracie knew a little about psychology, but she wasn't sure if he even considered Quinn a threat at this point or if Jaco just didn't like a reminder that his plan of execution had changed. He was supposed to deliver her and the formulas. But her negotiating the "plus a boyfriend" deal was not what he'd had in his mind.

"Don't worry, your boyfriend is going to live. The Chinese think he'll be a nice tool to get what they want from you."

Swaying from left to right, the truck made a turn. They were weaving in and out of traffic, but Gracie had no idea exactly where to. From the number of starts and stops, Gracie could infer their general location from her internal map of downtown Chicago.

The truck had been stopped for more than the typical 30 to 40 seconds. Jaco looked at his phone, read a quick text, then stood and opened the crate with the crowbar. From inside, he pulled out a high-end, slick-looking black plastic case. It was the length of a rifle case, only five times as thick. He carefully laid the case on the truck floor. Painted in white block letters on it was the word "MANPAD."

Jaco walked over to Quinn and pulled him to his feet. Not really trying to be too gentle about it, he dragged him to the wooden crate, then put him inside of it.

Jaco took the top panel and with the back side of his crowbar pounded the case shut.

He looked to Gracie. "He's the full package, isn't he?"

"You said he would be safe."

"I'll poke holes in it and put some lettuce in there." he knocked on the top panel of the box with the crow bar for good measure.

Jaco motioned for Gracie to come sit on the crate. She did.

"Do you know what this is?" Jaco asked.

"A Taser."

"I'm guessing you're smart enough to know exactly what these 50,000 volts will do to your nervous system."

Gracie nodded.

"That door's going to open, and me, you, and your boyfriend are going to go for a short walk to our boat. If you cooperate, everyone will be fine, you'll go to China and have the full support of your new country to cure cancer and save the world and all that. There's a good chance we will walk by several people in this high-traffic area, your instinct will be to scream for help. Your mind will demand for you to yell out 'rape' or something cute like that. I want you to know the exact consequences if you do." Jaco's eyes narrowed to wicked slits and his eyebrows arched as he pointed the Taser at her forehead. "I'm gonna tase you right between those pretty eyes, and tens of thousands of volts will drop you like a burnt sack of potatoes, leaving you incapacitated for 30 seconds. In those 30 seconds, I'll dump your boyfriend into Lake Michigan, still in this box, then throw you over my shoulder and walk onto the boat."

Jaco continued to stare at her. "Now then, are we going to have a problem getting on this boat or do you understand me?"

Gracie ever so slightly shook her head, not making eye contact.

"I'd rather gag you and stuff you in a crate like your boyfriend, but your host Mr. Zhou insisted on you being presented to him in a civilized manner. So, I'm going to ask you again, are we going to have a problem?"

"No," Gracie said.

Jaco put the Taser under her chin and lifted her face up. "I want you to look me in the eyes and say, 'No, I won't be a problem, Jaco. I don't want my actions to result in Quinn's drowning to death.'"

Jaco pushed the Taser even harder on her throat.

"No, I won't be a problem, Jaco." She turned away hard, trying to get the Taser off of her neck.

"All of it."

"I don't want my actions to result in Quinn's death."

"Good." Jaco put the Taser on his belt harness, concealing it under his sport coat, and pulling out a big knife. With this he cut the zip tie holding her hands behind her back.

Gracie raised her hands in front of her, opening and closing them to restore circulation.

Jaco unstrapped the dolly from the corner and glared back at her as he tilted the crate onto its side. Again, he wasn't gentle with the box as it slammed down on its side. Then he tilted one end off the floor and slid the dolly under the crate.

"Remember, your mind is going to tell you to do something stupid. Do yourself a favor. Don't listen to it."

83

Daylight spilled into the cargo box as the roll-up door was opened from the outside. Within a second, Gracie saw the massive Ferris wheel of Navy Pier. The driver had put the ramp on the rear of the truck. Jaco, ready to go, rolled the crate down off the truck. He then motioned for Gracie to come out.

The driver switched watches with Jaco. A Rolex for a couple hundred-dollar Fitbit-type watch.

The driver looked at his phone, then said, "A cool calm 56 beats a minute."

Moments later, Jaco rolled Quinn on the dolly with Gracie at his side. They walked onto Navy Pier. In front of them were 50 acres of parks, shops, restaurants, and family attractions that stretched 3,300 feet into Lake Michigan.

"Good afternoon," Jaco said with a smile to a passing family of four as he effortlessly weaved through the tourists.

On the horizon were a slew of boats. Having visited Navy Pier before, Gracie knew the usual boats, the architecture tour, the Seadog Speedboat, but past the Odyssey dinner cruise yacht, another yacht she'd never seen before was equal in size, docked 100 yards further down.

Her mind was screaming for her to do something. Seeing the yacht, it represented some kind of finish line. If she got on that boat, she knew she'd be gone forever.

She scanned the pier. A mixture of tourists and workers selling tickets for boat tours and street vendor types selling cotton candy and hot dogs.

Jaco grabbed her hand as the landscape of people spread to expose a Chicago PD K-9 unit headed towards them.

"Remember what I said," he muttered out of the side of his mouth as the officers approached.

Adrenaline flowed through her veins with the force of a tsunami.

Moments away from crossing paths with them, the K-9 veered a hard left toward teenage boys standing at the railing looking out onto the lake, taking a sudden interest in the skateboard one of them was holding.

Crap, she thought, all it's going to take is one of these kids to have a joint in their pocket and they're going to walk right by us.

The dog wasn't aggressive, but it wasn't leaving the teenagers. She and Jaco were now almost parallel with them, and in another couple of seconds they would pass.

Gracie turned and took a big breath, preparing to scream for help as loud as humanly possible.

That instant, the K-9 turned, and its dark eyes caught Gracie's. The connection was strong enough that she didn't feel a need to scream, and she didn't. The dog lost interest in the boys and beelined towards Gracie.

"Hello, officer," Jaco said.

The K-9 sniffed the crate. Gracie knew its moist black nose was going to set off the alarm bells any second.

"Your dog must have expensive taste," said Jaco. "Delivering a crate of Chateau Petrus for the yacht down at the end."

"He's partial to a fine red," the officer chuckled, pulling the leash of his dog to get him to move on.

Now or never.

"My name is Gracie Green, the terrorist on TV, and there's an FBI agent stuffed in that crate."

Instantaneously as she finished her sentence, Jaco lashed out and grabbed her arm in a viselike grip.

The officer didn't seem to have heard what she had said, still as calm as could be.

"I know who you are," the officer replied.

"Make sure to keep an eye out if anyone else is snooping around the yacht," said Jaco. "Especially the large black man."

"You bet," said the officer, tipping his cap, then turned and walked off in the opposite direction.

"Let go," Gracie said as the pressure of Jaco's grip felt like her forearm was about to break.

Jaco pulled her with his right hand, not letting go, and with his left rolled the crate on the dolly. "Stupid *kuchka*. I knew you wouldn't be able to resist." He leaned in and whispered. "For that little display, once we get in the yacht, I'm going to cut your boyfriend's chest open and have him bleed out right in front of you."

84

With its aroma of fresh pine and sage, and richly stained and glazed hardwood paneling, the interior of the yacht was nothing less than opulent. Dark, shiny, exotic panels alternated with artwork hand-etched in smoked glass. Beneath the glass floor was a series of round gray rocks, illuminated perfectly to bring out their dark beauty.

Jaco walked beside her while two men carried the crate Quinn was in behind them. The hall opened up to an expansive great room, almost all glass windows, with incredible views of the pier and Lake Michigan. On the foredeck landing area was a large helipad. A soft white circular couch with enough seating for 20 people surrounded the centerpiece of the room, a 3-foot-tall round fish tank that seemed to have a depth below the surface of the floor of at least a couple of feet. The exotic fish and coral were lit with interior lighting of an unnatural lavender hue. Lily pads with several blooming pink and white lotus flowers floated on top of the water. They were like nothing Gracie had ever seen. Each lotus had its own light pointed directly at it, bringing out every bit of its delicate beauty like sparkling diamonds in a jewelry store case.

The Asian man sitting on the couch, very relaxed, waited until Gracie entered the room and had a chance to fully absorb her surroundings. Then he stood with a comfortable smile. Dressed in a bespoke tailored three-piece suit and expensive Italian leather shoes, his dark hair combed to the side and held tight in place by product, he looked as dapper and fashionable as the yacht's interior.

"Welcome. I am Mr. Zhou," he said. He motioned to the couch. "Please sit."

Gracie stood. She looked at Zhou, then awkwardly at the box

Quinn was inside.

Zhou snapped his fingers. Then projected his voice in a commanding way and said, "*Xiǎoxīn dǎkāi*".

Two men put the crate on the floor, the one retrieved the tools necessary, and opened the crate. They pulled Quinn out of the box and stood him straight up. As soon as the men let go of him, he lost his balance.

"Untie him," Mr. Zhou said.

Jaco's eyes narrowed and his face contorted as he prepared to bark out an objection, but then thought better of it.

The two men freed Quinn.

Mr. Zhou once again motioned for them to sit.

Gracie knew she shouldn't show any emotion toward Quinn, but she couldn't help herself. She gave him a big hug and whispered into his ear. "Hang in there."

"I missed your smile," he whispered back.

Gracie and Quinn sat on the white couch. It felt like she was engulfed in some type of goose down, so soft and comfortable, with a cool feeling to it. Upon further inspection, she realized there was actual cool air being pumped through the fabric of the couch.

Mr. Zhou sat at their three o'clock. He hit a button on a remote and a projector screen dropped down from the ceiling.

"I know this is not ideal," said Zhou, "but as you know, the most powerful people in the US framed you as a terrorist, blew up your lab, and now are trying to wipe you and your formulas off the face of this earth. They are not trying to steal your formulas, they are trying to destroy them, selfishly keeping them from the world. China would like to offer you the hand of friendship, Ms. Green."

The screen fully down, the projector illuminated it with a video of a research lab.

"As you can see, the lab you will be working in has the most sophisticated equipment in the world. Anything you need, including other brilliant minds, will be at your disposal, and there will be no expenses spared."

Gracie had to stop herself from being excited at what she was seeing, it was everything she'd dreamed of and more at her disposal.

Zhou hit another button and a house that looked more like a penthouse appeared on the screen.

"You will live a life of luxury—"

"As a prisoner," Gracie interrupted.

"That's not how we like to look at it. Miss Green, you've been compromised. Mr. Ivanov was hired to kill you and wipe your research off the face of the earth, until I hired him away from his last employer. I'd like you to think of it more as a witness protection program. New life, new identity; a total fresh start." He looked over at Quinn. "I understand you are quite fond of the FBI agent, so in giving you a companion we were hoping to be a nice perk."

"To breed me."

"No Ms. Green, to give you the opportunity to have a family, if you choose."

Jaco cleared his throat.

"Yes, Mr. Ivanov?" Zhou's tone showed he didn't like being interrupted.

"Don't get me wrong. I'm loving movie night here and your terrific speech to boot. But if you don't mind, I'd like my money, please. Oh, and a glass of your most expensive scotch while I waited would be nice."

"Mr. Ivanov, do you have the formulas?"

Jaco pulled out the flash drive.

Zhou nodded to one of the two men, who walked to Jaco and grabbed the drive. A waiter entered the room with a glass of brown liquor on a sterling silver tray.

Jaco took the drink. "That's more like it."

A young Asian man entered. His attire was super hip, baggy trousers, a graphic t-shirt that said *Midnight Occult Civil Servants,* his black hair sporting frosted tips. He carried a laptop covered with stickers almost as if he had sponsorship from skateboard brands and energy drinks.

The man grabbed the flash drive and sat next to Mr. Zhou. He plugged the drive into his laptop. As the drive was loading, he plugged ear buds into his ears.

He looked at the screen for a moment, then said something to Mr. Zhou in Chinese.

"Do you know the password?" Mr. Zhou asked.

Gracie shook her head no.

Zhou nodded to the two men—Gracie hadn't realized it, but they were standing directly behind her and Quinn. Without warning, they snatched Quinn out of his seat and pulled him over the back of the couch.

As they dragged Quinn, he didn't put up much of a fight. "Do you know anything about the box jellyfish?" Mr. Zhou asked.

Gracie took another look at the beautiful fish tank and spotted several of the clear bodies, shaped like boxes with glowing white tentacles hanging from their bodies.

"It is considered the most venomous creature on earth, even more so than a pufferfish," Zhou continued. "They say the body screams in pain even while unconscious from shock."

She opened her mouth and Zhou held up his hand.

"Please, Miss Green, what you'll learn about our relationship is; I will only accept your first answer. You should always be prepared to live with the consequences of it. Gentlemen?"

85

The two men had Quinn locked down from each side with viselike grips. Jaco stood and watched, sipping his scotch, one hand in his pocket, a wry smile on his face. Finally, he was getting to see the good stuff. He'd been itching to hurt someone all morning.

Gracie pleaded, "I shouldn't have lied to you. It won't happen again."

"Miss Green, please, I hate to see you like this. What I can promise you is I will never lie to you, but I don't want you to be misled by my hospitality. I am as disappointed as you are about this, but I know it is what is best for our partnership long term. Just know I have a wonderful dinner waiting for us once we set sail."

"I'll be fine, Gracie," Quinn yelled out, his face hovering over the water.

Mr. Zhou motioned to the young man with the laptop. "Mr. Feng here is one of our greatest hackers. Your friend will be submerged into the water for as long as it takes him to break the password code."

"Please don't."

"I'm a man who enjoys sport," said Zhou, and nodded his head.

Quinn's head was plunged into the water.

The hacker's hands came to life, dancing on the keyboard like a virtuoso pianist.

Air bubbles escaped from Quinn's mouth. Three jellyfish were within a foot of his face.

After seconds had passed, Gracie looked at Zhou, relaxed as could be. His dark brown eyes had the depth of dark, deep caves, and right there at that moment she realized there was nothing she could say to this man.

"Come on," Gracie yelled at the hacker.

It didn't seem as if it were possible for his fingers to move faster, but after the encouragement, they did.

"Sting him in the face," Jaco said, laughing.

Gracie looked on in absolute horror.

Quinn fought with all of his might, shaking his body, the remaining air bubbling fast from his mouth.

She turned to the hacker, who'd suddenly stopped typing. She sucked in a breath, held it, ready for him to say he was finished, but it was a cramp in his hand that had stopped him.

Enough games, Gracie hopped up and soccer kicked one of the men between the legs from behind. He fell to the ground.

Jaco put down his glass and grabbed her by the throat in a crushing grip.

Mr. Zhou yelled something in Chinese.

Like programmed robots, the remaining men holding Quinn let go as they simultaneously drew their handguns.

Almost like an illusionist with sleight of hand, Jaco's free hand somehow had drawn his weapon.

Two guns were pointed at Jaco's head, and his was pointed right between Zhou's eyes.

Quinn, on the floor, head soaked, gasped for air.

"Mr. Ivanov, you're being a rude guest," Zhou said.

"My money, and I'll kindly leave this party," Jaco said, cocking the hammer on his hand cannon.

"Done," the hacker said. "It's all here."

"If you kill her, our deal is off," Zhou said.

Jaco released Gracie, who fell to the floor, gasping for breath right next to Quinn. She looked at him. No stings.

"Our business is done, Mr. Ivanov." Zhou pointed to a large duffel bag in the corner of the room, "There is another ten million in cash, and the rest is in the account listed. The drive atop the cash has the decryption key which will open the account, and prove your ownership within twenty-four hours. Now if you'd be so kind, we're about to set sail."

Jaco continued to aim at Zhou. "All of it, Zhou."

"Eleven billion dollars doesn't fit in a briefcase, Mr. Ivanov."

Jaco hit a button on his watch. "Look at that, my heart rate is over 94." He made his way back to his scotch all the time tracing his weapon on Zhou.

"Not taking my word is the highest insult." Zhou's tone reflected a stern warning.

"This isn't personal, it's business. I've already been stiffed once."

"Then you'll have to come with us. Delaying our departure puts everything in jeopardy. Rains is surely going to be coming soon."

"If I know Peter Rains, right now he's putting together half a battalion." Jaco laughed to himself. "He's going to be super pissed. Oh, and just so you know? My guy is within 100 yards of here with a Russian Verba aimed right at this boat."

"You shouldn't bluff like this, Mr. Ivanov. Kindly disembark or come with us. Your money isn't going to be any good if you are dead."

Jaco pointed at the red laser dot shining bright on the wall. "That's a guidance system for the rocket, accurate enough to hit a moving chopper. It's not going to miss a stationary boat."

Mr. Zhou stared at Jaco, "I don't have time for games." He picked up the remote, turned back on the projection monitor, and turned it to Channel 23. A lady, sitting on the floor in a small room, every inch of everything in the room—including her clothing—was gray as ash.

"You scum sucking pig of the earth," Jaco growled as he recognized his sister.

"I told you in our first meeting, there would be consequences."

Jaco clicked his tongue, showing that same relaxation Zhou did earlier. "If this boat leaves this dock without me walking off it with my money in my account or if I don't check in every 10 minutes, there will be a hole blown in the side of this ship the size of a bus."

"Being difficult is not good for your or your sister's health, Mr. Ivanov."

Jaco harnessed his weapon. "Moral hazards of 11 billion, I guess. I'll just have to buy another sister."

Mr. Zhou got up to exit the room, "Please clean our guest up for lunch," he ordered to his men.

86

The late afternoon sun glistened off the small waves of Lake Michigan. Mack looked down at his watch—4:19 PM. Bic had decided for them to go south. They'd hit every Chicago harbor down from the Jackson Park Yacht Club right to the Hyde Park neighborhood. They were now about 15 minutes from the Indiana border.

"There's nothing here big enough to be what we're looking for," said Bic. "My contact was sure they'd be south."

"There's a good chance they're gone and are now floating somewhere in this effin' massive lake-ocean," said Mack.

Bic didn't show any emotion. He had the same feeling, but they couldn't give up. Gracie was the only family he had, and everything he'd done had been centered around her for the last twenty-five years. He didn't want to panic, but if they got in this lake, he was sure they would take Gracie by helicopter from the yacht to a private air strip, then put her on a jet to China.

"I can't let Sam and Caroline down," Mack said.

"We won't." Bic waved to their driver of the black car, waiting idly like he had at the last several ports.

Mack and Bic hurried into the back seat. "Go north, fast," Bic instructed.

Heading on side streets, the driver cut in and out, navigating potholes, streets under construction, and pedestrians who seemed to think they always had the right of way, walking in front of traffic almost as if they were daring drivers to hit them.

From the back seat they watched impatiently. The heavy traffic made it seem like everything was working against them. What possible chance would they have? It had been almost 10 hours since Jaco had taken Gracie away in the Suburban.

"Can I use your phone? I want to reach out to my connection at Langley," Mack asked.

Bic handed it to him and he dialed.

With the phone to his ear, waiting for an answer, he said, "First thing I'm going to do when this is over is get a new phone."

"Put it on speaker," Bic requested.

"Tom, it's Mack. We're looking for a big yacht at one of the Chicago harbors. I'm guessing it would not be a regular, so it would have needed to register or something like that recently to be able to dock somewhere. Also, this might be a long shot that they registered in their own name and not some type of shell company, but the actual owner of the boat is Chinese."

"Okay," said Tom, "I'm on it. Also, by the way, I looked at all the possible companies that have huge reasons to never want a drug with a cure to come on the market. There's one company in particular, Vintigen. Almost all their revenue is derived from cancer drugs. They spent about seven billion a year in R&D over the last five years and they've never found a cure, only expensive long-term treatments."

"Good to know, but right now we need to find that yacht. It has the scientist and all her formulas on board."

"Got it," Tom said, and disconnected the call.

"You a fan of conspiracy theories, Bic?"

Bic stared straight ahead. "Not really."

87

Gracie and Quinn had been placed in a small cabin room with the instructions to get dressed for dinner. The closet had ample high-end designer dress choices for Gracie, all with matching shoes and a single tailored black suit, white shirt and thin black tie for Quinn.

The waiter who had been delivering drinks had given them a little advice about Chinese customs in perfect English, delivered with an exquisite Received Pronunciation British accent, instructing that it would be wise to not insult Mr. Zhou at dinner. Neither Quinn nor Gracie thought it was worth getting dunked in the fish tank over their formal wear, so they both complied.

Gracie sat on the bed, waiting. She was dolled up in a red Vera Wang sleeveless cocktail dress that hugged her nicely. She didn't usually wear dresses that were so revealing, but all the dresses were fitted to her exact measurements, so she just went with it. The makeup at the sink looked like it could have come directly from her own home.

Quinn, in a black tuxedo with black satin peak lapels over a wing collar white shirt and silver cuff links and tuxedo buttons, looked more dapper than ever. In so many other circumstances, a bow tie seems ridiculous, but it gave Quinn a very distinguished look. He'd been restlessly inspecting the cabin for a way out for the last hour. "This porthole is two inches thick, probably stronger than steel."

"Can I ask you a crazy question?" Gracie finally asked nervously.

Quinn sat down next to her on the bed. "Sure anything." Quinn rested his hand on her thigh.

Gracie gazed into his eyes, waiting, gauging not only what his response would be but also if she was nuts to even be thinking this.

"Maybe Zhou's right. Going with him is what's best for me and the cure."

"That's because he's a cunning snake. Did you see what he did to me when he didn't get what he wanted?"

"I just want the cure to be available in the world; Zhou might be my best option to finish my work. And those facilities had everything I would need."

"Gracie, those facilities are prisons. And when you don't give them what they want, they have ways to make you."

"But we both want the same thing. And with what people here think about me and sending people like Jaco to kill me, it might not be such a bad thing to be tucked away somewhere extra safe."

Quinn, frustrated, took a deep breath, then spoke, "I know it sounds logical, but are you going to give them what they want if they decide you need to help develop an airborne version of some deadly virus."

"It's a no-win situation, isn't it?" Gracie said, sadness washing over her face.

Quinn smiled big, his eyes delving all over every part of her.

"What?"

"Look at it this way, if we go down, red is definitely your color."

Gracie looked to Quinn. His glossy blue eyes were still enough to escape from their harsh reality.

"I almost lost you three times today." She reached out for his hand.

"I'm not going anywhere."

Quinn's eyes told her he wanted more, he wanted every part of her as he slowly leaned in.

The kiss was deep instantly, with the kind of passion that came from not knowing if you were going to be alive in an hour.

A hard knock on their cabin door.

The two untangled.

Quinn still with his hands gently touching Gracie's face, "we're going to make it through this, I promise."

88

Mr. Zhou sat at the circular 12-chair dining room table in a flawless black tuxedo with a very formal shawl collar, a white shirt with a wing collar, and a vest. On the level directly below the main great room, the bottom of the fish tank from the floor above dropped three feet down from the ceiling. With hundreds of crystals at the bed of the tank, light refracted tens of thousands of ways into the dining room, serving as the table's chandelier. From the ceiling hung a half-dome made of nickel with sculpted patterns, the detail so fine it looked as if Michelangelo had been commissioned for the piece.

To Zhou's right, Jaco sat in an oversized sofa chair set against the wall next to a bank of windows. The view was of Navy Pier.

"You should have your money within the hour," Zhou said.

"This is a comfy chair," said Jaco. "How much is it?"

"Please do not ruin my dinner with Miss Green," Zhou said.

"I'll do my best, but I'm telling you, I'll be much nicer as a billionaire."

"Ahh, Mr. Ivanov, lots of money doesn't change anything. It merely magnifies who you already are."

Zhou's deadpan expression turned into a smile as Gracie walked down one of the two double staircases coming down into the room. Her radiant espresso black skin and red dress popped against the room's neutral colors.

Mr. Zhou stood. "China is going to fall in love with you."

Gracie got to the bottom step, and she allowed a small curve of a smile.

Mr. Zhou welcomed her as he pulled back the chair next to his. Gracie walked over and sat.

Quinn was then escorted down the stairs by two men and seated on the opposite side of the table, closest to where the servers were entering into the room.

Gracie gave Zhou an awkward look as they sat Quinn on the other side of this massive table.

"It's best for our dinner conversation," said Zhou. "We have many things to discuss. Our scientists have reviewed your formulas. They are brilliant." Zhou paused, and the politeness in his eyes changed to a dark, hardened glare. "But the most important compound is missing."

Gracie's heartbeat quickened as she took a sip of tea. "I know."

Zhou pushed a notepad with a pen in front of her. "Would you be so kind?"

She looked at Quinn and the two men behind him, flanked on each side. She realized what was about to happen.

She picked up the pen, feeling Zhou's glare burning into her like sunlight beaming through a powerful magnifying glass. Finally, she wrote.

Zhou grabbed the notepad and read, "RELEASE QUINN".

"I was hoping for a wonderful meal," Zhou said, pushing the pad back in front of Gracie.

"Me too." She pushed the pad back.

"Let's not make any decisions on an empty stomach," Zhou said.

Gracie nodded. "Thank you for considering."

"My pleasure. Let's eat."

The wait staff quickly filled the table with more food than 20 people could have eaten. Gracie recognized some things, but most she wasn't sure of. But what caught her eye was the man wearing a chef's hat pushing a stainless-steel table with what she could recognize as some type of bird on a wooden butcher's block.

The man stopped to Gracie's right and stood.

"Miss Green, our master chef has prepared *Běijīng kǎoyā*, or Peking duck as Westerners call it. It has been prepared using the *guà lú* method. In our culture there are recipes dating back to 1330. It is tradition for the chef to carve it in front of the diners."

"It looks delicious." She wasn't hungry, but still, she was trying to adjust to the new normal for about the tenth time in the last week.

The chef picked up the knife and, with skill and precision, quickly cut the duck. The duck was served with a sweet and garlicky dipping sauce.

As they ate, Zhou explained, "There are stages to this meal. While the duck is still warm, the skin's taste is at its best, but once it cools down, we switch from dipping sauce to making duck rolls."

Zhou moved one of the steamed pancakes to his empty plate. He placed a slice of duck and spring onions onto the fluffy cake. With his fork he stabbed a cucumber stick and held it for Gracie to see.

"The cucumber is usually eaten as a refreshment between duck rolls, but at times I can be a little impatient." He put the cucumber stick on top of the meat and rolled the pancake. "I like the instantaneous refreshment."

The chef cleared the scraps off his butcher block and placed a leather case onto the surface. He opened the case to reveal a vial and a syringe.

As the chef inserted the needle into the vial, Zhou said, "Have you ever heard of *gǔ?*"

Gracie shook her head.

"It's an ancient Chinese poison created by enclosing multiple venomous creatures into a box." The chef loaded the syringe as Zhou continued. "After these creatures devour one another, the one that is left after digesting all the toxins of the other creatures creates a super venom."

Mr. Zhou took a bite of duck, chewed his food, wiped his mouth with his napkin before putting it back on his lap. "Of course, this is an old Chinese wives tale. I'm sure Mr. Quinn won't be affected by the poison, unless the legends are true. Then I'm afraid his internal organs will liquefy while he vomits blood."

Gracie snatched the notepad and scribbled something onto it. It wasn't the real compound, but it was one of the ones she had tried and didn't work.

She pushed it back to Zhou.

He looked at the notepad, "You know what happens if I find out you're lying."

Gracie stared at Zhou.

Looking into his dark eyes, a thousand scenarios played out, all of them leading to her suddenly jumping out of her chair to stab him in the throat with her knife.

Which was exactly what she did.

At a speed faster than she could have imagined, Zhou deflected the knife and had her in his grasp.

"Your disobedience is unfortunate, Miss Green. How many times must we play out this petty defiance? I offer you the world, and you spit in my face."

Gracie turned away. Looking out the row of windows, what she saw on Navy Pier made her eyes widen.

Bic, walking with Mack on the pier, turned and looked directly into the main deck windows.

"I want Mr. Quinn alive," Mr. Zhou said looking out at the armed men approaching his yacht.

"Allow me," said Jaco, who walked over and delivered a right cross on the button of Quinn's chin, knocking him out cold.

"Back up to the main room," Zhou instructed, dragging Gracie with him.

One of the men grabbed Quinn by his foot and dragged him away.

Gracie was led by force into the main saloon, watching over her shoulder as Quinn's head bounced as he was dragged. As they entered, the young man with his laptop joined them. From his laptop he hit a button and the chandelier over the round fish tank lowered. The light dropped until it touched the bottom of the fish tank. The hacker typed in another command and the beautiful fixture detached itself from the two-by-two-foot square flat piece of shiny metal attached to a single steel cable that came from the ceiling.

Using a long hook, one of the men fished the cable over to the edge.

"Get on the platform," Zhou instructed Gracie.

Gracie hesitated, looking at the pool of jellyfish she'd be pulled above.

"Don't make me ask twice, Miss Green," Zhou said firmly.

89

Bic and Mack had entered through the lower deck of the yacht in the rear. Bic had been surprised that there was no resistance thus far. He knew that meant they were patiently waiting with a plan.

In the dining room they saw signs of a struggle. Eerily silent, standing under the glass ceiling of a fish tank, shadows that didn't seem to belong cast down from within the tank.

"Whatever's waiting for us is up there," Mack said, pointing to the double staircase.

They both were at the bottom of the steps, guns pointed up, ready to fire.

Mack tracked to the other set of the double staircase. Both men cautiously made their way up the stairs. Sweat clung to their foreheads, knowing at any moment all hell was going to break loose.

At the upper deck, still with all of his body concealed in the stairwell, Bic peered into the large room from between the glass panel of the railing and the floor. Gracie was suspended 10 feet in midair, standing on a small platform over the fish tank.

Jaco and another man were sitting on the circular couch. Two other men flanked on each side of the room were on one knee, their semi-automatic rifles pointed directly at Gracie.

"I am Mr. Zhou," the man said, staring directly at Bic. "Come join us."

After a moment, Bic came out of the stairwell, subtly motioning for Mack to stay put. Mack, gun pointed and concealed in the other stairwell, nodded.

"Unc, there are box jellyfish in the tank!" Gracie said, holding on as tight as she could to the cable while trying to keep her feet balanced as the small platform shook from side to side under her feet.

"Everything's going to be okay, Gracie."

"Listen to your uncle," Zhou said. "We all want the same thing."

Bic sat across from Zhou and Jaco.

"I know your friend with the dying wife is nearby too, so I'll speak loudly so he can hear." Zhou adjusted his jacket. "We are on the same side. Within 24 hours, you all can be in the full protection of the Chinese government. Mack, we would have Gracie in a lab, with everything on this earth she needs to save your wife. Bic, you are a wanted man, you can never live in the US without the chance of them hunting you down like a wild animal. Perhaps a rabid animal is the better metaphor, for they will extinguish you as fast as they would something with rabies. Come with me and all this goes away in the blink of an eye. For what Gracie is going to do for China, all of you will carry a high rank and will be treated like royalty, I give you my word."

"It's too good of a deal for a dog like him," Jaco spat.

"Mr. Ivanov, show some manners," Mr. Zhou said.

Bic dwelled on the offer. A lot of what he was saying made sense.

"Making a deal with the devil is never a good idea," Gracie said.

Bic was about to speak when his heart leapt as Gracie almost fell.

A sudden quick vision of Gracie underwater with jellyfish tentacles wrapped all over her dead body filled Bic's mind, he knew it wasn't real but he could feel something very wrong going on inside his body.

Then, out of the dark depths of the water, his father appeared. He grabbed Gracie and took her into the dark.

Bic tried to calm himself to speak, but it was too late to stop the attack.

He dropped to his knees, as his insides burned as if molten lava was flowing through him.

"Unc!" Gracie called out.

Struggling to breathe, Bic pulled out an EpiPen and plunged it into his leg.

Lost in a moment of distorted time perception, he wasn't sure if five or thirty seconds had passed.

Suddenly a burst of blood erupted from Bic's mouth, spraying red onto the fish tank glass and the off-white carpet.

"It's time to kill this freak of nature for good," Jaco stood and pulled out his weapon.

Mack opened fire, hitting Jaco in the arm before he could get off a shot.

Mack's second shot hit one of the two men aiming at Gracie.

His third shot, at Mr. Zhou, missed. Zhou dove for cover behind the fish tank wall.

The other man opened fire in Mack's direction. Bullets pulverized the wood paneling and shattered the glass rail.

Mack dove down the stairwell.

Bic, using everything he had, got to his feet and charged Jaco.

Like a middle linebacker, Bic left his feet tackling Jaco. His torpedo-like momentum took both men up and over the back of the couch.

Bic, on top of Jaco, blasted him in the face with a haymaker. Bic pulled back for another, but his nausea and swimming vision intensified; he grabbed his side.

Jaco threw a hard jab into Bic's midsection. On impact, his organs felt like a nuke had just detonated inside him.

He tried to suck in air, but his lungs had shut down and he collapsed to the side.

Jaco crawled on top of Bic.

"It's time to finish this." Jaco wrapped his fingers around Bic's neck and began to squeeze. "Just like death and taxes, this was inevitable." Jaco smirked as he squeezed harder.

"*Remember me? You sucker-punching scumbag!*" Quinn barreled through the double doors from the adjoining service area, charging at Jaco with a knife in his hand. He lunged at Jaco, cutting Jaco's forearm, as the latter redirected the blade, using Quinn's forward momentum to take him to the ground.

With Jaco and Quinn grappling on the floor, Bic grabbed the back of the couch and pulled himself up.

Mack exchanged fire with the man in the corner and also had Zhou pinned down on the other side of the fish tank.

Too weak to hop over the couch, Bic leaned forward and let gravity do the work. His massive body picked up speed, sending him over the couch and onto the floor.

Bic grabbed his gun, ignoring the searing pain inside him, and took dead aim at the man exchanging fire with Mack. Staring through the sight, he saw double. He covered one eye, and the two targets became one. He took the shot.

The bullet snapped into the man's chest, jolting his body hard to the left. Along with his body, his weapon spun up, firing a cluster of bullets in Gracie's direction.

One of the bullets grazed Gracie's leg and she lost her footing, sending her feet dangling in the air.

Holding all her weight with the grip of her fingers on a thin cable, she frantically tried to get her feet back on the platform. Her first hand came loose. And she fell.

A roar as loud as a thousand cannons erupted from Bic's chest as he leapt into the fish tank with a massive splash, catching Gracie in his arms.

Water waist high, Bic trudged through the tank.

He lost consciousness as he fell into the edge of the tank, dropping Gracie to the ground.

Gracie hopped up. With Bic's lower half submerged in the water and jellyfish everywhere, she tried with all of her might to pull him out, but she could not budge his massive body.

90

M r. Zhou had retrieved Jaco's gun, protected by everyone else's attention being divided. On the other side of the couch, Quinn and Jaco were scrapping on the floor like pit bulls.

Closing the gap, Zhou aimed in Gracie's direction. But his eyes looked past her.

Gracie turned in Mack's direction—her last chance to get out of this mess. What she saw crushed her.

Mack walked out of the stairwell with his hands up, one of Zhou's men behind him with a gun pointed at his back.

Zhou pulled Gracie from Bic.

He locked eyes with hers. "All this death, it will never end unless you let me help you."

Gracie looked at Bic. He still wasn't moving, and she saw no sign of breath.

She looked back at Zhou and nodded. Zhou reached out for her hand, and she accepted. He walked her towards Quinn and Jaco.

Jaco had Quinn in a rear naked choke hold. Quinn was about to lose consciousness.

Zhou aimed at the men locked together on the floor as Gracie gasped. "You have violated the terms of our agreement." The shot rang out. Jaco's head snapped to the right as it caught the bullet.

"To your feet, Mr. Quinn," Zhou instructed. "That was long overdue. My apologies you have had to suffer the attention of that repellant man."

Quinn rolled off Jaco's dead body.

Two more of Zhou's men appeared. He barked instructions, "Yóutǐng qǐháng. Xiànzài."

They listened then promptly left.

Outside, the men unhooked ropes from the docks.

"The deal stands," Mr. Zhou said as he and Gracie walked toward Mack.

"All of it?" Mack asked.

"Yes," Zhou replied.

A soft beeping noise suddenly persisted behind them. Gracie looked to Quinn, then she zeroed in on where the noise was coming from. Jaco's wrist.

"His heart rate monitor," she yelled as, visible through the glass, a bright white light with a trail of smoke jetted over Lake Michigan, climbing with a rainbow arc before taking a sharp turn down toward the yacht.

The missile smacked into the cabin with a thunderous explosion, one room away from where they stood.

A fiery ball of yellow fire tore the double doors off their hinges, along with part of the wall. The blinding flash shattered the windows as the supersonic shockwave blew everyone onto the floor.

With her ears ringing, barely able to balance herself on her hands and knees, Gracie's eyes were glued to the gun Zhou had dropped to the floor.

Zhou, lying face down on the floor, started to recover, and his hand instinctively reached for his weapon.

Gracie focused on her target and lunged.

91

Gracie, Zhou, and Quinn stood in a triangle.

Gracie widened her eyes as she pointed the gun at Zhou. She handed it off to Quinn. "You're better with these things than I am."

"You don't know what you're doing!" Zhou lunged for the weapon.

Quinn snatched the gun and pointed it at Zhou's face. "Hands on your head. *Now*."

Quinn spun Zhou, then grabbed the back of his shirt, walking towards Mack and Zhou's men on the floor. On the way, he shot Zhou's man in the back of the head. He then pressed the barrel against Zhou's temple. "Call your tech boy with the formulas."

Gracie went to Bic. She saw the jellyfish's tentacles wrapped around Bic's forearm. "Quinn, help me get him out, he's getting stung."

"He's gone, Gracie, let him go."

She ignored him, still trying to help Bic.

Quinn grabbed Gracie and pulled her up to him. He aimed his gun at Mack.

"Sorry, bud, can't trust anyone. Make your way here, leave the weapon on the floor."

"Quinn, you're scaring me," Gracie said.

"We can't trust anyone, darling."

He'd never called her 'darling' before.

At point blank range, Mack had no choice but to follow Quinn's orders. He walked towards Quinn with his hands up. "How's your niece doing?"

Quinn smirked, "If I had one, she'd be great."

"Quinn, please tell me what's happening," Gracie pleaded from within his grasp.

The young man entered the room from the staircase, opposite side of the explosion.

"Go ahead and put the computer and the flash drive on the couch."

The kid followed the order.

"Get your phone out and dial 703-552-5752. Put it on speaker."

After a moment, they heard, "Rains speaking."

"It's Quinn. I have the target. Jaco's dead. Need to be extracted ASAP at Navy Pier. You can't miss it. There's a 100-foot mega-yacht on fire."

"The extraction team will be there in five."

"Make it two," said Quinn, and shot the hacker in the chest.

Gracie stared at the young man, then Mr. Zhou.

"I'm sorry I allowed this man to break your heart," said Zhou. "That was not my intention."

"And they say chivalry is dead." said Quinn. He snapped a round into Zhou's head. The bullet exited out the back, spraying the white couch in an abstract mist of red bone, brain matter, and blood.

"There's going to be a special place in hell for you," Mack said.

"It's not going to be easy, but duty calls." Quinn took dead aim at Mack.

Mack had nowhere to go. Quinn had him at point blank range.

"Listen, Quinn," Mack said, "even if you don't have a niece with cancer, at some point—"

Quinn shot Mack in the chest. He fell to the floor.

"Good thing that I have a spare bottle of the pills," Quinn said proudly.

Gracie couldn't feel anything except for the unbearable pain of betrayal. It was Quinn all along on the inside playing her. She quickly flashed back. The bad guys had somehow been one step ahead of their every move, using her to find and destroy all remains of her formula.

She stared at Bic. "Sorry for not trusting you, Unc," she whispered.

Mack stirred on the floor.

Quinn flipped Mack onto his back with his foot, "I forgot about that lame ass vest. Let's see what happens when I put one in your head."

As the hammer snapped forward, Gracie sprung up, knocking Quinn's arm upward.

The bullet missed Mack by millimeters, slicing his cheek like a knife.

"You *bitch!*" Quinn threw her to the floor. "Okay then, you first. Rains wanted you dead before I was picked up."

"Everything about you is revolting," Gracie snarled.

"Don't take it personal, darlin', you were a nice piece of ass. Under other circumstances, we might have had a go at it." Quinn took dead aim at Gracie.

Like a crocodile springing from a river's edge, Bic exploded towards Quinn.

With a jelly fish in his hand, he slapped the cube-sized invertebrate onto Quinn's face.

Quinn screamed in agony as Bic pulled him into the tank, body-slamming him into the water, pushing his body under.

As quick as Bic came to life, his battery quickly ran out of juice. He staggered back to the tank's edge.

Mack ran up to help pull Bic out of the tank.

"We have to get out of here!" he said to Gracie. "I got Bic, you grab the formulas!"

92

The speedboat bounced at high speed, smacking down on the waves with a steady, rhythmic clap. As luck would have it, the super yacht had a speedboat for a dinghy. Mack and Gracie had to carry Bic into the boat. By the time they'd made it to the lower deck launch area, Bic was falling in and out of consciousness. They'd sat him in the back of the speedboat, and he hadn't moved from there since.

Gracie had instructed Mack to head south to Jackson Park harbor. About ten miles south, the University of Chicago hospital was a couple of blocks from the lake. There Bic could get world-class medical care. It was getting dark. Mack hugged the shoreline, using the streetlights on Lake Shore Drive as a guide.

"Anna's mom, you did it." Mack hollered over the sound of the motor and waves.

"How do you know Diana?" Gracie yelled as the wind blew in their faces.

"I met her a couple of weeks ago. You cured her, she was cancer free!"

"I had suspected Anna would try, but I didn't want to know if she did, since it would jeopardize the company. She's such a great lady. I can't wait to see her."

Gracie looked out at the skyline, where the lights outlined hundreds of different buildings, all shapes and sizes. She sucked in the cool lake air in appreciation of the moment of confirmation. She had cured cancer.

"Did she have any side effects?"

"No, she was perfect."

"You keep saying *was*."

"How fast do you think you can make more pills?"

"I don't know, why?"

"My wife, Caroline. She's on hospice, fighting for her life. She is being driven here to meet with us and I need you to save her."

"There's a research lab about a block away from the hospital. With all my formulas, depending on what they have in the lab, I can come pretty close, maybe."

"I hope so. See if Bic's phone still works. If it does, he should have a contact named Tony Parelli in there. I want you to text him where we are going to be."

Gracie went to the back of the boat. She rubbed Bic's head. His eyes seemed lifeless, his pupils filling them. Gracie wanted him to blink or focus on her. She was sick to her stomach thinking about the number of things that could be wrong with Bic, including severe brain damage.

"Unc, you still with me?"

Bic did not respond.

"It's okay, you rest. We're going to the hospital."

Gracie reached into his inside jacket pocket, grabbed his phone. It seemed to be working fine. She used his thumb to unlock the iPhone and went to texts, Tony was the last one. She texted him a quick recap of what had happened, where she was taking Bic and where they'd be.

Gracie gave Bic a big hug and kiss on the forehead.

Gracie stood next to Mack, her black hair blowing in the wind, "Do you have anyone you can call to help us?"

"After what happened with Quinn, I have no idea who to trust." Mack kept the steering wheel steady.

"I can't believe I fell for him. He played me."

"You and me both, sister. Don't beat yourself up about it. He got what he deserved."

"Karma has a funny way of paying you back," Gracie said, then pointed, "There's the harbor, pull under Lake Shore Drive."

Mack turned the boat, slowing down to coast under the bridge into the lagoon.

Off to the north about 3 miles, in the sea of darkness over Lake Michigan, lights from multiple helicopters shone as they glided toward them.

"They're coming," Gracie said.

"I count four of them. They notified the cavalry." Mack

reaccelerated the boat. "Our only chance is to get to land and become invisible."

93

Mack raced past several rows of docked boats. At high speed, he entered a small canal that led to the oval-shaped lagoon, and after a sharp turn he headed directly west for the bank.

He throttled the boat wide open. The bow jumped into the air high enough to clear the bank of rocks lining the lagoon edge. The hull smacked into the rocky shoreline, and its forward momentum launched the boat onto the grass. Dirt was thrown everywhere at impact, the front end stopping feet from S. Cornell Drive, a north and south road that hugged the lagoon.

Bic's body had been flung to the floor. Gracie tried in vain to lift him up. "There's no way we can carry him."

"We got him here, didn't we?" Mack growled like an Olympic weightlifter as he grabbed Bic and clean jerked him to his feet then dragged him out of the boat.

Gracie grabbed the laptop.

Holding Bic under his arms, Mack backpedaled, dragging him towards the street.

From the north, a set of headlights came down Cornell Drive.

"We need to stop that car," Mack said, panting. "There's no way I'll be able to drag him to the hospital."

Gracie leaped out onto the road, flagging the car down.

The car stopped, and she yelled out, "We need your help, our friend is sick."

The headlights were high and bright. It wasn't just any car, it was a black Suburban.

Two men got out of the car while a second black Suburban pulled up to the parked car's passenger side, its light casting the shadow of a man in a dark suit, white shirt, black tie.

"At last we meet." The man approached Gracie and extended his hand. "Peter Rains."

Gracie took a step back, holding onto the laptop as if she were protecting her baby.

"Don't worry, I don't bite."

A chopper from above lit up the whole street to reveal two additional Suburbans, with men pouring out of them like army ants. Before she could think to run, they had her pinned down in every direction.

Mack watched in terror, still in the concealment of the bushes. He had to do something and *now*.

He pulled out the EpiPen Bic had given him and he stabbed it into Bic's thigh.

Seconds later, no response from Bic.

Mack pleaded as he tried to shake him awake. "Come on Bic, *No ma la den, no ma la den,*" he said, repeating the phrase he'd heard from Bic's days in Vietnam. "We need the Black Ghost. We need him now."

Still no response. Mack placed Bic on the ground at the base of a large tree. He knew this was all on him. Caroline, Gracie, and the cure that could save millions would either stay alive or be killed forever, right here, right now.

He went north, concealed by the heavy brush dividing the lagoon and the street. By his count, there were nine men he would have to deal with, using only a handgun. They were more than likely heavily armed. *I am so going to die.* He thought, but didn't slow down.

His only chance was to snatch Gracie out of there, and to do that he needed to take out one guy, the driver of Peter Rains' vehicle. He could then take the vehicle and speed off, assuming he could also get Gracie in there with him.

He crawled as close as possible to the edge of the bush cover. Like a leopard, his success would rest on the element of surprise.

Apparently, there was a better leopard in the forest. Before Mack was able to spring his plan into action, he felt the cold hard steel of an assault rifle press up against his temple.

"Shit."

"I'd say more like deep shit," the man said with a smirk.

94

The man was dressed in all black, with a strong jawline. He prodded Mack in the back with the barrel of his rifle, pushing him out onto the road towards Gracie.

"Quinn said you were like a harmless puppy, but I guess he was wrong." Rains said when he saw him.

"Overconfidence leaves a huge blind spot, especially when it comes to harmless puppies."

Rains considered Mack for a moment. "I usually don't take things personally, but he was my number one asset. The kid was like a damn vampire, a stone-cold killer concealed by a beautiful inviting shell."

The man raised his rifle to point blank at Mack's head. "Should I take him out?"

"Not until I find out what the hell these news choppers are doing here," said Rains.

Mack looked up. Four choppers were circling. He had assumed they were with Rains when he first saw them from the speedboat, but in fact they were all the major news networks circling, taping them right now.

Rains made a call. "I've got news choppers above us; I need someone to get them out of here now!"

As Rains listened to his phone, Mack thought he heard something—a branch, maybe? —back in the direction he'd left Bic.

"The media, we own them. Don't they know that?" Rains hung up his phone. "Party's over. We're on live TV right now. We need to load them up."

"We're not going anywhere. If you're going to shoot us, you'll have to do it right here," Mack said.

"Grab them," said Rains. "We'll lose the choppers, then take care of business."

Three of the men approached Gracie and Mack.

Mack prepared himself to fight for Caroline's life. He wasn't sure what was up with the news choppers, but his instincts told him not to let them take them away from this site.

Mack stepped in front of Gracie, corralling her behind him with his arm. He took a quick glance in the direction he had left Bic, thinking to himself, *Okay, big guy, now would be a nice time to jump into this fight.*

"Let's do this," he said.

The first man stepped forward to throw a right cross. Mack ducked then came back with an uppercut, connecting with the man's jaw and snapping his head back.

Fully engaged with the man he'd just punched, Mack didn't pay attention to the other two men who had come up behind him. They grabbed him by his arms, one on each side, and the man he'd just punched returned the favor as he put all of his weight behind a shot to Mack's stomach. Mack gasped as he felt like his guts had been smashed together.

"Mack!" Gracie yelled out as another man grabbed her.

The next shot was a right cross. The man's fist smashed into Mack's jaw. Blood sprayed from Mack's mouth.

Mack tried to break free, but the two men holding him were locked on.

The man holding Gracie dragged her over next to Rains. He snatched the laptop from her and handed it to his boss.

"You ready to get into the SUV now?" Rains asked.

Mack looked toward the lagoon, blood trickling down his lip, praying with all his might that Bic would erupt onto the scene like hellfire.

"Not unless it's in a body bag," Mack slurred.

One of the men kicked down on Mack's knee, chopping him to the floor.

Feeling as if his leg had been just snapped in two, a pain greater than his physical wounds overtook him.

He cried out in agony as he realized he had failed his soulmate.

The men holding Mack raised him up a little, just the right angle as the third man slammed his fist across Mack's jaw again. His head snapped sideways, blood sprayed from his mouth, his face numbed with pain.

Discombobulated from the blow, he slurred, "I'm—"

"Knock that punk out already," said Rains.

The man wound up for the final blow.

"*I'm sorry, Caroline,*" Mack mumbled through a mouthful of blood.

"I'm right here," A familiar female voice called out.

95

A bright light beamed into Mack's face.

He peered into the persistent light and saw the outline of a woman. She came closer. He wasn't sure if the light was coming from a separate source or the figure itself was emitting it. Was this real?

The figure grew closer still, then at her side, another figure, also female, and dressed in a red suit, appeared, holding a microphone.

"Caroline?"

A sudden clarity came to Mack. It was Caroline, and she was alive, and standing with an anchor woman for a local Chicago news station. The light was from the camera crew behind Caroline and the other woman, and the red light on the news camera was running live.

She was alive, and she'd brought the news with her.

"This is homeland security business," Peter Rains barked, flashing his badge. "Turn the camera off and vacate the premises immediately as we apprehend this terrorist."

His shiny badge was as ineffectual as a rubber knife. Chicago PD swarmed in like wasps. Dozens of men in uniform came onto the scene, heavily armed, far outweighing the manpower of Rains and his team.

The anchorwoman, her voice confident and strong, began the interview. "I'm here with F.B.I. Agent Caroline Foxx Maddox, who just days ago was on hospice care and unconscious, at the final days of her life from her losing battle with cancer. Can you tell me what happened?"

Mack could see Caroline was still frail, but when he saw the green sparkle that had returned to her eyes, he knew that the impossible had happened. Where had it come from? How had it happened?

"Yes, Dr. Gracie Green, the young lady right there, cured me of stage four terminal cancer. I'm here today as living proof that she has found a cure for cancer. The accusations against her and her company being a front for terrorists are absolutely false. Peter Rains was hired to make her look like a terrorist so they could wipe her and her company off the face of this earth."

Rains walked closer to the camera as he addressed everyone, "This woman is a terrorist who is responsible for the biggest attack in Chicago's history—killing your mayor and several officers in the process."

"Terrorists don't cure cancer," Caroline retorted. "And agents follow procedure, unlike you."

Mack broke away.

He stumbled over to Caroline and cradled her in his arms, staring into her eyes in utter amazement and an appreciation unmatched by anything he'd ever felt in his life.

"I thought I was too late," he said, eyes gleaming with water.

"I'm right where I'm supposed to be. You're a mess, by the way."

"Don't make me cry," he said. "It hurts."

"Okay," said Rains, "we're leaving. You all can have your say at the trial when Ms. Green has her due process."

"I know men like you," said Caroline. "Your definition of due process is much different than for the rest of us."

"Well, unless anyone wants to commit a federal offense, we are taking the terrorist into custody," Rains said. He walked towards his vehicle, and the man holding Gracie followed.

Mack released Caroline, but before he could take a step, the two men who were holding him down got in front of him.

Mack wasn't sure what to do, but he was sure that if Rains took Gracie away they'd never see her alive again.

His heart leaped into full throttle as he prepared to plow through the two men ahead of him as Gracie neared.

Unexpectedly, a hardened looking Chicago cop with a shotgun stepped into the path of the man dragging Gracie.

"Out of the way," the man holding Gracie said.

"My mother's dying of cancer," the cop said, not showing any sign of moving out of the way.

"My auntie, she has cancer, too," another cop said as he chambered a bullet and pointed it at Peter Rains.

"We are federal agents, with the full authority of the United States of America. You will all be facing jail time. Now step aside or face the consequences."

Another cop, a Hispanic man, short with a stout build, tears running down both sides of his face, spoke up, "Nobody is taking this lady except us today. If there is even a chance she can save my baby girl, I don't care who you are, time to throw down or get the hell out of our town." The man pointed his shotgun at Rains.

Metal clanked as Rains' men and the Chicago PD pointed weapons at one another.

"You have all made the worst move of your careers. There *is* no cure for cancer." Rains pointed at Caroline. "I have no idea who this crazy broad is, but you all just fell for the biggest scam in history. There is no cure for cancer and there never will be."

Rains walked toward his Suburban. His men followed suit, heading back to their vehicles.

Gracie ran to Mack and Caroline and embraced them both.

The Chicago PD formed a protective circle around them. No one was getting near them on this night.

"How did this happen?" Gracie asked.

"I'm not sure," said Caroline. "The man who helped me was one of Bic's friends. He said Bic gave him the pills he had found on one of the terrorists who had blown up your building."

"Unc," Gracie yelled out.

"I left him in the bushes," said Mack and pointed. "He was in pretty bad shape."

The Chicago PD escorted them to the bushes.

96

The black Suburban headed north on Lake Shore Drive.

"If it's the last thing I ever do, I'm going to ruin every person's life who was there, all of them," Rains yelled in the direction of his driver. "Don't they know I will have her in custody by tomorrow morning? Those bottom dwellers have no idea who runs things."

He looked over at his driver. "What's that look for, Parks?"

"Sir, look at your phone. This thing went viral. I don't think there's any chance in hell we're walking in there with paperwork and walking out."

Rains pulled up his phone and looked at his news feeds. It was everywhere. It even had its own hashtag on Twitter. #SaveTheCure had nine hundred thousand followers in a matter of twenty minutes.

Rains' phone rang. The caller ID read Colton Nash.

"Colton," Rains answered the phone. "Everything will be okay. It's just going to be a little messier than what we'd like... No... hey! Listen... don't you threaten me, I'll make your ass disappear before you go to bed tonight!"

Rains hung up the phone. "*Dammit!*"

The driver stopped at a red light at the intersection of Lake Shore and East Roosevelt Road.

Rains watched the traffic from Roosevelt come out into the intersection, turning left to head north on Lake Shore Drive in front of them. His mind was spinning, trying to gain clarity on his next move. He knew it would be big, but it had to be the right one.

His driver turned on the radio. Mozart's *Jupiter Symphony*, 4th movement.

Rains sat in stillness, waiting for the light to change. The perfect run of notes started to give him some clarity on his next move.

The light on Roosevelt turned yellow, then red.

In that frozen second between the lights changing, two massive arms sprung from the back seat, snapping the driver's neck in a motion as fluid as the arrangement of instruments in the classical masterpiece.

The glowing eyes from the back seat, drowned in a sea of darkness, flicked from his driver to Rains. Rains hadn't thought he would be afraid of the devil when he met him, but now he knew he was wrong.

Bic snatched Rains from the front seat into the back.

"It's pork chop eatin' time."

He put Rains to sleep with a quick right to the chin.

97

24 hours later

Between the chopper blades sweeping through the air, *thwup, thwup, thwup,* and his teeth chattering uncontrollably from the cold, Peter Rains couldn't hear much.

He sat with his arms tied behind his back, peering out onto a giant white page of nothing, a wasteland of white for as far as the eye could see in every direction.

His breath turned to vapor with each exhale. The tip of his nose had been numb seemingly minutes after he was taken from a jet onto the chopper. It had been 24 hours since being knocked out cold in his car.

Bic sat across from him in brittle silence, heavily dressed, a thick jacket with a hood outlined in brown fur over his head.

Bic had not answered any of his other questions yet, but he figured he'd ask him again. "Why are we in the Arctic?"

Bic didn't even look in his direction. He continued to peer out the windows on his side of the chopper. Occasionally, he lifted a pair of binoculars to his face, lowering them with a satisfied look.

Rains would have paid big money to know what was inside the two large Yeti coolers. He was pretty sure they weren't bringing booze to an Eskimo party.

The chopper's forward momentum stopped for the first time. Hovering over the area, Rains still couldn't see anything other than a whiteout.

Bic stood and pulled Rains to his feet. He then grabbed the long line of rope. At its end, he took the carabiner and attached it to Rains' harness.

"If you're going to hang me from a helicopter in this icebox, spare us all the antics. I'll freeze to death in seconds. Just throw me from the chopper and get it over with."

"Your blood will be pumping plenty hard to keep you from freezing," Bic said.

"What do you want?" Rains asked.

"Names," Bic replied.

"I can give you a lot of things, but I can't give you that," Rains replied.

Bic opened the cooler. Immediately the cabin filled with a pungent gasoline smell. He reached in with both hands and pulled out a four-foot plump dark gray seal. At first glance, Rains thought it was dead, but when he looked closer to see cables coming out of both sides, he realized it was fake.

Bic put the seal on Rains' back, and, with three sets of cables, high, mid, and low, he secured the seal tightly. Bic gave a tug. The seal didn't budge.

The chopper descended.

Rains looked out the window, and in the sea of white, he saw an off-white mass with a long neck and black snout.

"You're going to feed me to a polar bear?" His voice cracked.

Bic pulled out a knife. Rains' heart jackhammered as Bic cut the zip ties around his legs.

Bic opened the door. The frigid cold howled into the cabin, stinging any skin exposed to it.

"Colton Nash will sing like a bird," Rains said, not because he thought this would change his fate one bit, but because in his final move, he wanted everyone to get taken down with him.

"I know," said Bic, and pushed Rains out of the chopper.

Rains hung suspended in the air with a seal strapped to his back. As luck would have it, he faced the direction of the polar bear. Fifty yards away, the large mammal watched with curiosity.

Rains began to scream. Warmth spread down both legs.

He suddenly dropped to about four feet off the ground. He could just see Bic, and the flash of the knife, and the line was cut. He fell, slamming belly down onto the frozen snow.

He tried to will himself to die as he heard the chopper fly away.

Instinct kicked in a moment later, and he hopped to his feet.

Hot, primal fear coursed through him. The bear was walking towards him then stopped still, its nostrils chuffing thick gouts of steam.

Rains turned and ran, making sounds he'd never made before.

After 25 yards of sprinting with the seal on his back, his chest started to feel like a block of ice. With each breath, the pain in his chest increased.

He looked back, his sprint now a struggling jog.

The massive bear was running straight at him.

Rains stopped running. *No use,* he thought. *Maybe it won't be... that bad.*

Standing his ground, the massive white-furred locomotive kicked into high gear.

The clumsiness suddenly turned fluid as the largest land carnivore on earth sprung to its hind legs, at ten feet tall. The bear dropped its claw-filled hands, smashing Rains to the icy ground.

Claws embedded into his flesh. With a thousand pounds holding him down, the bear's elongated muzzle with its slightly arched snout reared up. The bear growled, flashing its dagger-like canines, and chomped down onto Rains' head.

Epilogue

Two Months Later

Gracie and Bic again stood in the impressive atrium at UChicago Medicine's DCAM research facility to celebrate the green light from the FDA for Phase 1 human trials. Caroline and Mack were also there with them, also accepting public recognition of the accomplishment. After Colton Nash, the CEO of Vintigen, had been arrested, he did indeed sing like a bird, turning everyone in for a deal and clearing Gracie Green's name. The university gave its full support and use of its lab facilities to Gracie until Greentech could rebuild its research lab. Mack and Caroline had become Greentech's first official investors.

The day Colton Nash was arrested and the cure was validated, Vintigen's stock crashed from 127 dollars to 14 dollars a share. Mack had shorted Vintigen and two other major cancer drug companies using put options after seeing proof that Diana Graham, Anna's mother had been cured. He bought 4,500 Vintigen options contracts with a strike price of 80 dollars. In one day his 36,000-dollar investment turned into almost 30 million.

Gracie raised her glass. "I want to thank everyone for making this possible. You all are responsible for this day."

Mack leaned over and kissed Caroline on the cheek.

"I'm still not sure how exactly you got your hands on the pills," Gracie said to Bic.

"Dumb luck," Bic said with a smile. "I had thrown one of the terrorists to the ground and it sounded like he had a box of Tic-Tacs in his front pocket. Curiosity got the best of me and I had to have a look. Then, as God would have it, I wound up in the same hospital as Caroline a couple of days later."

Bic's phone pinged. He looked at it and his face changed.

"What is it?" Gracie asked.

"Nothing."

"No secrets, Unc. You promised."

"It's Hawk."

"Is he okay?"

"He's doing better every day."

"Tell him I said hi and I wish he were here."

Bic texted the message.

Bic read his reply. "He says he's livin' on a prayer. He's half way to recovery and he'll make it he swears."

"That sounds just like Hawk," she said.

"Just like him," Bic said.

She stared at him a moment.

"What?" he said.

"I know that face. I've seen it before. You get that look and then you disappear. Not this time!"

"I need to take care of some unfinished business," Bic said.

"No," Gracie said.

"He's killing me. I have to."

"Who's killing you?"

"My father."

Bic hugged everyone.

Mack looked at Caroline for a long moment, eyes locked, then she nodded yes.

"I'm coming with you," Mack said.

"Not your fight," Bic said as he turned to walk away.

"I owe you everything, so it *is* my fight," Mack said.

"Mine too," Caroline added.

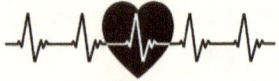

The dark and shadowy corridor of trees was illuminated by slivers of the moonlight cutting through the canopy. Men, hunched and loping, hurried towards the African voodoo drum music coming from the end of the tunnel.

Torches surrounded the altar made from a large tree stump covered in white painted symbols.

Clarence Green stood in front of 30 men, their eyes burning with religious fervor. The music stopped, and the men waited in pin drop silence.

"The dark horse is coming," Clarence Green announced, raising his hands high into the air. His eyes glared bright. "Whosoever takes the head of this man... will receive the gift of eternal life!"

THE BEGINNING...

Acknowledgments

The positive feedback and support of the Black Ghost series has been tremendous. Much appreciation to my great family and amazing friends. Each time someone embraces the journey of these characters I am truly inspired — this feeling never gets old.

To my wife, Jennifer, thank you for being such an integral part of this journey. Without you it would not be the same. We'll do it all. Everything. On our own.

To my children, Sofia, Freddie and Charlie, for helping me mail the signed copies. So far, we've only sent a couple of books to the wrong person. ☺

To my mom, you are still the smartest person I know. That is pretty good since I've been blessed with knowing a lot of smart and talented people. Like Einstein, you too have challenges with the simplest things, like figuring out how to end a facetime call.

To my sister Nina Hunter for always helping with your amazing graphic design talents. The Black Ghost deleted scenes pdf you created is awesome, thank you!

To my brother-in-law Dr. Tim Hughes for always being a great resource with your medical knowledge.

To my family and friends, again thank you for being the foundation to help share this series with the world of thriller readers.

To Linda Harris, thank you for the timely beta read and great feedback.

To all the gifted professionals who contributed to making this novel its best version of itself. Keith Olexa, Paul Lorello and Peter J. Wacks. Thank you for your care and expertise with this novel.

Thanks Dane Low for the great cover art, you nailed it again.

Much gratitude to Erik Gevers, you are so much more to this book than just the impeccable formatting.

Special recognition to Peter J. Wacks for continuing to help me in so many ways with this series. I appreciate your friendship.

"A reader lives a thousand lives before he dies..."
George R.R. Martin

I'm eternally grateful to YOU for reading THE CURE. I hope you had an amazing journey reading it. I'd love to hear about it!

If you haven't got your free deleted/altered chapter PDF from the first BLACK GHOST novel, readers have been giving great feedback and are loving the extra material. You can either reach out to me directly at freddie@freddievillacci.com or go to my website at freddievillacci.com and sign up for the newsletter. I will be excited to send these fifty-one pages of extra scenes for your enjoyment.

Signed copies of BLACK GHOST and THE CURE in paperback or hardcover are available at the website, freddievillacci.com.

Any feedback or questions feel free to email me at freddie@freddievillacci.com, It would be an honor to hear from you.

I am forever thankful you lived another life through reading the second book, THE CURE, in the BLACK GHOST THRILLER SERIES.

Also, please review the book on Amazon, if you liked it ☺ *, that would be greatly appreciated!*

REVENGE

The third book in the BLACK GHOST THRILLER SERIES
Coming soon…

I know Bic still hasn't confronted his father…
Readers have been dying for resolution…
But I promise…
The wait will be worth it…
In the third book, REVENGE, in the Black Ghost Series…
It is on like Donkey Kong between Bic and his father!

Currently the name of the Third book is REVENGE. It is simple and it is what the book is about, Bic seeking revenge with his father Clarence for killing his mother and ultimately changing Bic's life's path to eventually become a highly functioning serial killer. I am not 100% sold on the name, I like it, but I'm wondering if there is something better.

I would encourage anyone who has read the first two BLACK GHOST books to email me at freddie@freddievillacci.com with your ideas for the title options instead of REVENGE. If your idea is used instead of REVENGE, I will give you props in the acknowledgement and also send you first edition signed copies of the first three hardcover books in the BLACK GHOST THRILLER series.

About the Author

Freddie Villacci, Jr. was born and raised in Wood Dale, Illinois. He earned a degree in marketing from Berry College, while playing baseball. At the age of nineteen he began to invest in the stock market and continued on with a career in the insurance and financial services industry.

Besides books, he also fuels his creativity writing movie scripts and songs. FACELESS, an independent movie is due out in 2021.

Freddie loves being out in the sun, especially playing baseball and golf with his daughter and twin boys. He and his wife, Jennifer, have a passion for supporting charities that help children.

Freddie would love to connect with his readers at www.freddievillacci.com.

www.ingramcontent.com/pod-product-compliance
Lightning Source LLC
Chambersburg PA
CBHW051950240626
47153CB00005B/1700